Edited by Eric Reynolds — Designed by Jacob Covey
Production by Paul Baresh — Promoted by Jacq Cohen — Published by Gary Groth

Fantagraphics Books Inc.
7563 Lake City Way NE, Seattle, WA 98115
www.fantagraphics.com

Subscribe to *NOW*: Visit www.fantagraphics.com/now for details.

ISBN 978-1-68396-399-8
Library of Congress Control Number: 2018949686
First printing: July 2021
Printed in Canada

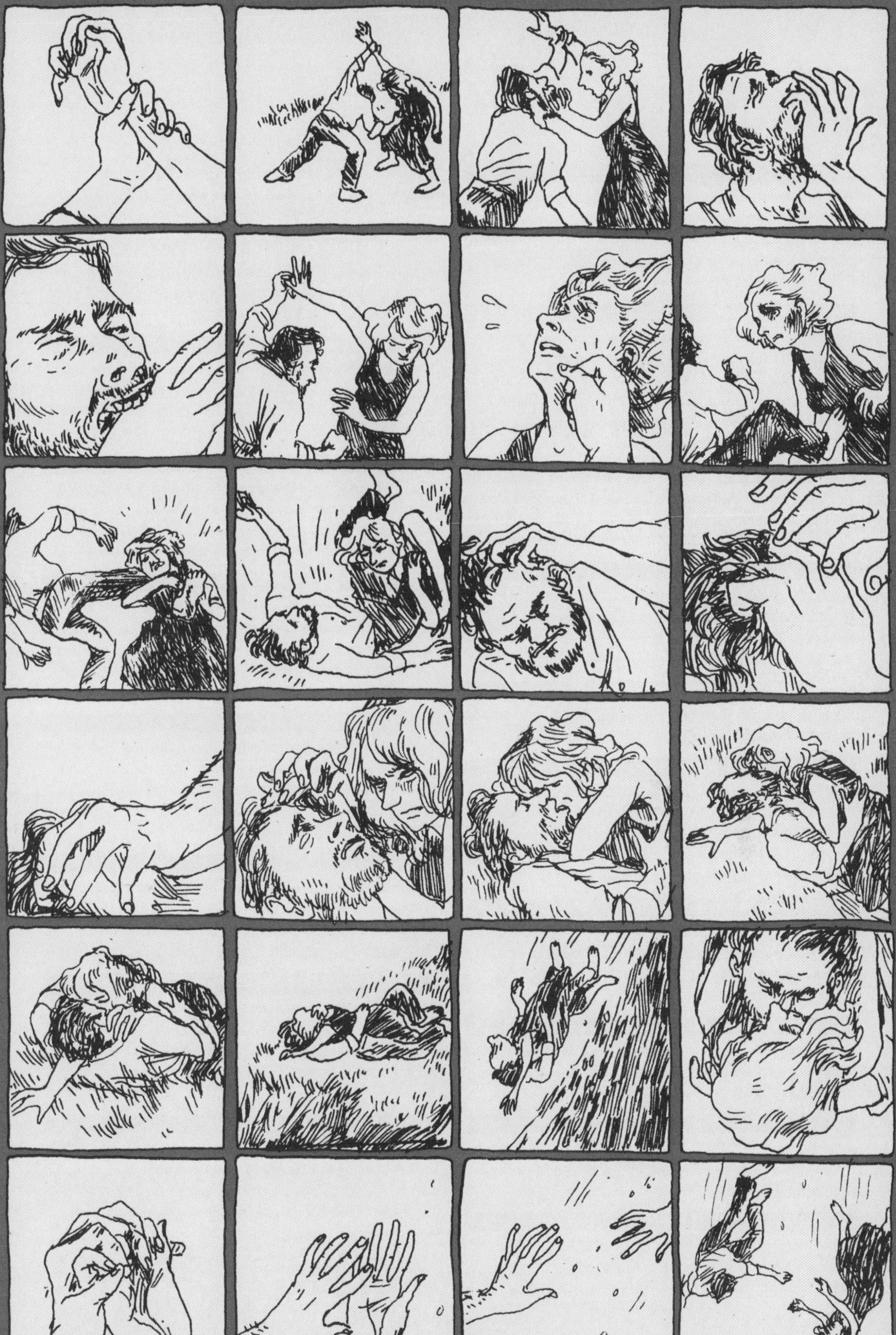

About the Contributors

INSTAGRAM: @REBECCAMORGAN10

Rebecca Morgan hails from central Pennsylvania, and works in painting, drawing, and ceramics that subvert stereotypes of Appalachia. Her work previously appeared on the cover of the very first issue of *NOW* ("Plan B on Easter Sunday").

INSTAGRAM: @THORAZOS

Julia Gfrörer is the author of the graphic novels *Black Is the Color* (2013), *Laid Waste* (2016), and most recently, *Vision* (2020), all from Fantagraphics. She lives on Long Island, where she maintains an extensive collection of black cardigans. Gfrörer pronounces her name "gruh fare" but you can say it however you like.

TIMLANEILLUSTRATION.COM

Tim Lane lives in Washington, D.C. He is the author of the books *Abandoned Cars* (2010), *The Lonesome Go* (2014), and *Toybox Americana* (2020), all from Fantagraphics.

JACOB-WEINSTEIN.COM

Jacob Weinstein is the co-author and illustrator of FreeDarko's two books, *The Macrophenomal Pro Basketball Almanac* and *The Undisputed Guide to Pro Basketball History*. He lives in New York.

INSTAGRAM: @WEI_SS_MAN

Steven Weissman is an East Hollywood hodad and author of many books for Fantagraphics and others.

INSTAGRAM: @M.S.HARKNESS

M.S. Harkness is a cartoonist based out of the American Midwest. She's the author of the acclaimed memoir *Tinderella* (2018) and most recently, *Desperate Pleasures* (2020), both from Uncivilized Books. She enjoys competitive weightlifting.

INSTAGRAM: @WALT_HOLCOMBE

Walt Holcombe is the author of the book *Things Just Get Away From You* (Fantagraphics, 2007). He lives in Los Angeles and storyboards for animation. He wishes he could draw comics faster.

INSTAGRAM: @THEO_ELLSWORTH_

Theo Ellsworth's new graphic novel, *Secret Life* (an adaptation of a short story by Jeff VanderMeer), is out in September 2021 from Drawn and Quarterly.

INSTAGRAM: @JOAKIMDRESCHER

Joakim Drescher (b.1986) is best known for his books in the motel universe series. He currently lives and works in Copenhagen, Denmark.

INSTAGRAM: @ROCCCCHI_SILVIA

Silvia Rocchi is an award-winning Italian cartoonist and illustrator who has written and drawn several graphic novels and short stories published in Italy. She started doing comics co-funding the experimental comics collective La Trama. She lives and works in Bologna, Italy, and wishes to thank Frank Santoro for helping edit her story.

INSTAGRAM: @ALEXNALL0

Alex Nall is a cartoonist and teaching artist living in Chicago. His books include *Lawns* and *Are Comic Books Real?* published by Kilgore Books.

INSTAGRAM: @HARTLEY._.LIN

Hartley Lin is behind the ongoing comic book experiment called *Pope Hats*. His collection *Young Frances* (AdHouse) won the 2019 Doug Wright Award for Best Book. He lives in Montreal.

INSTAGRAM: @INKWEED76

Chris Wright lives and works in Richmond, VT. He is the author of the book *Blacklung* (Fantagraphics, 2012) and has been finishing a new collection of drawings and stories for the past two years. www.hoboink.com.

INSTAGRAM: @NOAHVSCOMICS

Noah Van Sciver is the prolific author of several acclaimed graphic novels, including *The Complete Works of Fante Bukowski* and, most recently, *Please Don't Step On My JNCO Jeans* (both from Fantagraphics). He lives in South Carolina.

INSTAGRAM: @OKEJTJEJGORSINGREJ

Cecilia Vårhed is a cartoonist active in Stockholm, Sweden. She's a general goods vendor at the local food store and collects celebrity receipts. Her comics revolve around people who can't leave each other alone, liars, weaklings, and cool friends.

Richard Sala was the acclaimed and beloved creator behind dozens of books and comics in his remarkable career (see page 98 for a more comprehensive list). He passed away in 2020.

INSTAGRAM: @KARLSTEVENSART

Karl Stevens is a comic strip artist based in Boston. His work has appeared in *The New Yorker*, *The Village Voice*, and *The Boston Globe*, amongst other places. His most recent book is *Penny: A Graphic Memoir* from Chronicle Books.

INSTAGRAM: @NICKFROMISLANDS

Nick Thorburn is a Canadian cartoonist, writer, and musician living in Los Angeles. He has fronted numerous bands, including Islands, the Unicorns, and Human Highway. His debut graphic novel, *Penguins*, was published by Fantagraphics in 2018.

WWW.FANTAGRAPHICS.COM/SERIES/NOW

For more issues of *Now* visit the web.

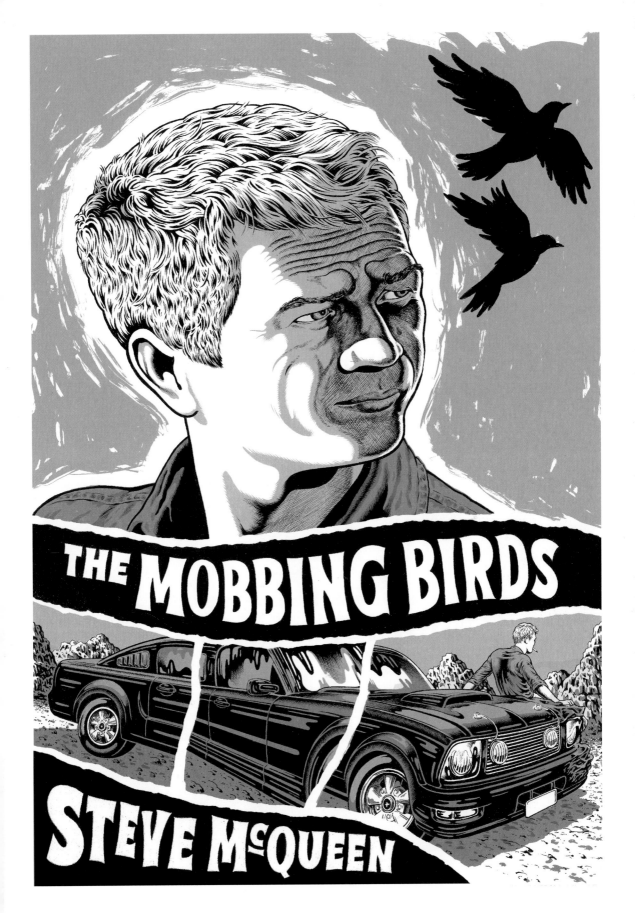

THE MOBBING BIRDS

STEVE McQUEEN

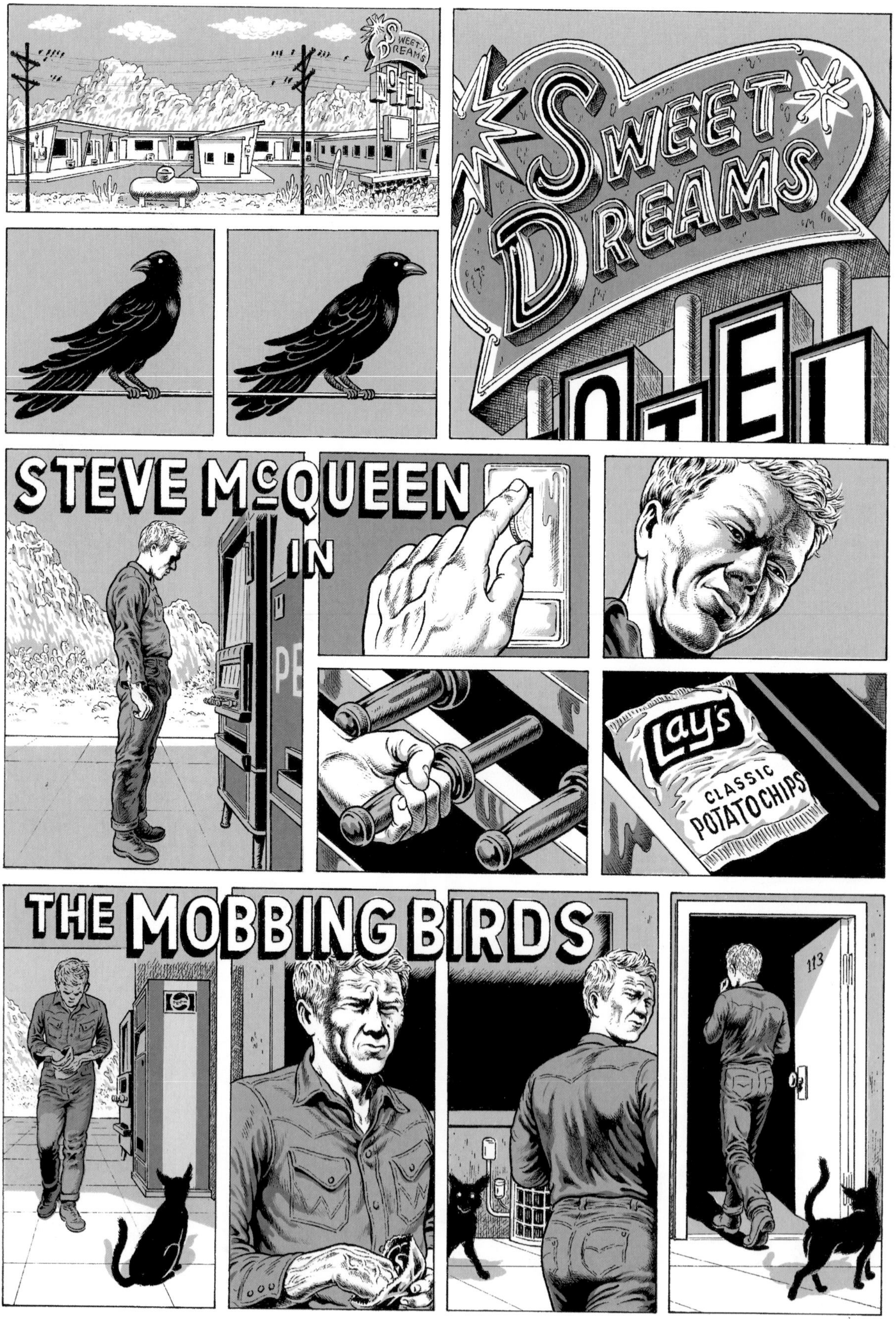
SWEET DREAMS
MOTEL
SWEET DREAMS
STEVE McQUEEN
IN
Lay's
CLASSIC
POTATO CHIPS
THE MOBBING BIRDS
113

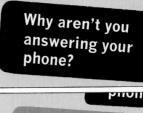

Why aren't you answering your phone?

You know why

I need to see you

In town

WTF!?!

. . .

Where are you?

I'm here

In town

. . .

What the fuck is wrong with you?!

Where's here?

WTF!?!

wrong with you?!

. . .

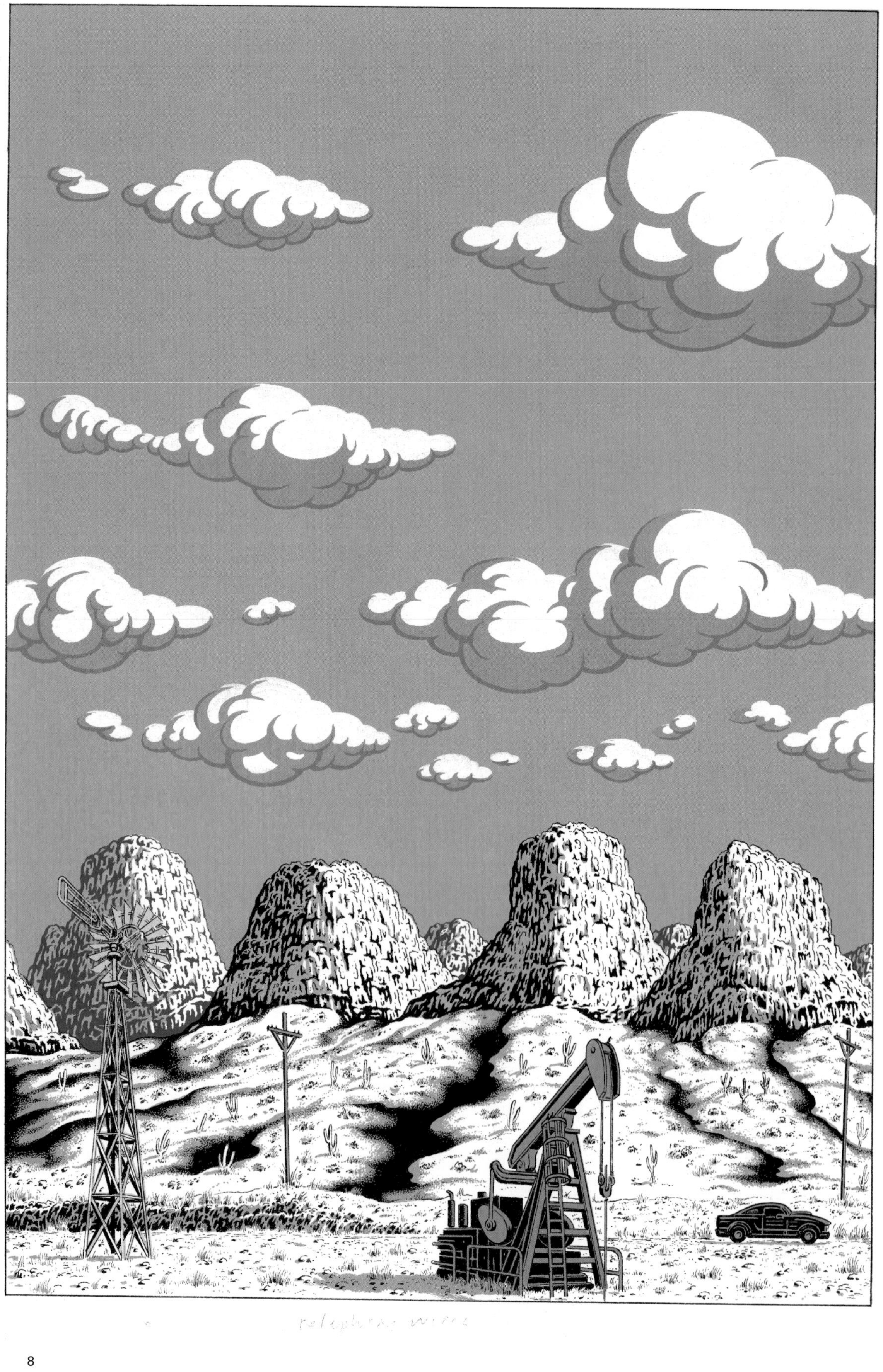

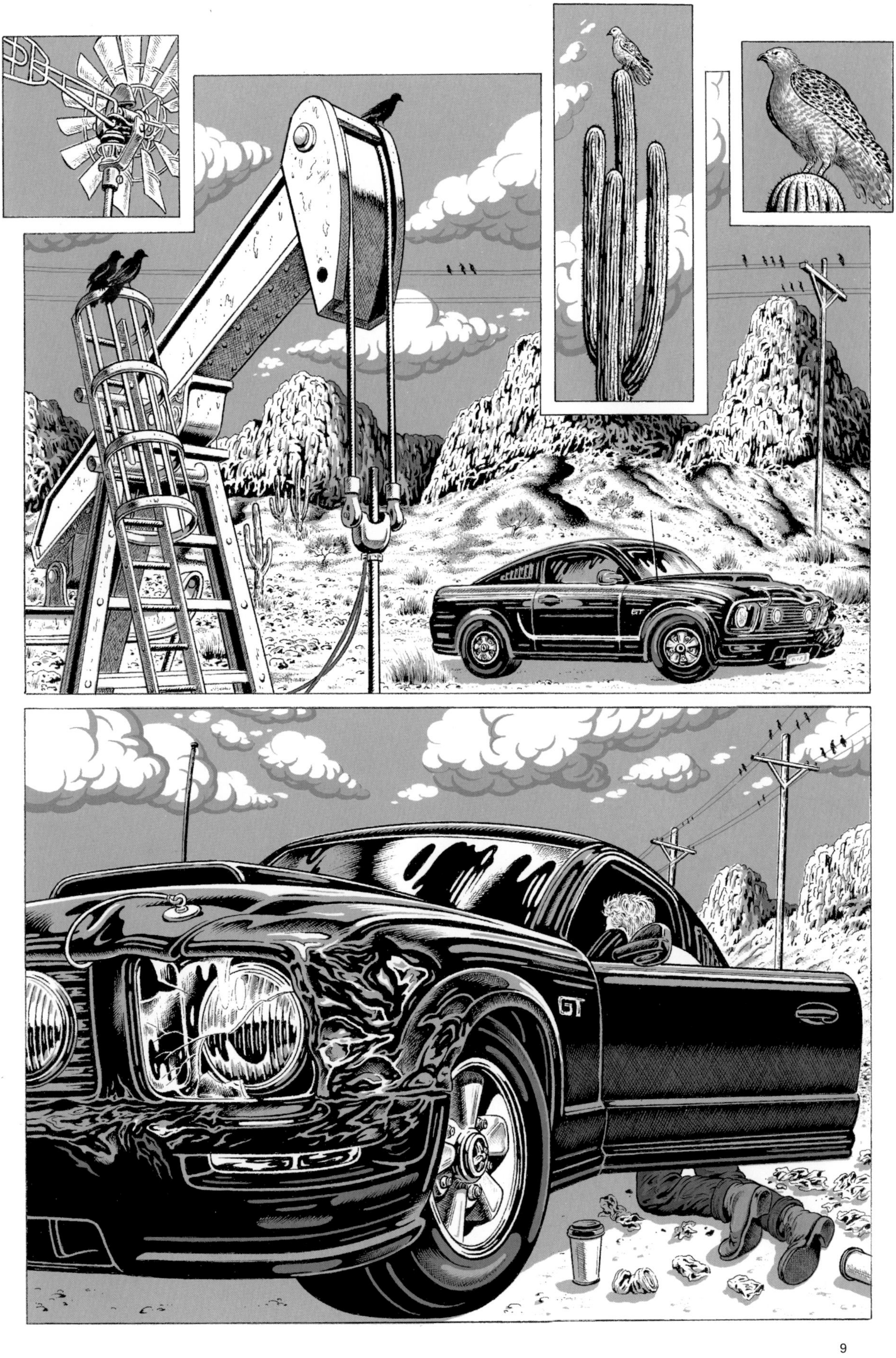
GT

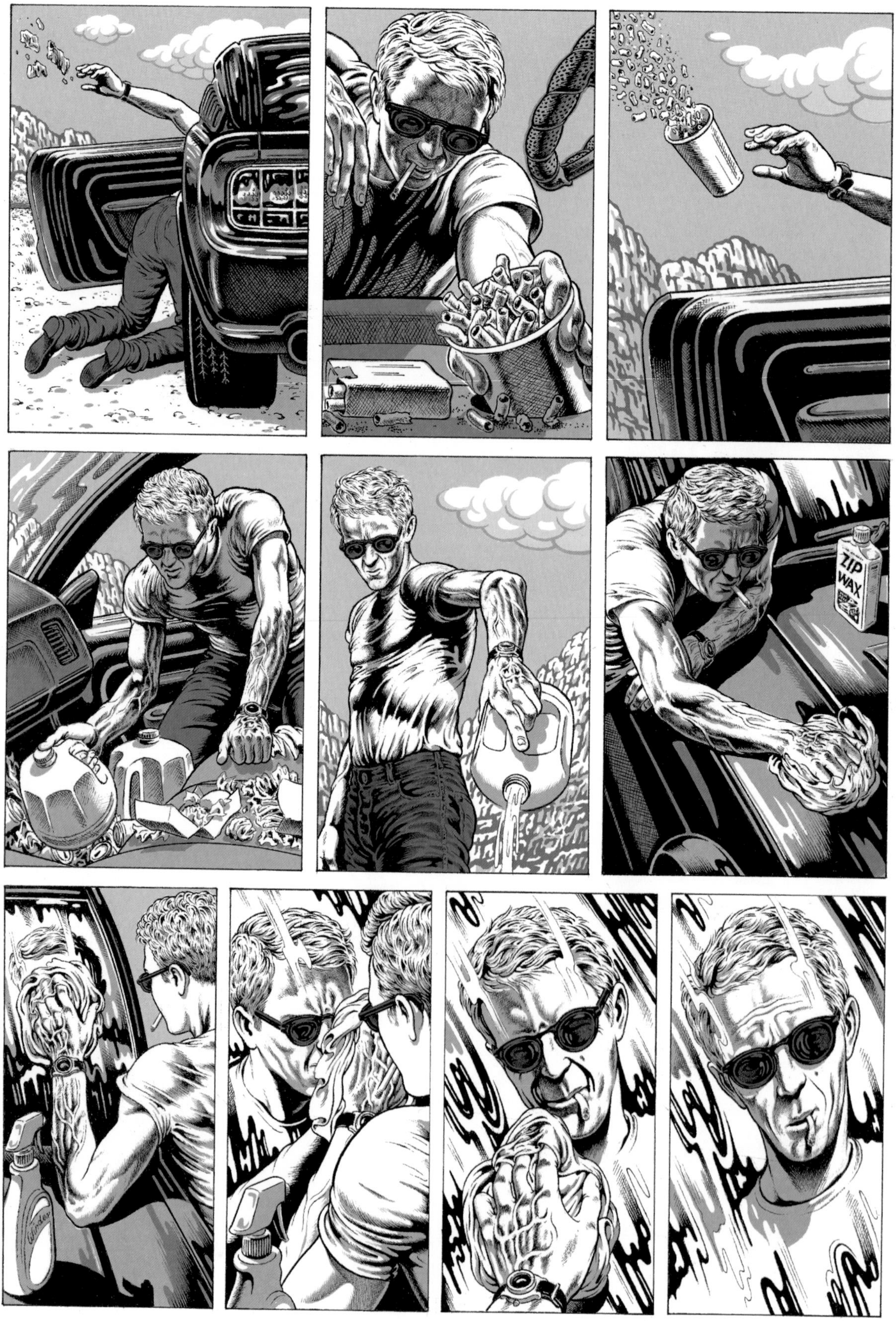
ZIP
WAX

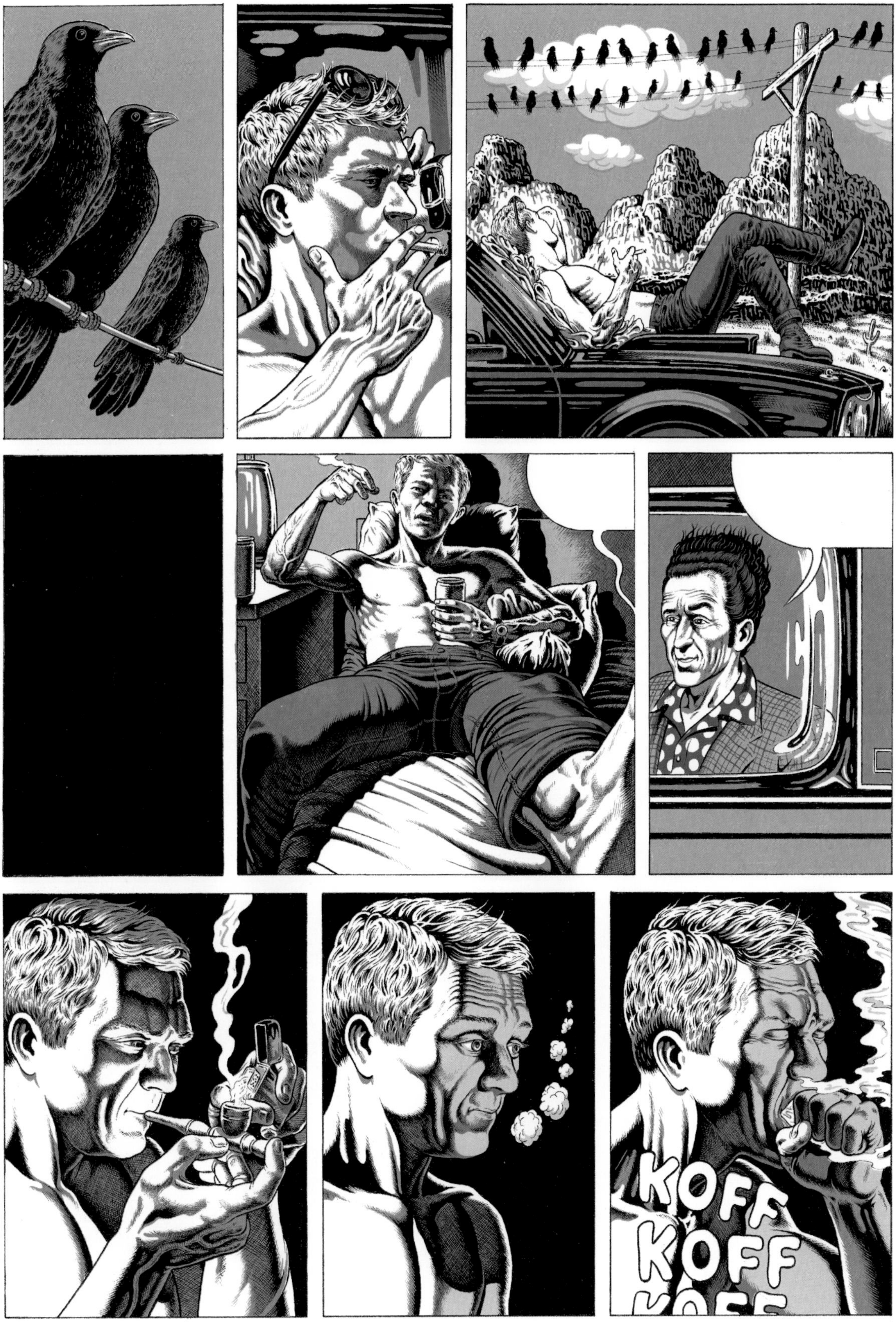
KOFF
KOFF

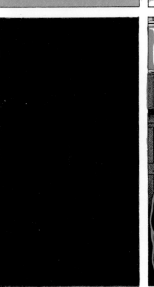

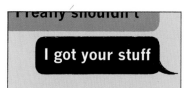

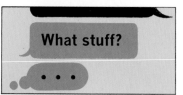

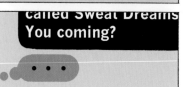

Will you come see me?

I got your stuff

Where EXACTLY are you?

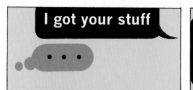

see me?

. . .

I got your stuff

. . .

Some old motel called Sweat Dreams. You coming?

see me?

I really shouldn't

What stuff?

. . .

called Sweat Dreams
You coming?

. . .

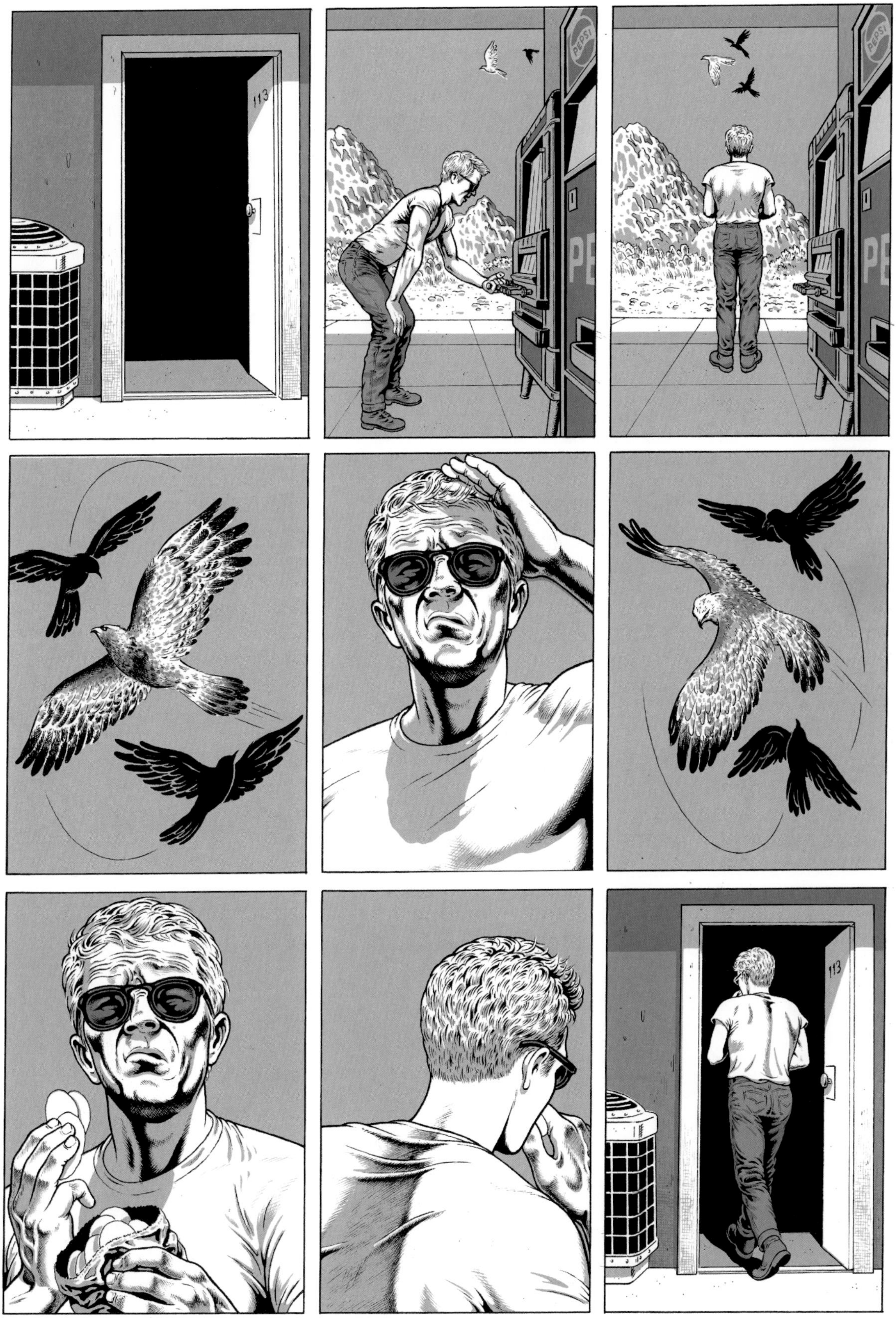
113
PEPSI
PEPSI

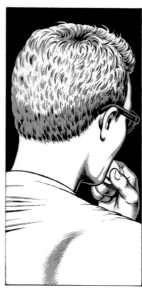

STAND DOWN, TRASH! STAND THE FUCK DOWN!

YOU UNDERSTAND?

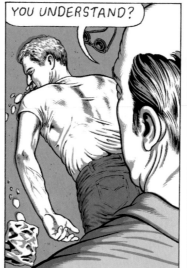

YOU UNDERSTAND?

YES!

SAY IT!

I UNDERSTAND!

stupid fuck...

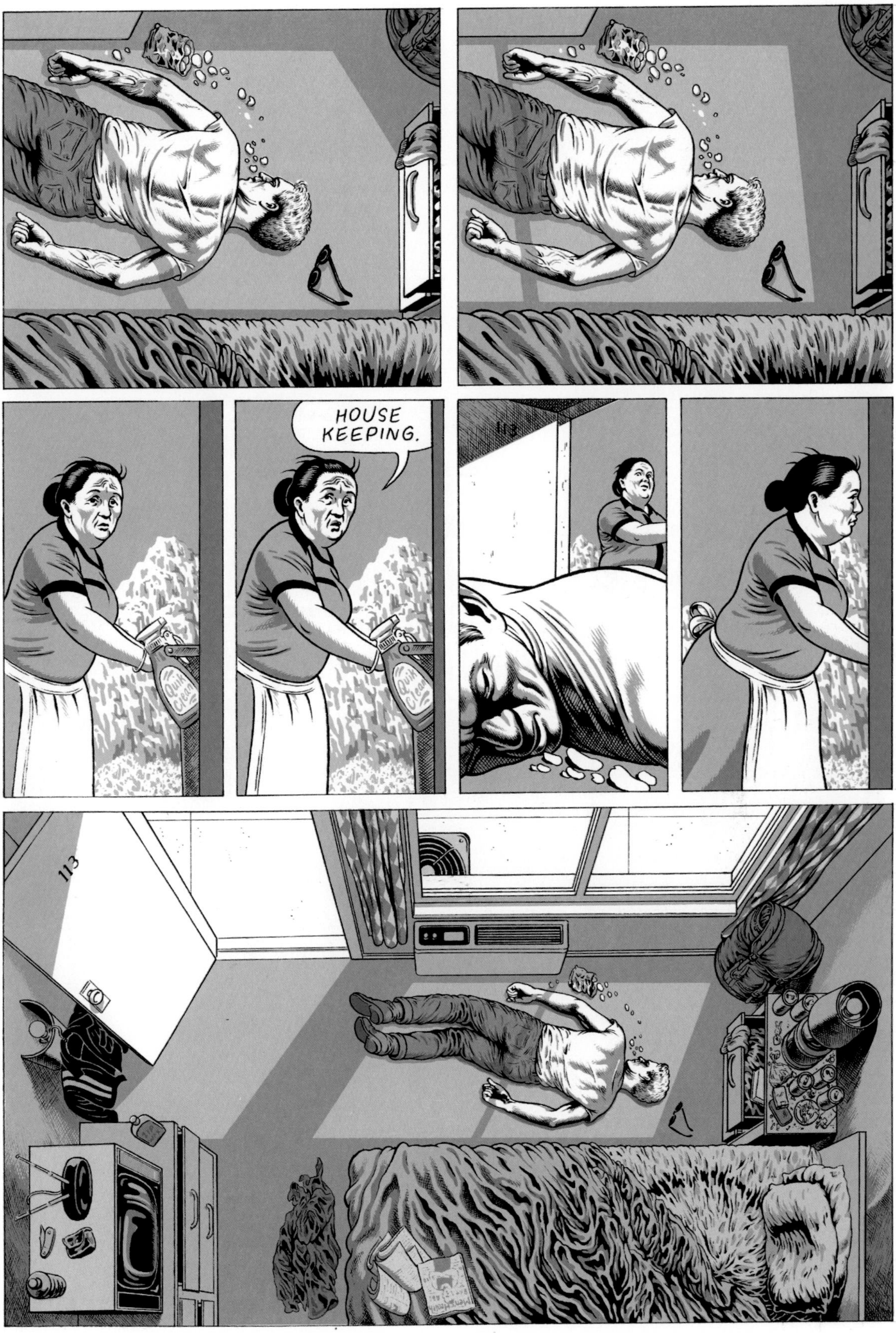
HOUSE KEEPING.
Quik Clean
113

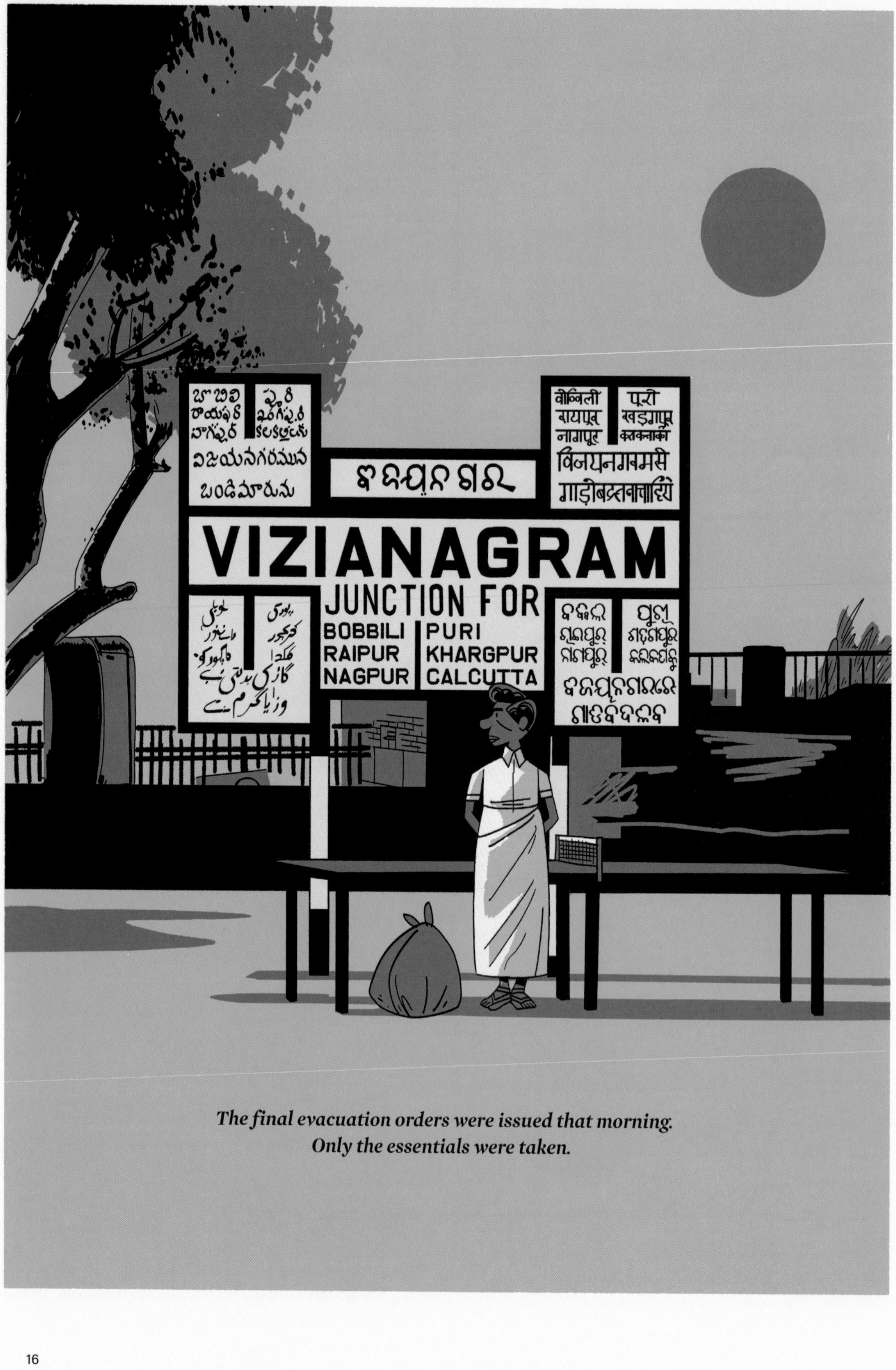
VIZIANAGRAM
JUNCTION FOR
BOBBILI
RAIPUR
NAGPUR
PURI
KHARGPUR
CALCUTTA

The final evacuation orders were issued that morning.
Only the essentials were taken.

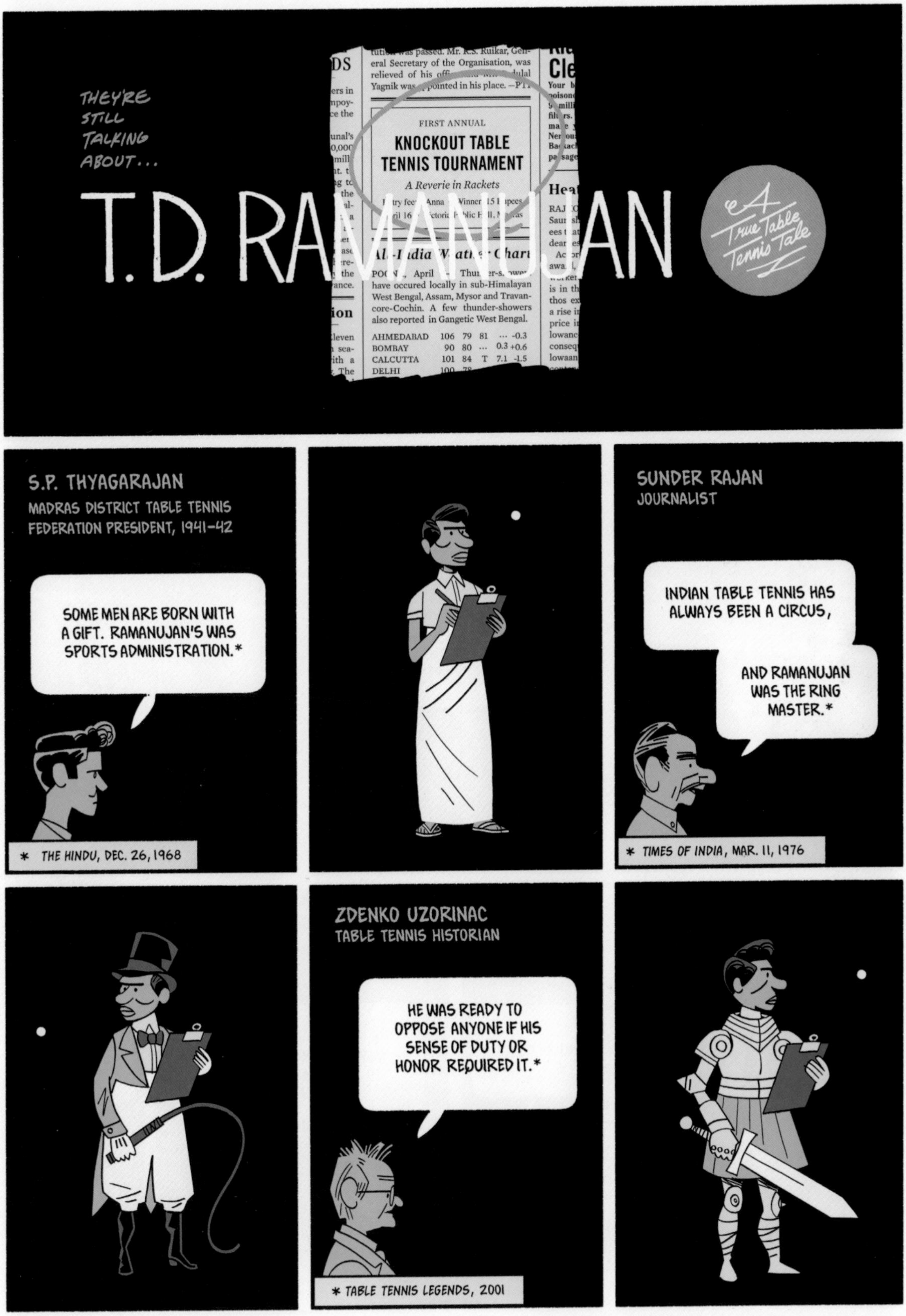

THEY'RE STILL TALKING ABOUT...
T.D. RAMANUJAN
eral Secretary of the Organisation, was
FIRST ANNUAL
KNOCKOUT TABLE TENNIS TOURNAMENT
A Reverie in Rackets
have occured locally in sub-Himalayan
West Bengal, Assam, Mysor and Travan-
core-Cochin. A few thunder-showers
also reported in Gangetic West Bengal.
AHMEDABAD 106 79 81 ... -0.3
BOMBAY 90 80 ... 0.3 +0.6
CALCUTTA 101 84 T 7.1 -1.5
DELHI
A True Table Tennis Tale
S.P. THYAGARAJAN
MADRAS DISTRICT TABLE TENNIS FEDERATION PRESIDENT, 1941–42
SOME MEN ARE BORN WITH A GIFT. RAMANUJAN'S WAS SPORTS ADMINISTRATION.*
* THE HINDU, DEC. 26, 1968
SUNDER RAJAN
JOURNALIST
INDIAN TABLE TENNIS HAS ALWAYS BEEN A CIRCUS,
AND RAMANUJAN WAS THE RING MASTER.*
* TIMES OF INDIA, MAR. 11, 1976
ZDENKO UZORINAC
TABLE TENNIS HISTORIAN
HE WAS READY TO OPPOSE ANYONE IF HIS SENSE OF DUTY OR HONOR REQUIRED IT.*
* TABLE TENNIS LEGENDS, 2001

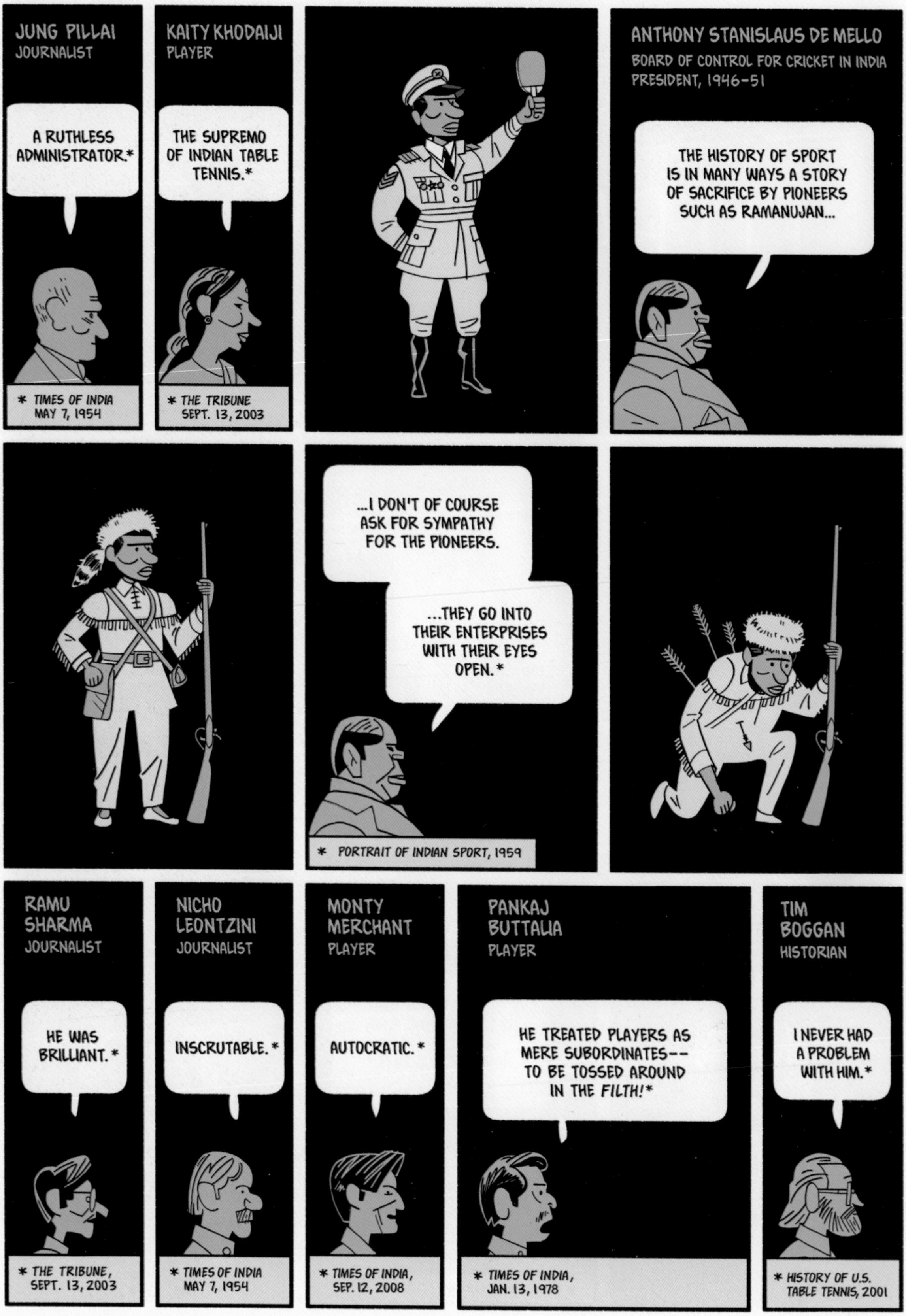
JUNG PILLAI
JOURNALIST
A RUTHLESS ADMINISTRATOR.*
* TIMES OF INDIA MAY 7, 1954
KAITY KHODAIJI
PLAYER
THE SUPREMO OF INDIAN TABLE TENNIS.*
* THE TRIBUNE SEPT. 13, 2003
ANTHONY STANISLAUS DE MELLO
BOARD OF CONTROL FOR CRICKET IN INDIA PRESIDENT, 1946-51
THE HISTORY OF SPORT IS IN MANY WAYS A STORY OF SACRIFICE BY PIONEERS SUCH AS RAMANUJAN...
...I DON'T OF COURSE ASK FOR SYMPATHY FOR THE PIONEERS.
...THEY GO INTO THEIR ENTERPRISES WITH THEIR EYES OPEN.*
* PORTRAIT OF INDIAN SPORT, 1959
RAMU SHARMA
JOURNALIST
HE WAS BRILLIANT.*
* THE TRIBUNE, SEPT. 13, 2003
NICHO LEONTZINI
JOURNALIST
INSCRUTABLE.*
* TIMES OF INDIA MAY 7, 1954
MONTY MERCHANT
PLAYER
AUTOCRATIC.*
* TIMES OF INDIA, SEP. 12, 2008
PANKAJ BUTTALIA
PLAYER
HE TREATED PLAYERS AS MERE SUBORDINATES-- TO BE TOSSED AROUND IN THE *FILTH!**
* TIMES OF INDIA, JAN. 13, 1978
TIM BOGGAN
HISTORIAN
I NEVER HAD A PROBLEM WITH HIM.*
* HISTORY OF U.S. TABLE TENNIS, 2001

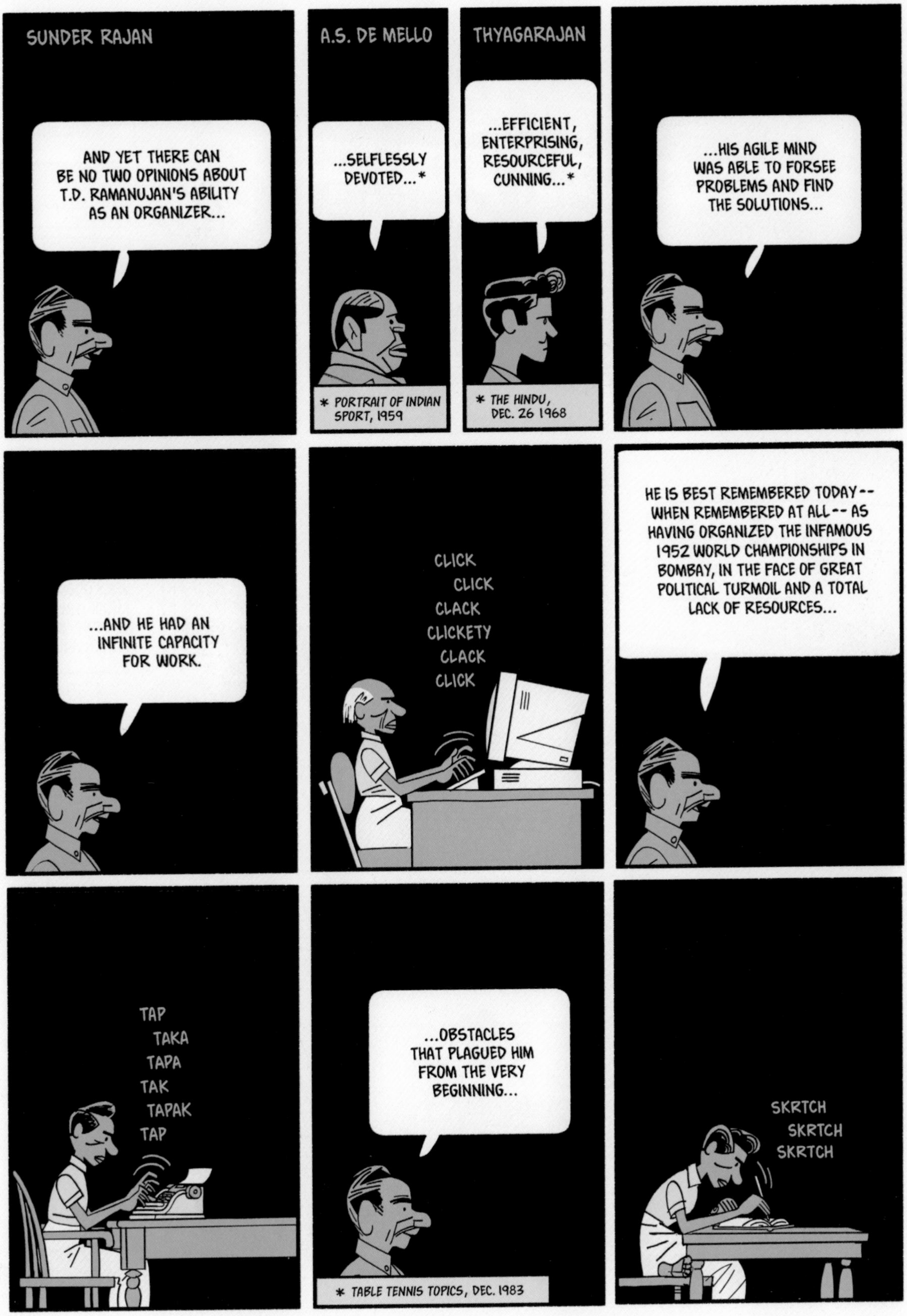
SUNDER RAJAN
AND YET THERE CAN BE NO TWO OPINIONS ABOUT T.D. RAMANUJAN'S ABILITY AS AN ORGANIZER...
A.S. DE MELLO
...SELFLESSLY DEVOTED...*
* PORTRAIT OF INDIAN SPORT, 1959
THYAGARAJAN
...EFFICIENT, ENTERPRISING, RESOURCEFUL, CUNNING...*
* THE HINDU, DEC. 26 1968
...HIS AGILE MIND WAS ABLE TO FORSEE PROBLEMS AND FIND THE SOLUTIONS...
...AND HE HAD AN INFINITE CAPACITY FOR WORK.
CLICK CLICK CLACK CLICKETY CLACK CLICK
HE IS BEST REMEMBERED TODAY-- WHEN REMEMBERED AT ALL-- AS HAVING ORGANIZED THE INFAMOUS 1952 WORLD CHAMPIONSHIPS IN BOMBAY, IN THE FACE OF GREAT POLITICAL TURMOIL AND A TOTAL LACK OF RESOURCES...
TAP TAKA TAPA TAK TAPAK TAP
...OBSTACLES THAT PLAGUED HIM FROM THE VERY BEGINNING...
* TABLE TENNIS TOPICS, DEC. 1983
SKRTCH SKRTCH SKRTCH

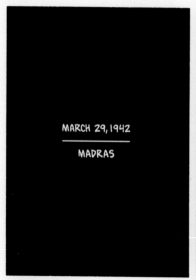

MARCH 29, 1942

MADRAS

SKRTCH
SKRTCH
SKRTCH

RAMANUJAN?

T.D. RAMANUJAN? DO YOU HAVE THE ANSWER?

SKRTCH
SKRTCH
SKRTCH

$1-p = 4.6$

SKRTCH

THE POPULATION GROWTH RATE WILL EXCEED FOOD SUPPLY BY 4.6% IN A MALTHUSIAN MODEL.

VERY GOOD. AND IF THE VALUE OF 'X' IS UNKNOWN?

GAH! ECONOMICS.

THE 'DISMAL SCIENCE' INDEED. WERE WE PUT ON THIS EARTH MERELY TO CALCULATE THE RATE OF OUR OWN MISERY?

DO YOU READ THE PAPERS T.D.? HALF THE WORLD AT WAR, FAMINE IN BENGAL, 3.5 MILLION ALREADY DEAD IN EUROPE...

3.6 MILLION.

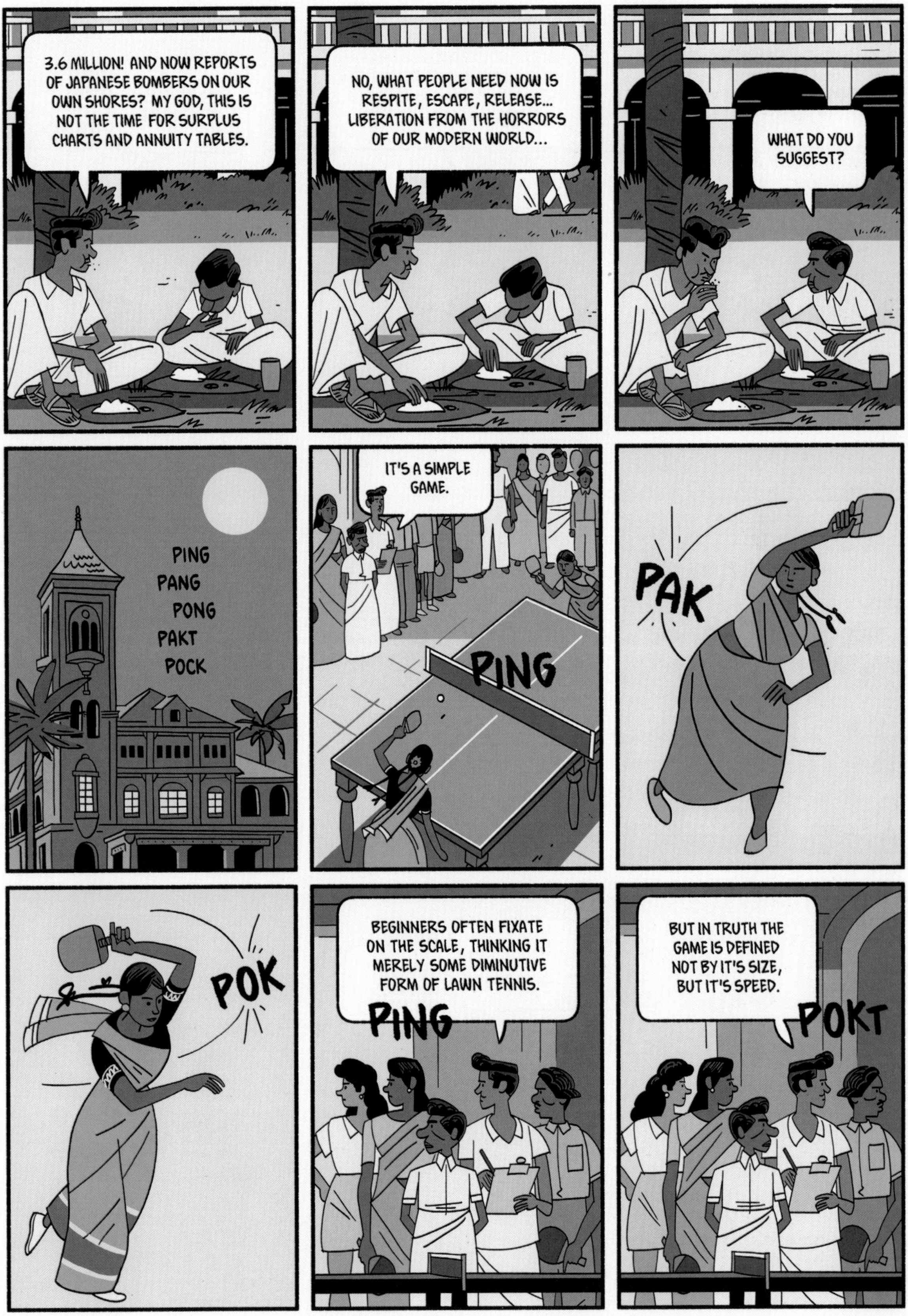
3.6 MILLION! AND NOW REPORTS OF JAPANESE BOMBERS ON OUR OWN SHORES? MY GOD, THIS IS NOT THE TIME FOR SURPLUS CHARTS AND ANNUITY TABLES.
NO, WHAT PEOPLE NEED NOW IS RESPITE, ESCAPE, RELEASE... LIBERATION FROM THE HORRORS OF OUR MODERN WORLD...
WHAT DO YOU SUGGEST?
PING
PANG
PONG
PAKT
POCK
IT'S A SIMPLE GAME.
PING
PAK
POK
BEGINNERS OFTEN FIXATE ON THE SCALE, THINKING IT MERELY SOME DIMINUTIVE FORM OF LAWN TENNIS.
PING
BUT IN TRUTH THE GAME IS DEFINED NOT BY IT'S SIZE, BUT IT'S SPEED.
POKT

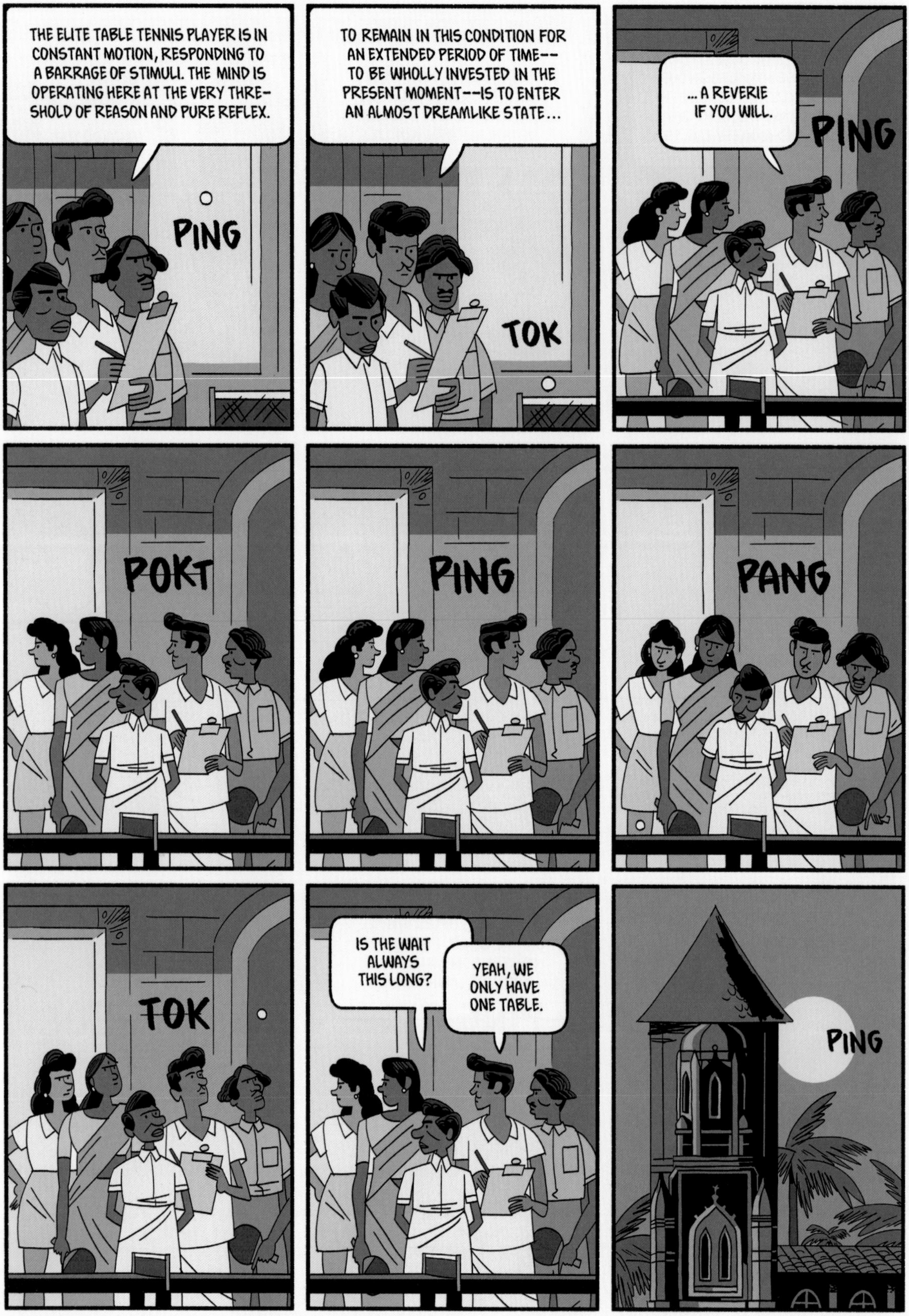
THE ELITE TABLE TENNIS PLAYER IS IN CONSTANT MOTION, RESPONDING TO A BARRAGE OF STIMULI. THE MIND IS OPERATING HERE AT THE VERY THRESHOLD OF REASON AND PURE REFLEX.
PING
TO REMAIN IN THIS CONDITION FOR AN EXTENDED PERIOD OF TIME--TO BE WHOLLY INVESTED IN THE PRESENT MOMENT--IS TO ENTER AN ALMOST DREAMLIKE STATE...
TOK
...A REVERIE IF YOU WILL.
PING
POKT
PING
PANG
TOK
IS THE WAIT ALWAYS THIS LONG?
YEAH, WE ONLY HAVE ONE TABLE.
PING

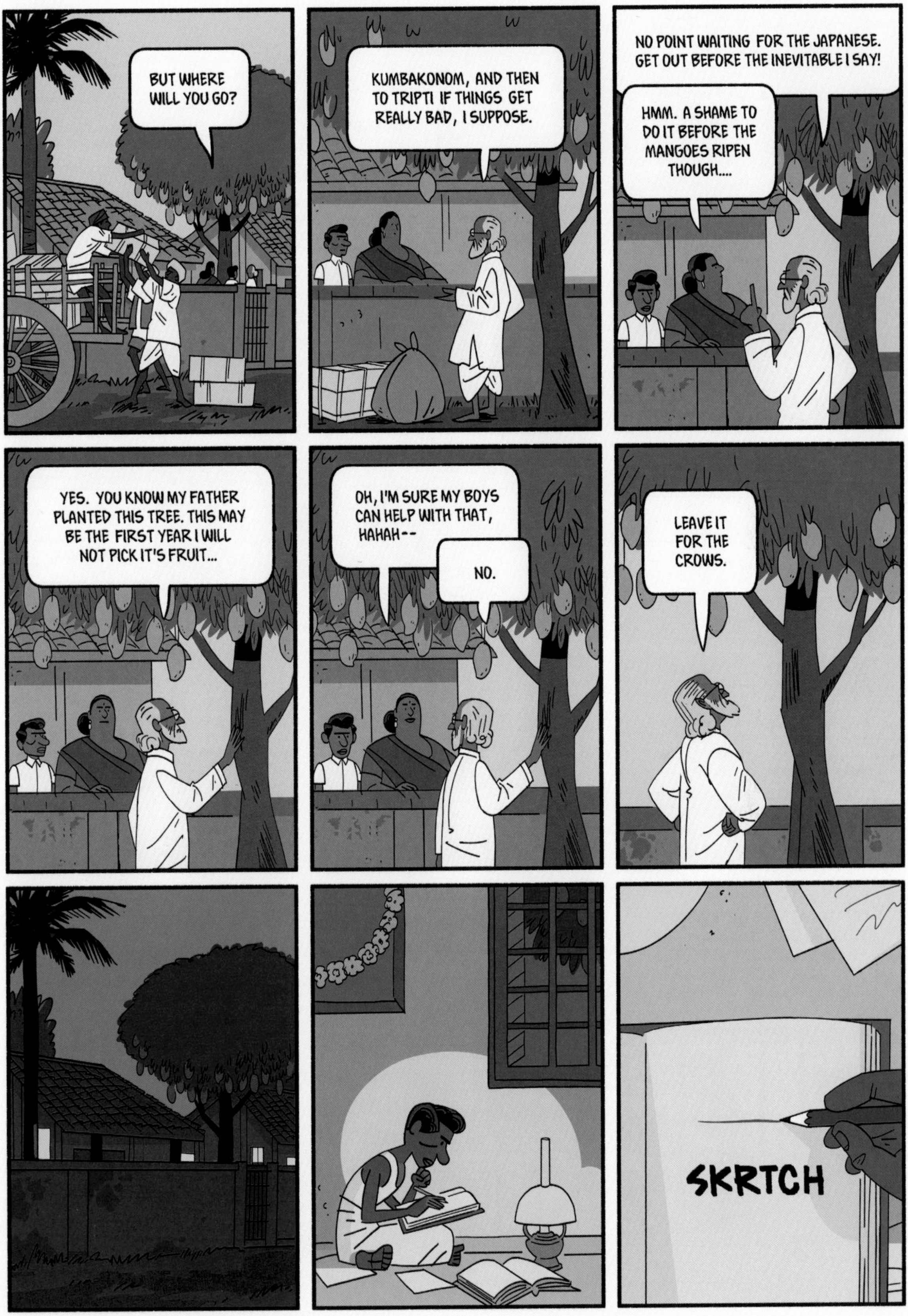
BUT WHERE WILL YOU GO?
KUMBAKONOM, AND THEN TO TRIPTI IF THINGS GET REALLY BAD, I SUPPOSE.
NO POINT WAITING FOR THE JAPANESE. GET OUT BEFORE THE INEVITABLE I SAY!
HMM. A SHAME TO DO IT BEFORE THE MANGOES RIPEN THOUGH....
YES. YOU KNOW MY FATHER PLANTED THIS TREE. THIS MAY BE THE FIRST YEAR I WILL NOT PICK IT'S FRUIT...
OH, I'M SURE MY BOYS CAN HELP WITH THAT, HAHAH--
NO.
LEAVE IT FOR THE CROWS.
SKRTCH

MARCH 30, 1942
SKRTCH
SKRTCH
SKRTCH
SKRTCH
RAMANUJAN?
15 min for best of 3
25 min for best of 5
SPACE
10' MINIMUM
5' MIN
REVENUE
- DUES
Knockout
2
15
4
13
6
11
8
9
200 WATT
3'10"
2ND
Round Robin: N/2(N-1)
Knockout: N-1?
SKRT--
UH...
ROAR!
THEY SHOT THEM IN BERLIN, YOU KNOW.
AFTER THE BOMBING THEY SHOT THE ENTIRE ZOO. ONLY FITTING THAT HAVING UNLEASHED OUR BESTIAL NATURE, WE MUST THEN PROTECT OURSELVES FROM THE BEASTS.
YOU SHOULD SWITCH TO A KNOCKOUT TOURNAMENT.
EXCUSE ME?
IF YOU SWITCH TO A KNOCKOUT FROM A ROUND ROBIN, YOU CUT THE NUMBER OF GAMES IN HALF.
ZOO

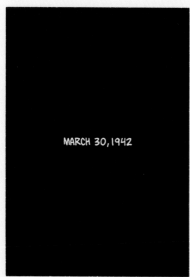

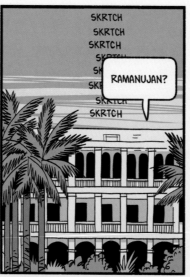

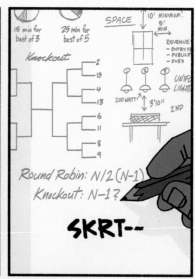

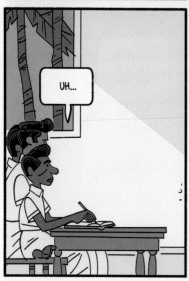

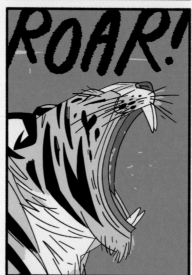

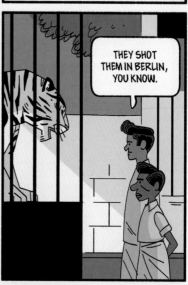

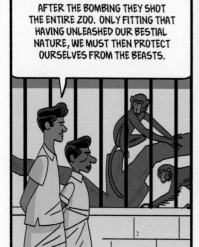

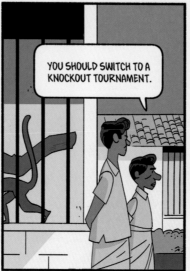

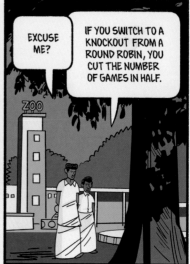

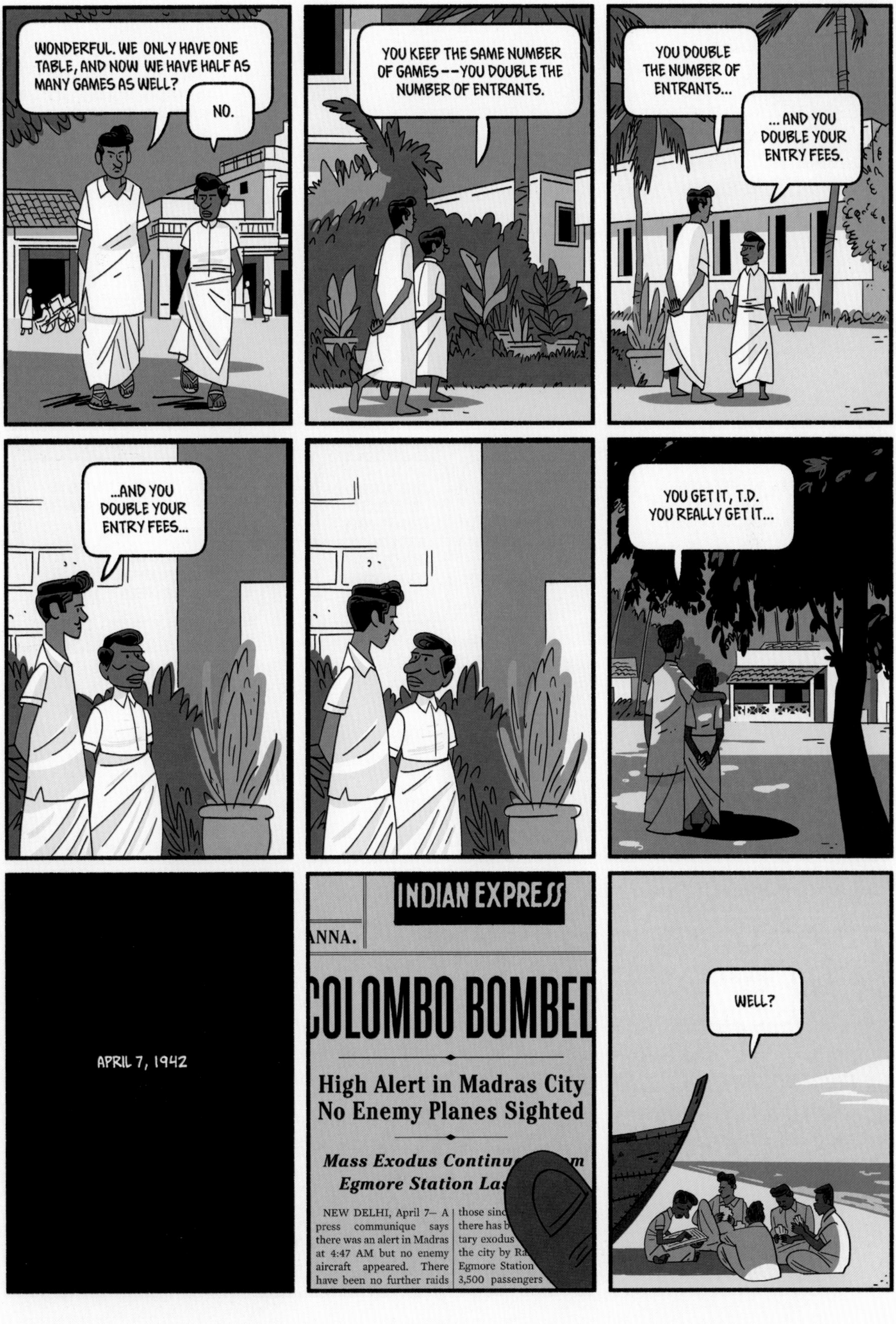
WONDERFUL. WE ONLY HAVE ONE TABLE, AND NOW WE HAVE HALF AS MANY GAMES AS WELL?
NO.
YOU KEEP THE SAME NUMBER OF GAMES--YOU DOUBLE THE NUMBER OF ENTRANTS.
YOU DOUBLE THE NUMBER OF ENTRANTS...
... AND YOU DOUBLE YOUR ENTRY FEES.
...AND YOU DOUBLE YOUR ENTRY FEES...
YOU GET IT, T.D. YOU REALLY GET IT...
APRIL 7, 1942
INDIAN EXPRESS
ANNA.
COLOMBO BOMBED
High Alert in Madras City
No Enemy Planes Sighted
Mass Exodus Continu
Egmore Station La
NEW DELHI, April 7— A press communique says there was an alert in Madras at 4:47 AM but no enemy aircraft appeared. There have been no further raids
those sinc
there has b
tary exodus
the city by Ra
Egmore Station
3,500 passengers
WELL?

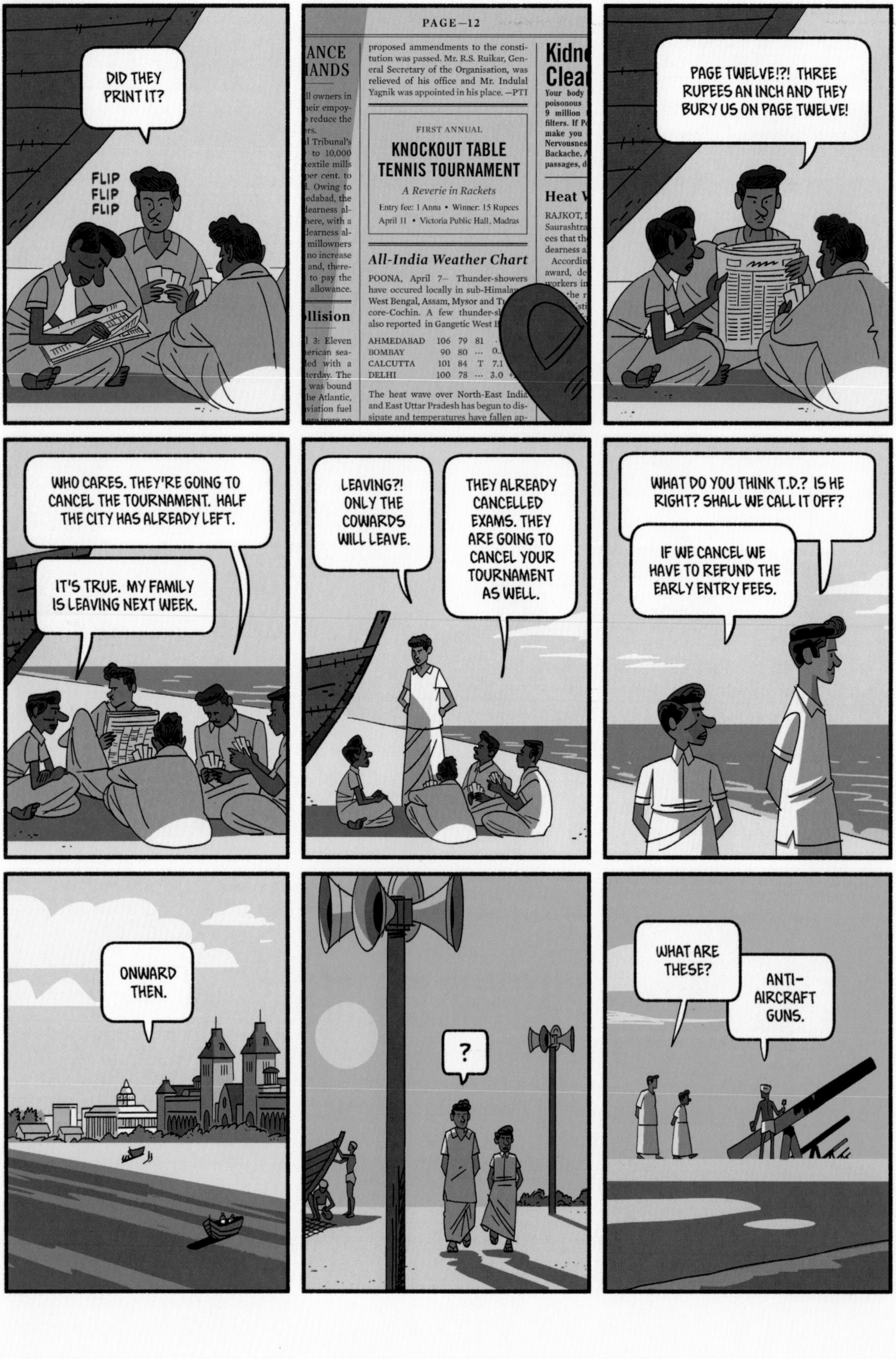
DID THEY PRINT IT?
FLIP FLIP FLIP
PAGE—12
proposed ammendments to the constitution was passed. Mr. R.S. Ruikar, General Secretary of the Organisation, was relieved of his office and Mr. Indulal Yagnik was appointed in his place. —PTI
FIRST ANNUAL
KNOCKOUT TABLE TENNIS TOURNAMENT
A Reverie in Rackets
Entry fee: 1 Anna • Winner: 15 Rupees
April 11 • Victoria Public Hall, Madras
All-India Weather Chart
The heat wave over North-East India and East Uttar Pradesh has begun to dissipate and temperatures have fallen ap-
PAGE TWELVE!?! THREE RUPEES AN INCH AND THEY BURY US ON PAGE TWELVE!
WHO CARES. THEY'RE GOING TO CANCEL THE TOURNAMENT. HALF THE CITY HAS ALREADY LEFT.
IT'S TRUE. MY FAMILY IS LEAVING NEXT WEEK.
LEAVING?! ONLY THE COWARDS WILL LEAVE.
THEY ALREADY CANCELLED EXAMS. THEY ARE GOING TO CANCEL YOUR TOURNAMENT AS WELL.
WHAT DO YOU THINK T.D.? IS HE RIGHT? SHALL WE CALL IT OFF?
IF WE CANCEL WE HAVE TO REFUND THE EARLY ENTRY FEES.
ONWARD THEN.
?
WHAT ARE THESE?
ANTI-AIRCRAFT GUNS.

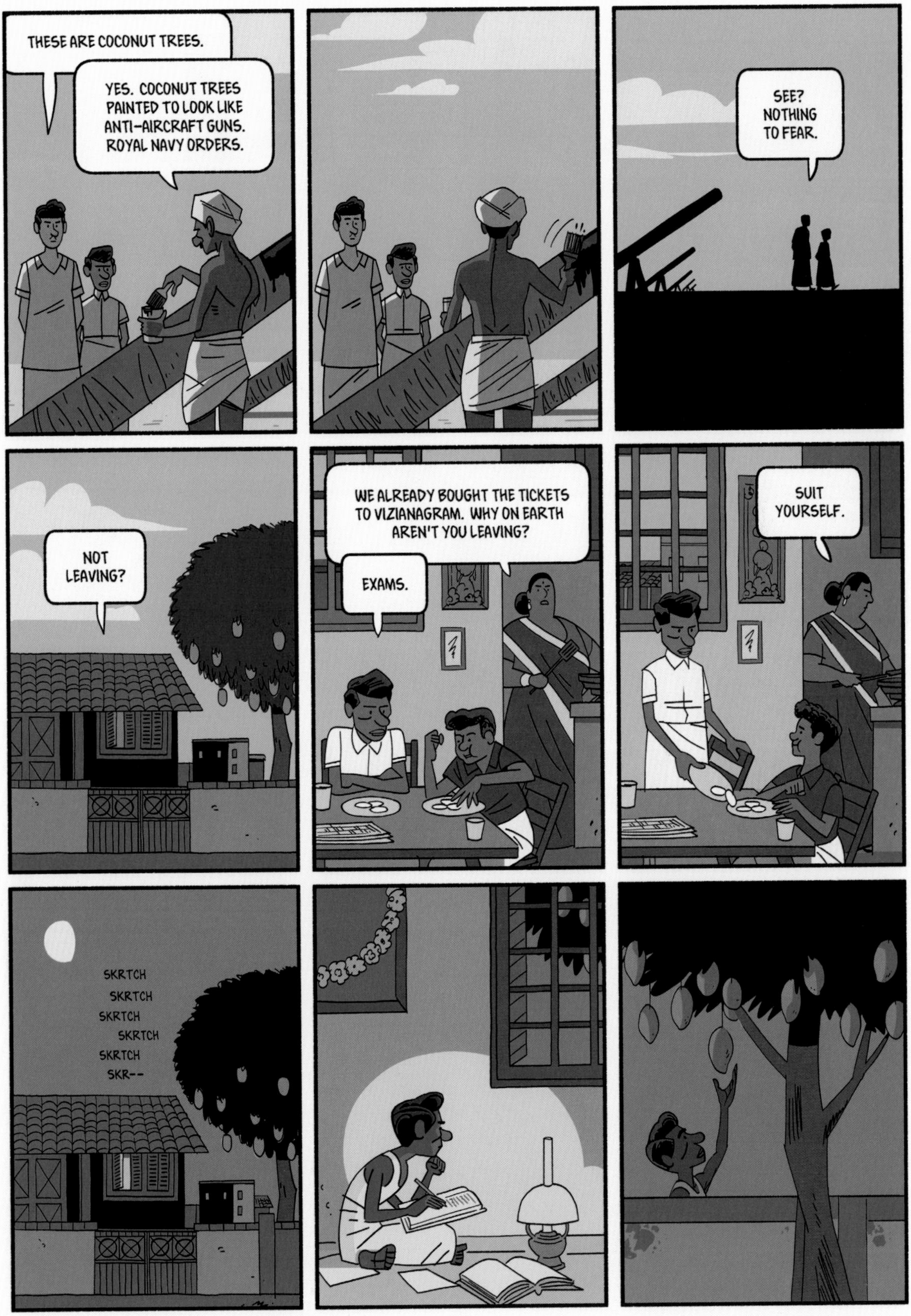
THESE ARE COCONUT TREES.
YES. COCONUT TREES PAINTED TO LOOK LIKE ANTI-AIRCRAFT GUNS. ROYAL NAVY ORDERS.
SEE? NOTHING TO FEAR.
NOT LEAVING?
WE ALREADY BOUGHT THE TICKETS TO VIZIANAGRAM. WHY ON EARTH AREN'T YOU LEAVING?
EXAMS.
SUIT YOURSELF.
SKRTCH
SKRTCH
SKRTCH
SKRTCH
SKRTCH
SKR--

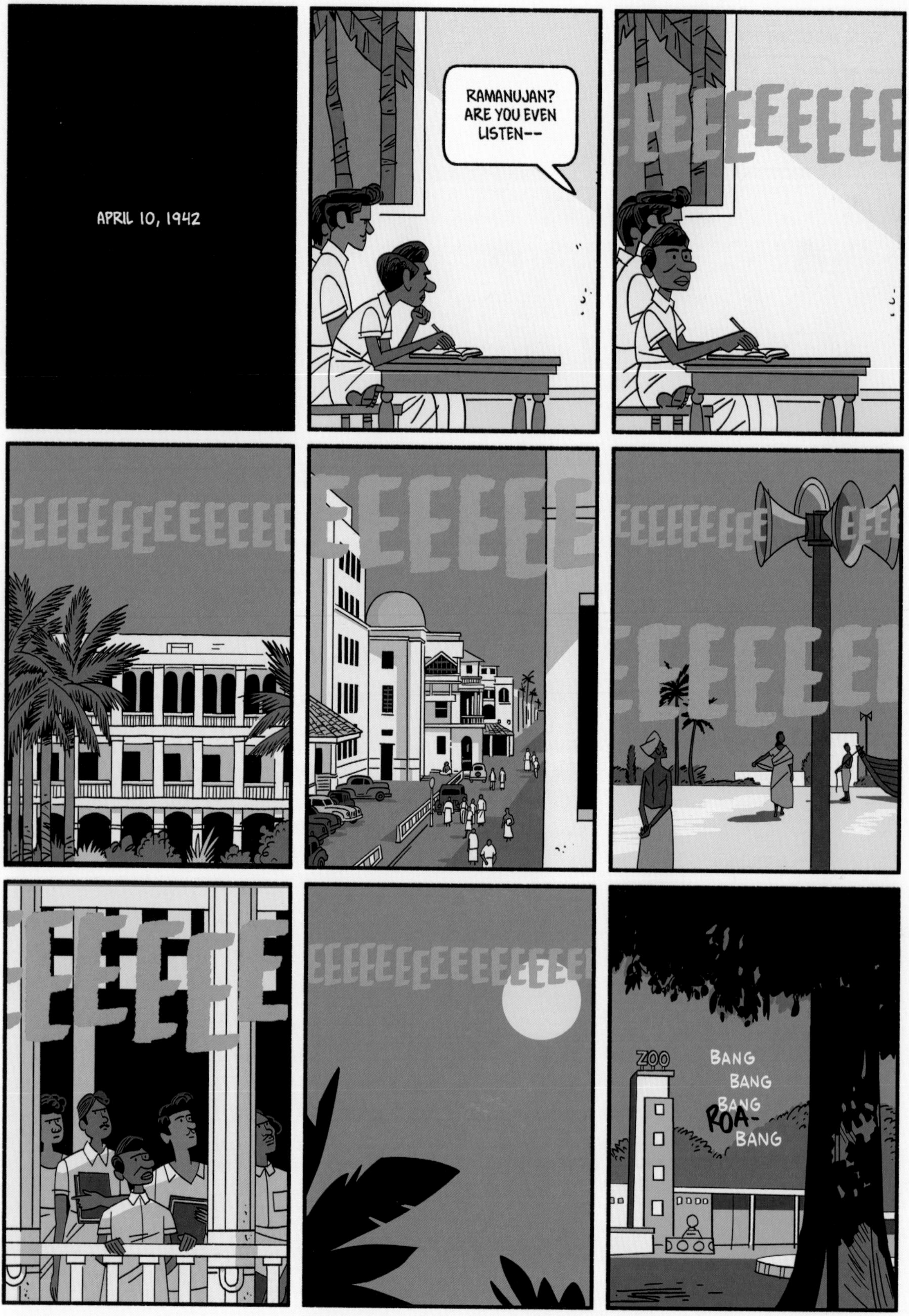
APRIL 10, 1942
RAMANUJAN? ARE YOU EVEN LISTEN--
EEEEEEEEE
EEEEEEEEEEEEE
EEEEE
EEEEEEEEE
EEEEEE
EEEEEE
EEEEEEEEEEEEEEE
ZOO
BANG
BANG
BANG
ROA-
BANG

APRIL 11, 1942

THIS IS BARBARISM.

NO, THIS IS A CITY MANDATE. ALL NON-ESSENTIAL ACTIVITY HAS BEEN CANCELLED.

CLICK

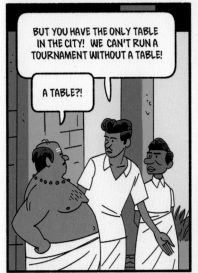

BUT YOU HAVE THE ONLY TABLE IN THE CITY! WE CAN'T RUN A TOURNAMENT WITHOUT A TABLE!

A TABLE?!

MADRAS MAY BE UNDER ATTACK AND YOU BOYS ARE CRYING OVER A TABLE! WHY, IF THE FUTURE OF THE NATION RELIES ON THE LIKES OF YOU TWO, GOD HELP US ALL.

AND YET, I SEE YOU HAVE FAILED TO CANCEL THE CRICKET MATCH?

CRICKET, IS AN ESSENTIAL ACTIVITY!

TABLE TENNIS IS ESSENTIAL!

TABLE TENNIS IS THE DEFINITION OF NON-ESSENTIAL!

REVERIE IS THE FIRST CASUALTY OF WAR, T.D.

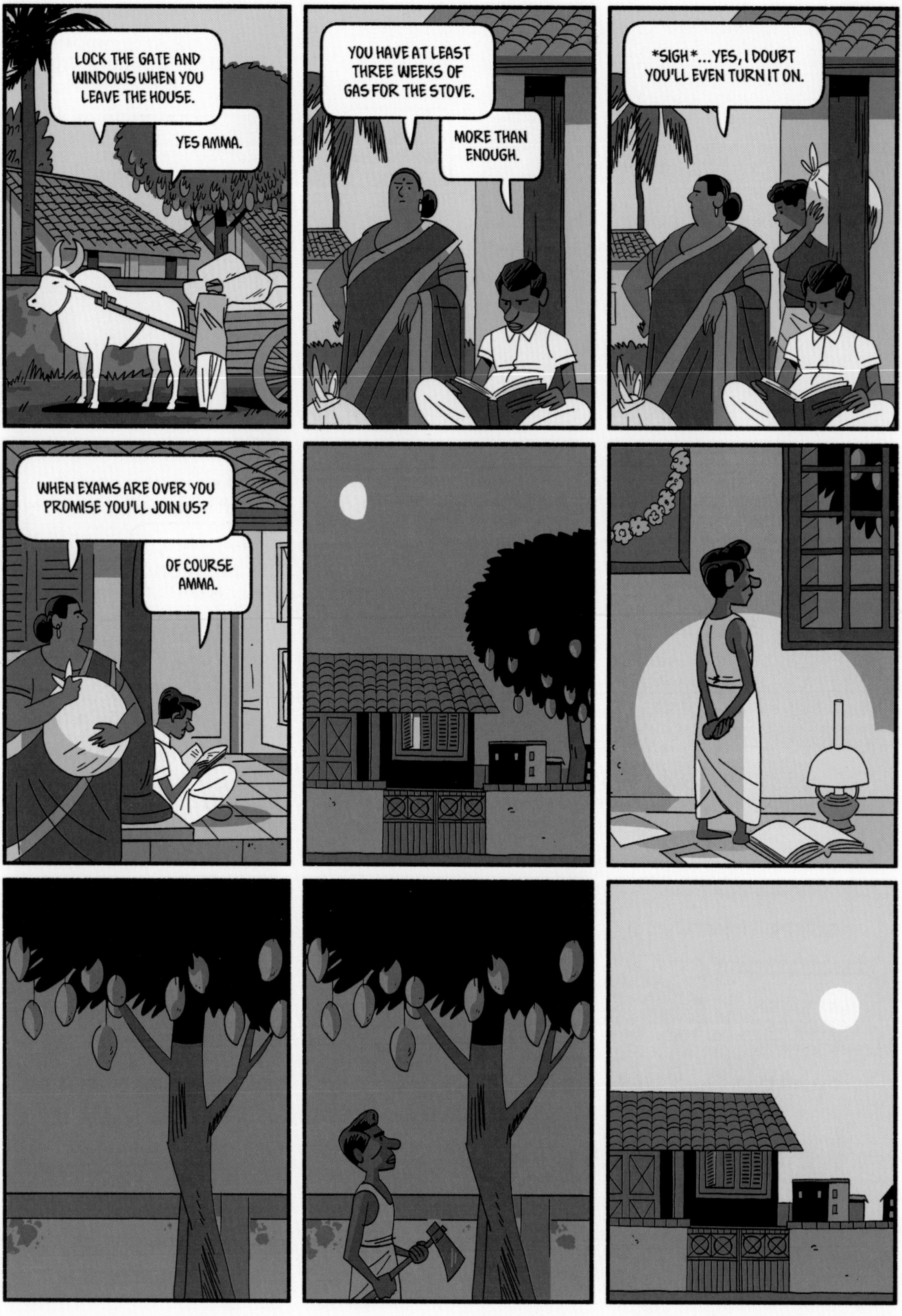
LOCK THE GATE AND WINDOWS WHEN YOU LEAVE THE HOUSE.
YES AMMA.
YOU HAVE AT LEAST THREE WEEKS OF GAS FOR THE STOVE.
MORE THAN ENOUGH.
SIGH... YES, I DOUBT YOU'LL EVEN TURN IT ON.
WHEN EXAMS ARE OVER YOU PROMISE YOU'LL JOIN US?
OF COURSE AMMA.

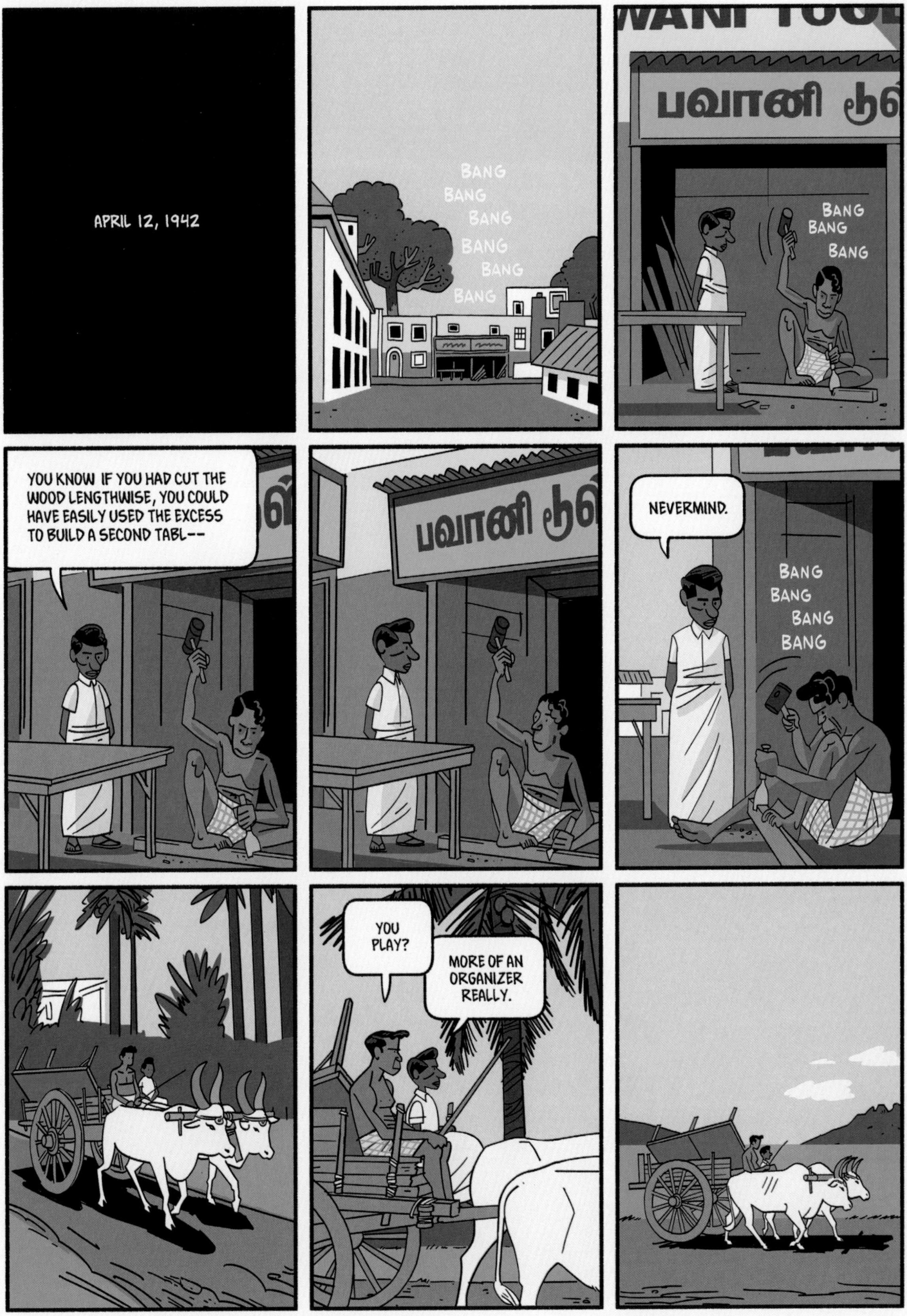
APRIL 12, 1942
BANG BANG BANG BANG BANG BANG
பவானி
BANG BANG BANG
YOU KNOW IF YOU HAD CUT THE WOOD LENGTHWISE, YOU COULD HAVE EASILY USED THE EXCESS TO BUILD A SECOND TABL--
பவானி
NEVERMIND.
BANG BANG BANG BANG
YOU PLAY?
MORE OF AN ORGANIZER REALLY.

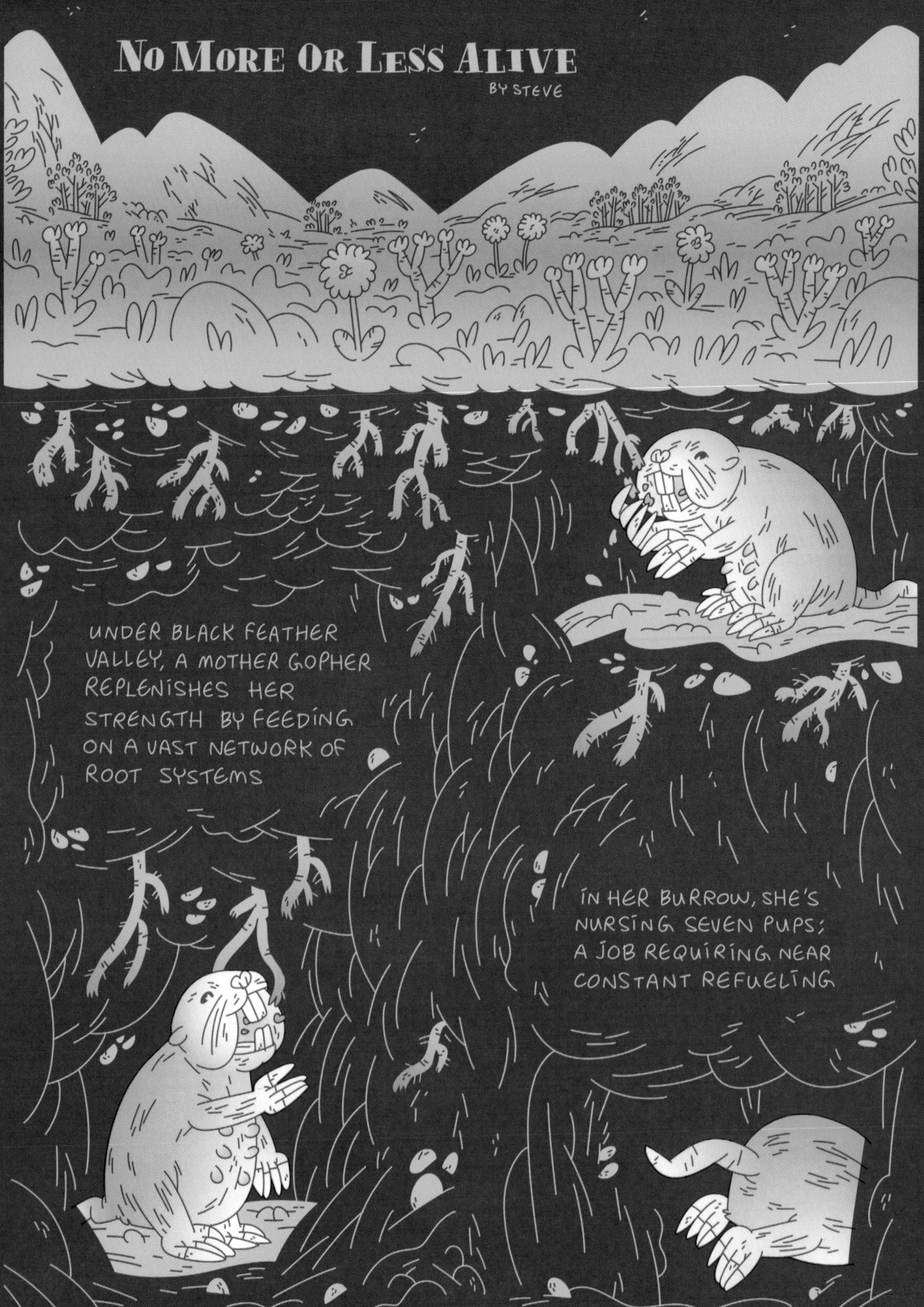

NO MORE OR LESS ALIVE
BY STEVE
UNDER BLACK FEATHER VALLEY, A MOTHER GOPHER REPLENISHES HER STRENGTH BY FEEDING ON A VAST NETWORK OF ROOT SYSTEMS
IN HER BURROW, SHE'S NURSING SEVEN PUPS; A JOB REQUIRING NEAR CONSTANT REFUELING
IT ALSO REQUIRES VIGILANCE; SHE'S STRAYED AS FAR AND FOR AS LONG AS SAFETY ALLOWS

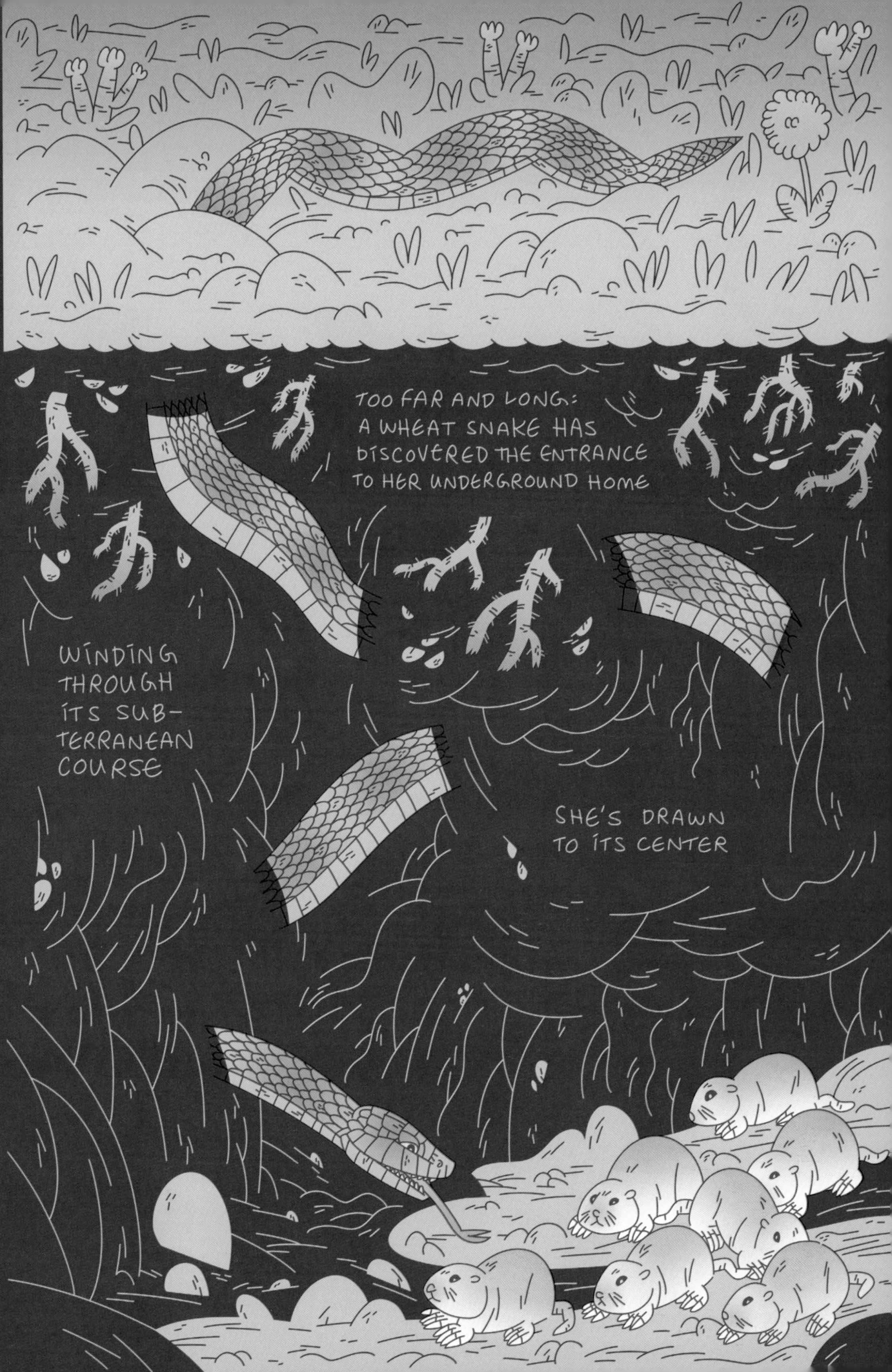
TOO FAR AND LONG: A WHEAT SNAKE HAS DISCOVERED THE ENTRANCE TO HER UNDERGROUND HOME
WINDING THROUGH ITS SUB-TERRANEAN COURSE
SHE'S DRAWN TO ITS CENTER

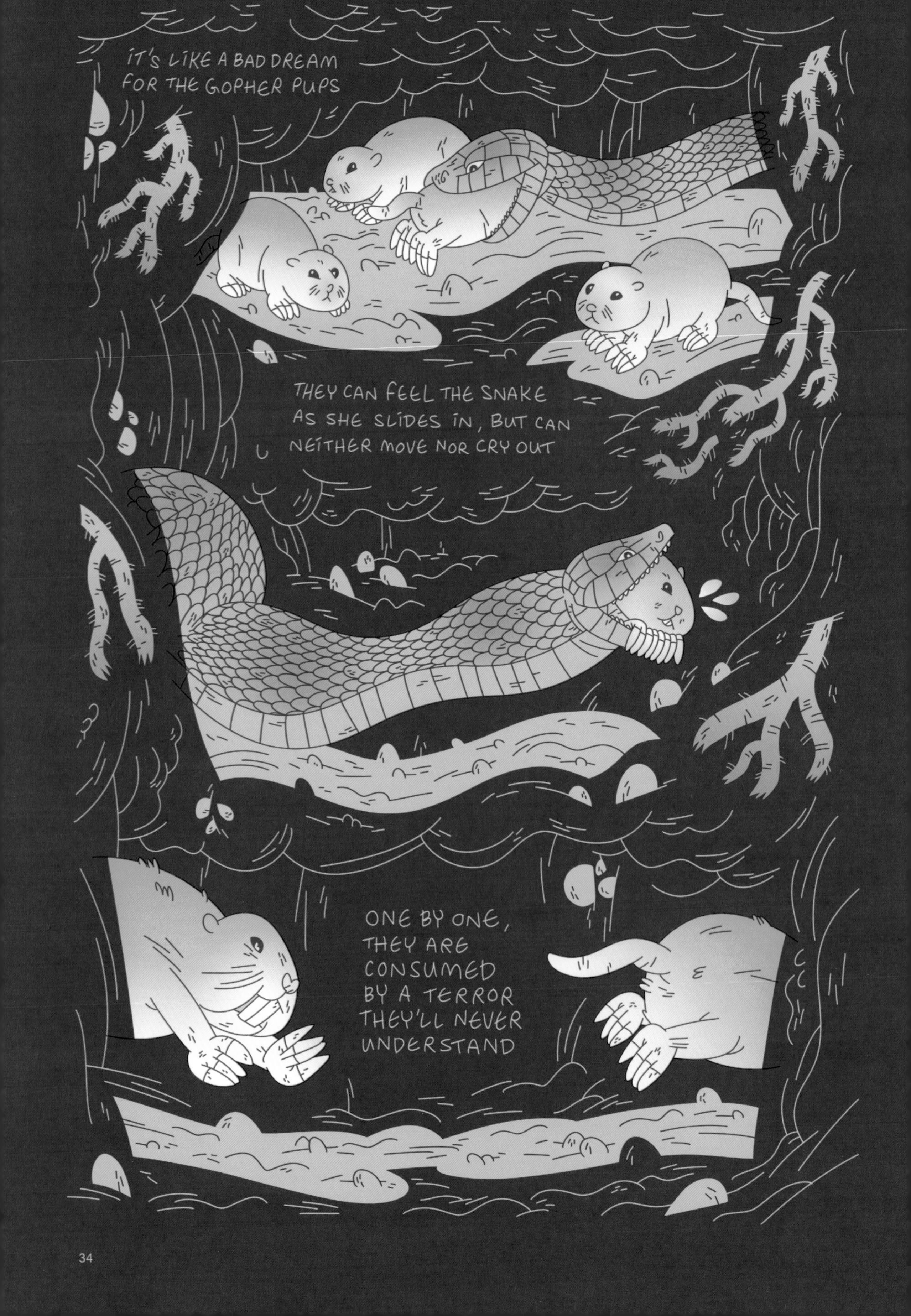
IT'S LIKE A BAD DREAM FOR THE GOPHER PUPS
THEY CAN FEEL THE SNAKE AS SHE SLIDES IN, BUT CAN NEITHER MOVE NOR CRY OUT
ONE BY ONE, THEY ARE CONSUMED BY A TERROR THEY'LL NEVER UNDERSTAND

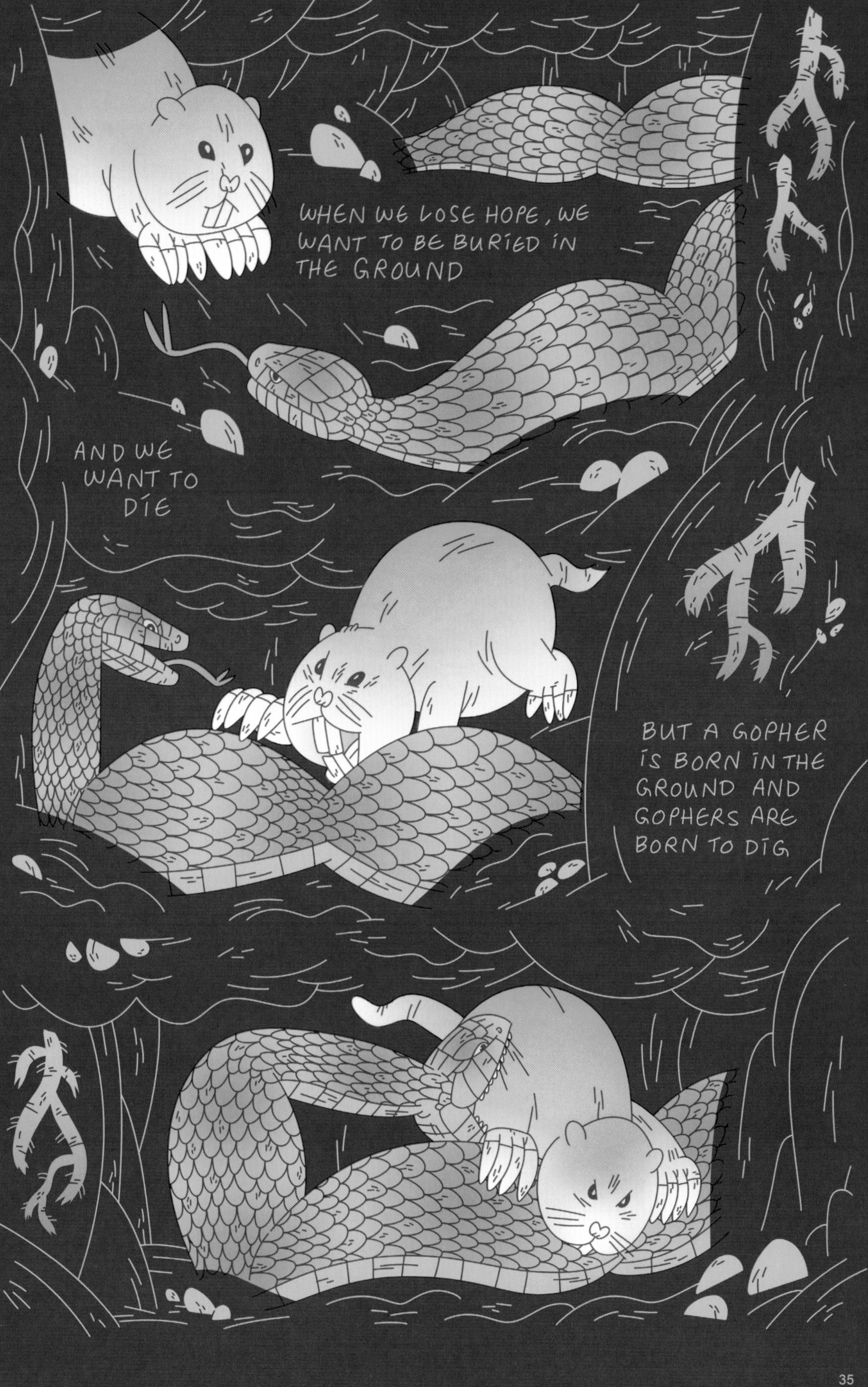
WHEN WE LOSE HOPE, WE WANT TO BE BURIED IN THE GROUND
AND WE WANT TO DIE
BUT A GOPHER IS BORN IN THE GROUND AND GOPHERS ARE BORN TO DIG

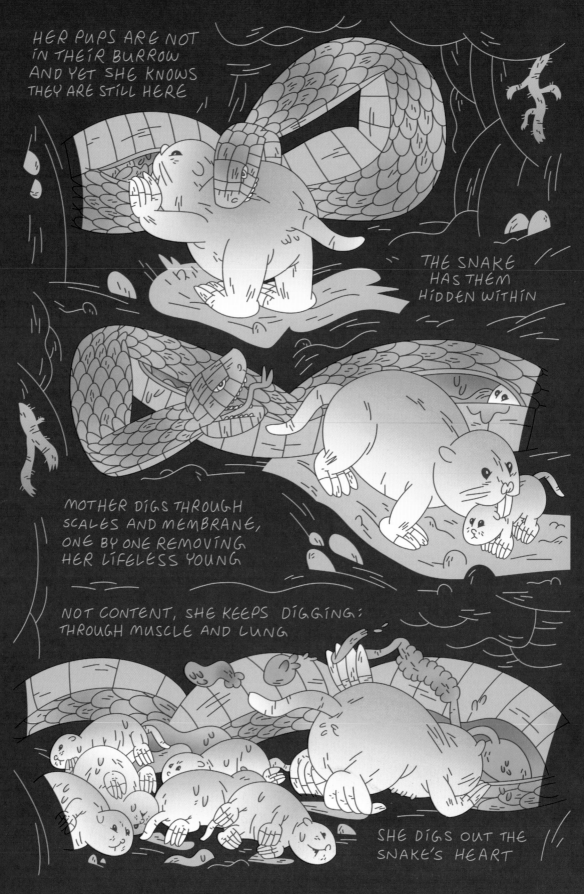

HER PUPS ARE NOT
IN THEIR BURROW
AND YET SHE KNOWS
THEY ARE STILL HERE

THE SNAKE
HAS THEM
HIDDEN WITHIN

MOTHER DIGS THROUGH
SCALES AND MEMBRANE,
ONE BY ONE REMOVING
HER LIFELESS YOUNG

NOT CONTENT, SHE KEEPS DIGGING:
THROUGH MUSCLE AND LUNG

SHE DIGS OUT THE
SNAKE'S HEART

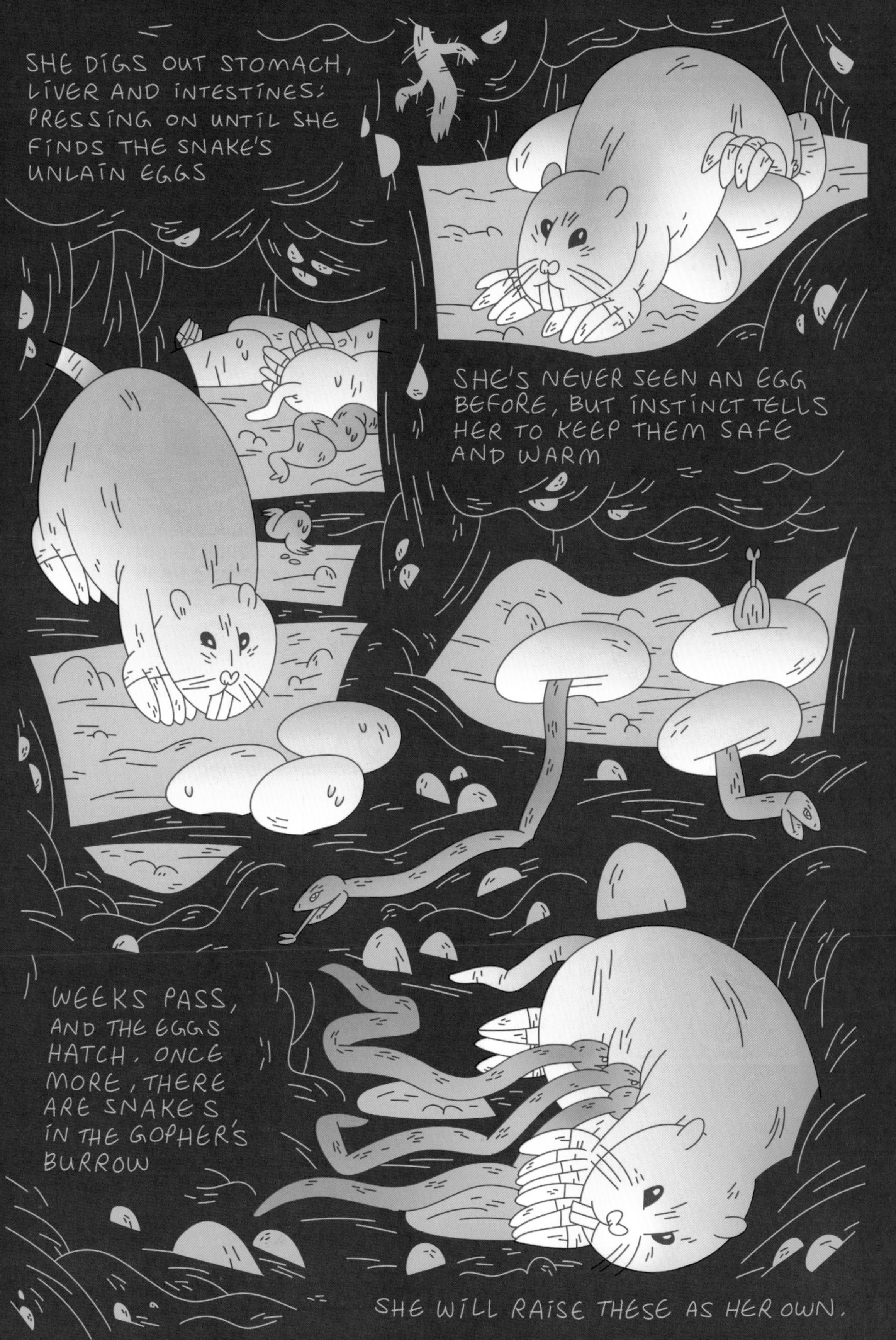
SHE DIGS OUT STOMACH, LIVER AND INTESTINES: PRESSING ON UNTIL SHE FINDS THE SNAKE'S UNLAIN EGGS
SHE'S NEVER SEEN AN EGG BEFORE, BUT INSTINCT TELLS HER TO KEEP THEM SAFE AND WARM
WEEKS PASS, AND THE EGGS HATCH. ONCE MORE, THERE ARE SNAKES IN THE GOPHER'S BURROW
SHE WILL RAISE THESE AS HER OWN.

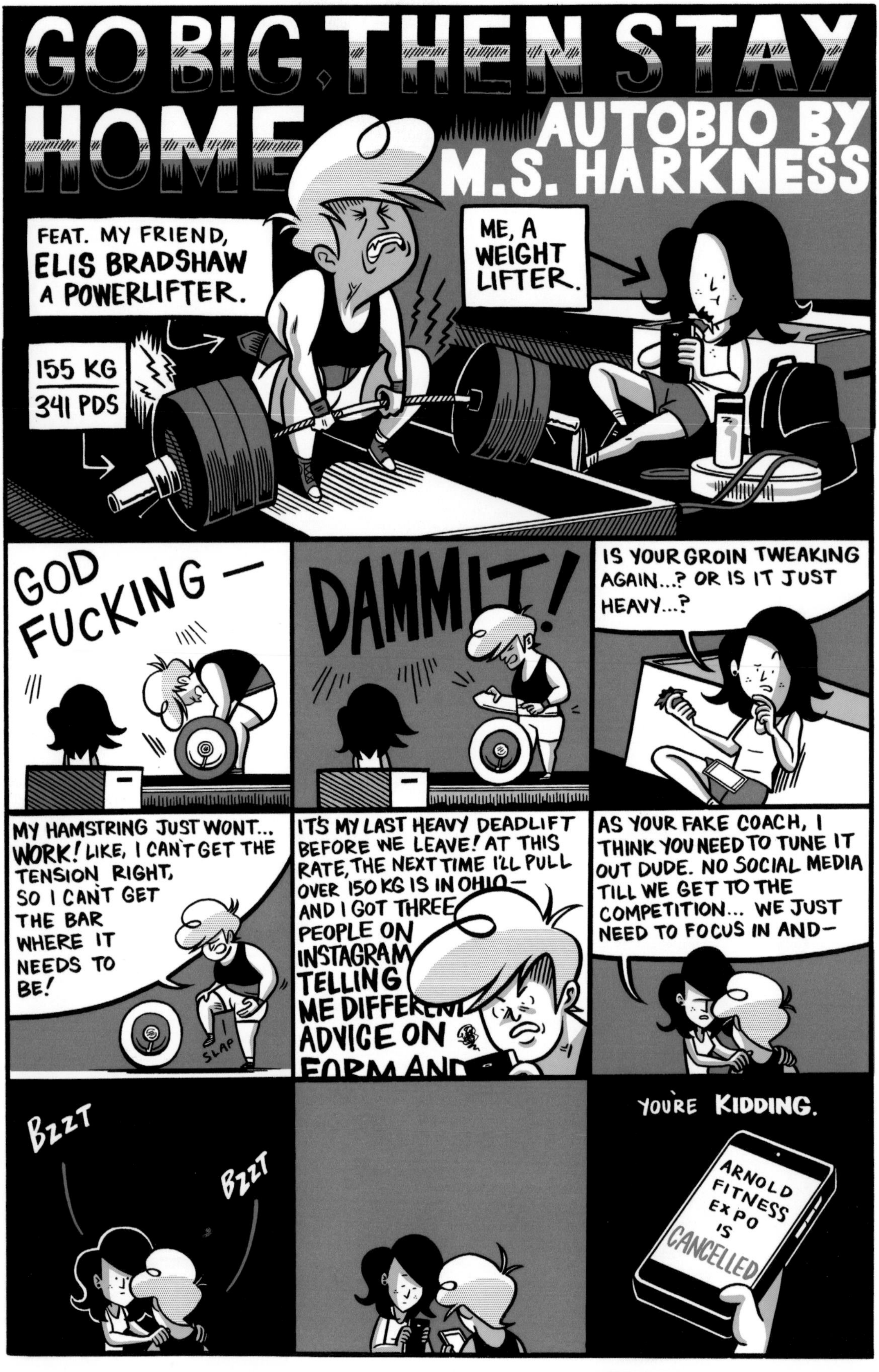
GO BIG, THEN STAY HOME
AUTOBIO BY M.S. HARKNESS
FEAT. MY FRIEND, ELIS BRADSHAW A POWERLIFTER.
155 KG
341 PDS
ME, A WEIGHT LIFTER.
GOD FUCKING—
DAMMIT!
IS YOUR GROIN TWEAKING AGAIN...? OR IS IT JUST HEAVY...?
MY HAMSTRING JUST WONT... WORK! LIKE, I CAN'T GET THE TENSION RIGHT, SO I CAN'T GET THE BAR WHERE IT NEEDS TO BE!
SLAP
IT'S MY LAST HEAVY DEADLIFT BEFORE WE LEAVE! AT THIS RATE, THE NEXT TIME I'LL PULL OVER 150 KG IS IN OHIO— AND I GOT THREE PEOPLE ON INSTAGRAM TELLING ME DIFFERENT ADVICE ON FORM AND
AS YOUR FAKE COACH, I THINK YOU NEED TO TUNE IT OUT DUDE. NO SOCIAL MEDIA TILL WE GET TO THE COMPETITION... WE JUST NEED TO FOCUS IN AND—
BZZT
BZZT
YOU'RE KIDDING.
ARNOLD FITNESS EXPO IS CANCELLED

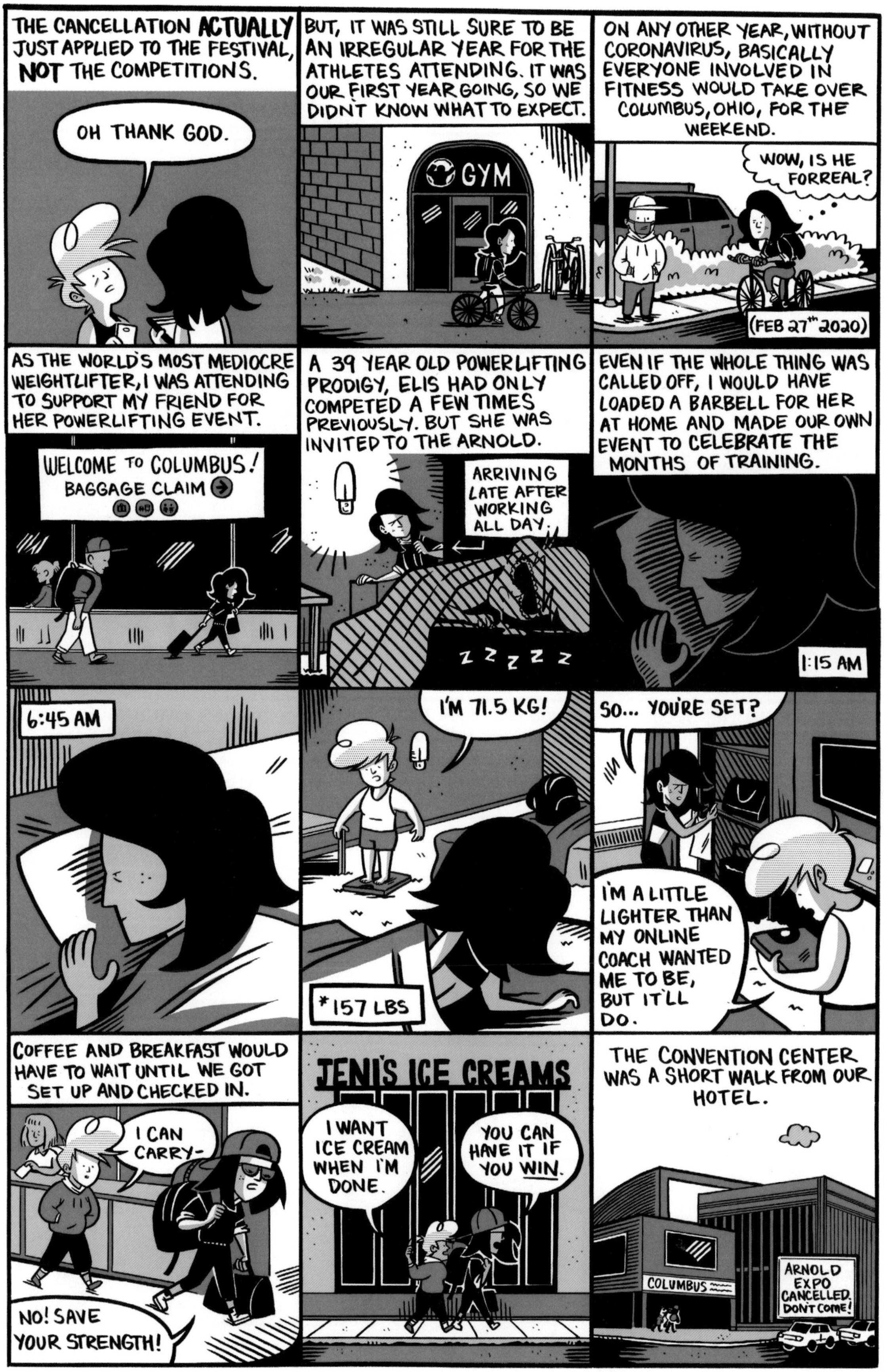
THE CANCELLATION ACTUALLY JUST APPLIED TO THE FESTIVAL, NOT THE COMPETITIONS.
OH THANK GOD.
BUT, IT WAS STILL SURE TO BE AN IRREGULAR YEAR FOR THE ATHLETES ATTENDING. IT WAS OUR FIRST YEAR GOING, SO WE DIDN'T KNOW WHAT TO EXPECT.
GYM
ON ANY OTHER YEAR, WITHOUT CORONAVIRUS, BASICALLY EVERYONE INVOLVED IN FITNESS WOULD TAKE OVER COLUMBUS, OHIO, FOR THE WEEKEND.
WOW, IS HE FORREAL?
(FEB 27th 2020)
AS THE WORLD'S MOST MEDIOCRE WEIGHTLIFTER, I WAS ATTENDING TO SUPPORT MY FRIEND FOR HER POWERLIFTING EVENT.
WELCOME TO COLUMBUS!
BAGGAGE CLAIM
A 39 YEAR OLD POWERLIFTING PRODIGY, ELIS HAD ONLY COMPETED A FEW TIMES PREVIOUSLY. BUT SHE WAS INVITED TO THE ARNOLD.
ARRIVING LATE AFTER WORKING ALL DAY.
Z Z Z Z Z
EVEN IF THE WHOLE THING WAS CALLED OFF, I WOULD HAVE LOADED A BARBELL FOR HER AT HOME AND MADE OUR OWN EVENT TO CELEBRATE THE MONTHS OF TRAINING.
1:15 AM
6:45 AM
I'M 71.5 KG!
*157 LBS
SO... YOU'RE SET?
I'M A LITTLE LIGHTER THAN MY ONLINE COACH WANTED ME TO BE, BUT IT'LL DO.
COFFEE AND BREAKFAST WOULD HAVE TO WAIT UNTIL WE GOT SET UP AND CHECKED IN.
I CAN CARRY-
NO! SAVE YOUR STRENGTH!
JENI'S ICE CREAMS
I WANT ICE CREAM WHEN I'M DONE.
YOU CAN HAVE IT IF YOU WIN.
THE CONVENTION CENTER WAS A SHORT WALK FROM OUR HOTEL.
COLUMBUS
ARNOLD EXPO CANCELLED. DON'T COME!

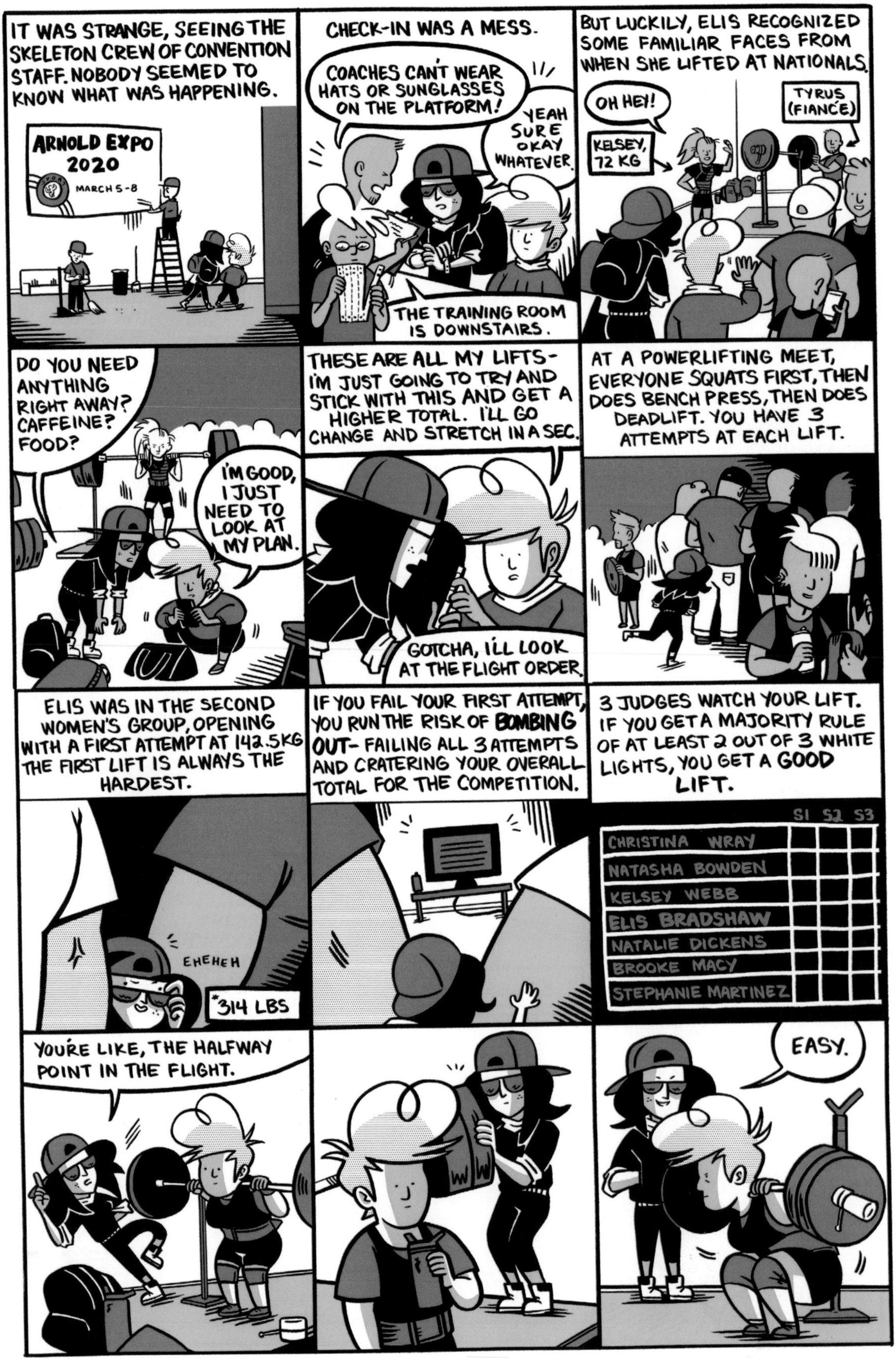
IT WAS STRANGE, SEEING THE SKELETON CREW OF CONVENTION STAFF. NOBODY SEEMED TO KNOW WHAT WAS HAPPENING.
ARNOLD EXPO 2020
MARCH 5-8
CHECK-IN WAS A MESS.
COACHES CAN'T WEAR HATS OR SUNGLASSES ON THE PLATFORM!
YEAH SURE OKAY WHATEVER.
THE TRAINING ROOM IS DOWNSTAIRS.
BUT LUCKILY, ELIS RECOGNIZED SOME FAMILIAR FACES FROM WHEN SHE LIFTED AT NATIONALS.
OH HEY!
TYRUS (FIANCE)
KELSEY, 72 KG
DO YOU NEED ANYTHING RIGHT AWAY? CAFFEINE? FOOD?
I'M GOOD, I JUST NEED TO LOOK AT MY PLAN.
THESE ARE ALL MY LIFTS- I'M JUST GOING TO TRY AND STICK WITH THIS AND GET A HIGHER TOTAL. I'LL GO CHANGE AND STRETCH IN A SEC.
GOTCHA, I'LL LOOK AT THE FLIGHT ORDER.
AT A POWERLIFTING MEET, EVERYONE SQUATS FIRST, THEN DOES BENCH PRESS, THEN DOES DEADLIFT. YOU HAVE 3 ATTEMPTS AT EACH LIFT.
ELIS WAS IN THE SECOND WOMEN'S GROUP, OPENING WITH A FIRST ATTEMPT AT 142.5KG THE FIRST LIFT IS ALWAYS THE HARDEST.
EHEHEH
*314 LBS
IF YOU FAIL YOUR FIRST ATTEMPT, YOU RUN THE RISK OF BOMBING OUT- FAILING ALL 3 ATTEMPTS AND CRATERING YOUR OVERALL TOTAL FOR THE COMPETITION.
3 JUDGES WATCH YOUR LIFT. IF YOU GET A MAJORITY RULE OF AT LEAST 2 OUT OF 3 WHITE LIGHTS, YOU GET A GOOD LIFT.
S1 S2 S3
CHRISTINA WRAY
NATASHA BOWDEN
KELSEY WEBB
ELIS BRADSHAW
NATALIE DICKENS
BROOKE MACY
STEPHANIE MARTINEZ
YOU'RE LIKE, THE HALFWAY POINT IN THE FLIGHT.
EASY.

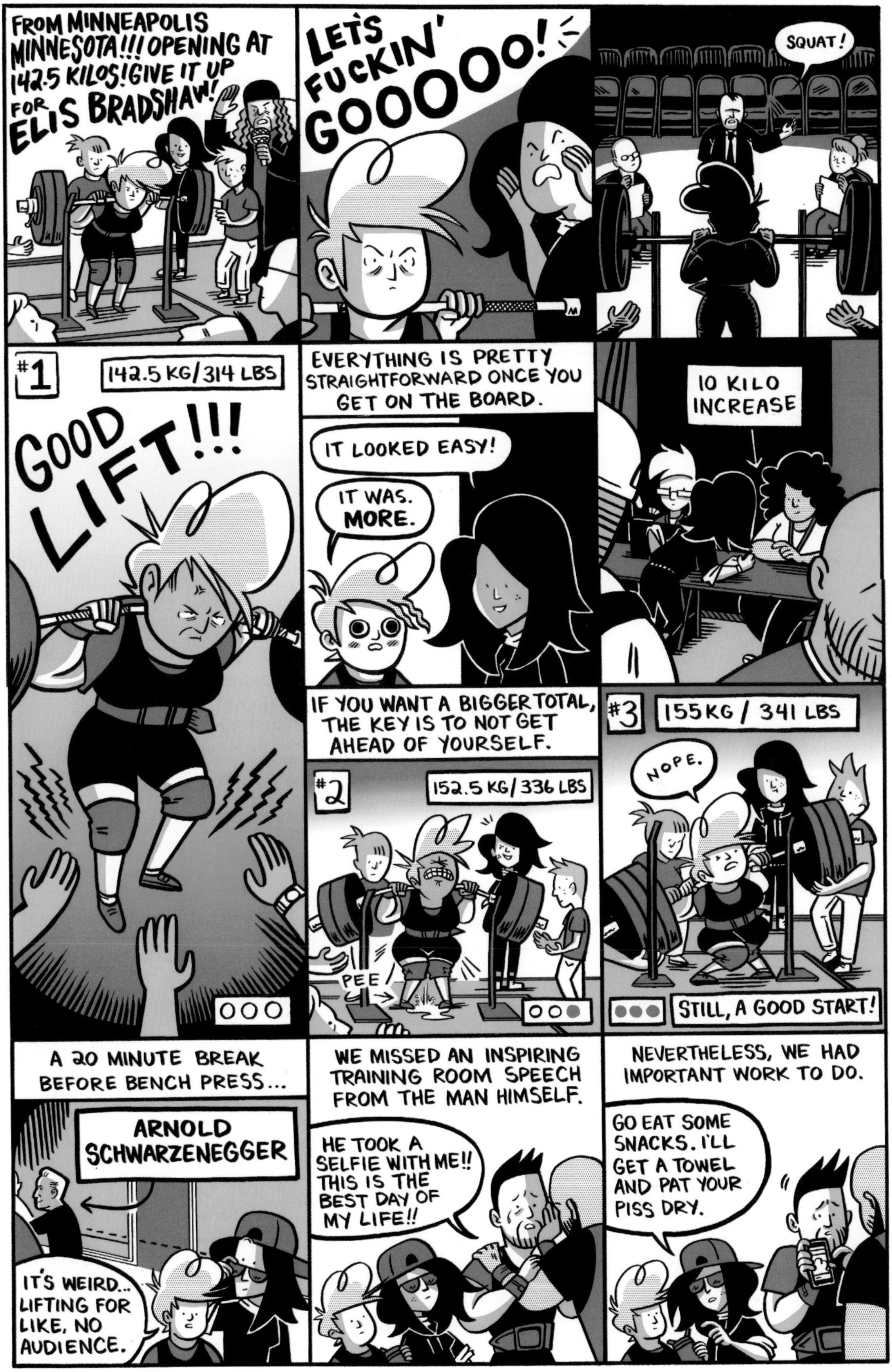
FROM MINNEAPOLIS MINNESOTA!!! OPENING AT 142.5 KILOS! GIVE IT UP FOR ELIS BRADSHAW!
LET'S FUCKIN' GOOOOO!
SQUAT!
#1
142.5 KG/314 LBS
GOOD LIFT!!!
EVERYTHING IS PRETTY STRAIGHTFORWARD ONCE YOU GET ON THE BOARD.
IT LOOKED EASY!
IT WAS. MORE.
10 KILO INCREASE
IF YOU WANT A BIGGER TOTAL, THE KEY IS TO NOT GET AHEAD OF YOURSELF.
#2
152.5 KG/336 LBS
PEE
#3
155 KG / 341 LBS
NOPE.
STILL, A GOOD START!
A 20 MINUTE BREAK BEFORE BENCH PRESS...
ARNOLD SCHWARZENEGGER
IT'S WEIRD... LIFTING FOR LIKE, NO AUDIENCE.
WE MISSED AN INSPIRING TRAINING ROOM SPEECH FROM THE MAN HIMSELF.
HE TOOK A SELFIE WITH ME!! THIS IS THE BEST DAY OF MY LIFE!!
NEVERTHELESS, WE HAD IMPORTANT WORK TO DO.
GO EAT SOME SNACKS. I'LL GET A TOWEL AND PAT YOUR PISS DRY.

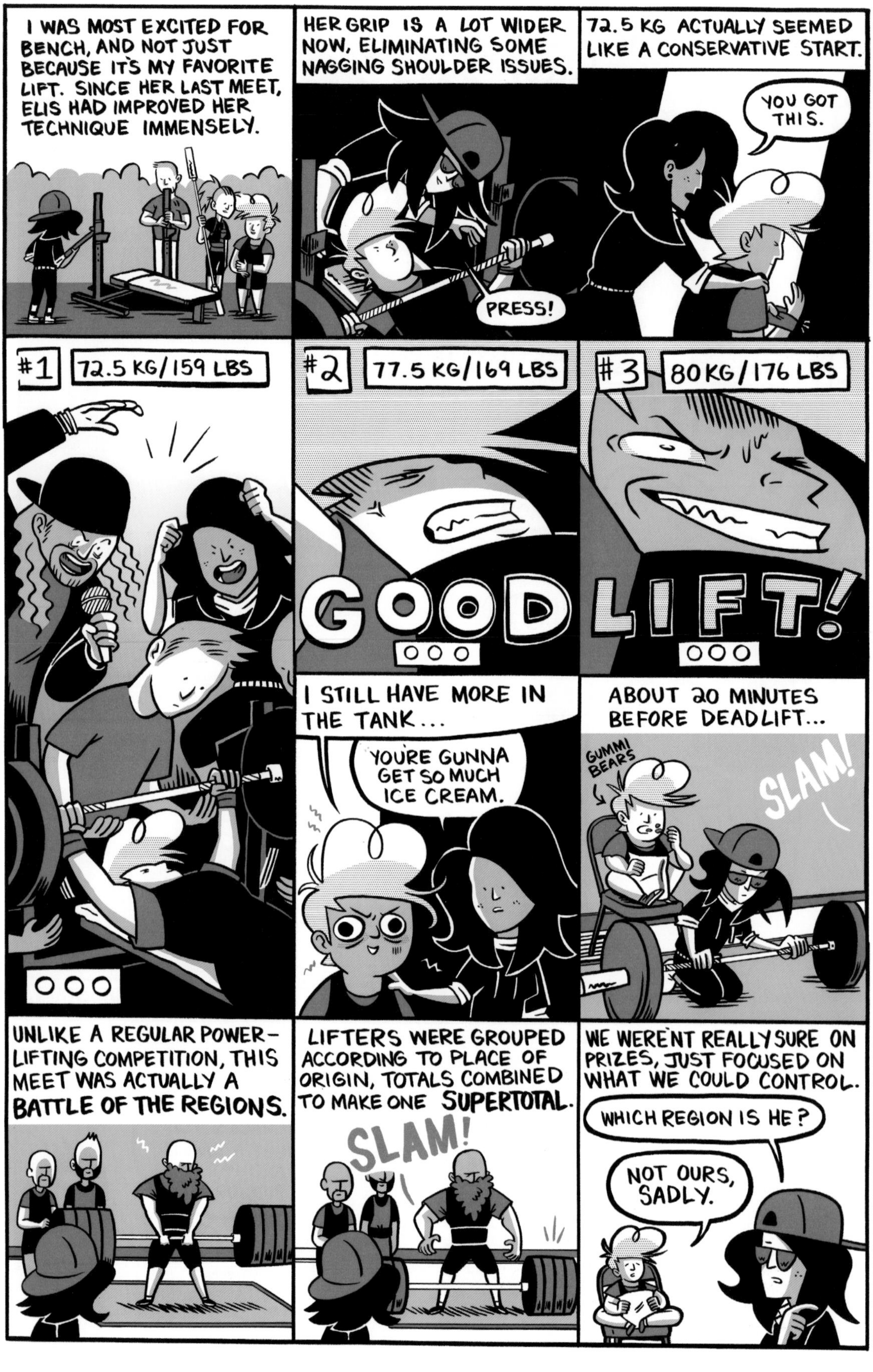

I WAS MOST EXCITED FOR BENCH, AND NOT JUST BECAUSE IT'S MY FAVORITE LIFT. SINCE HER LAST MEET, ELIS HAD IMPROVED HER TECHNIQUE IMMENSELY.
HER GRIP IS A LOT WIDER NOW, ELIMINATING SOME NAGGING SHOULDER ISSUES.
PRESS!
72.5 KG ACTUALLY SEEMED LIKE A CONSERVATIVE START.
YOU GOT THIS.
#1
72.5 KG/159 LBS
#2
77.5 KG/169 LBS
#3
80 KG/176 LBS
GOOD LIFT!
I STILL HAVE MORE IN THE TANK...
YOU'RE GUNNA GET SO MUCH ICE CREAM.
ABOUT 20 MINUTES BEFORE DEADLIFT...
GUMMI BEARS
SLAM!
UNLIKE A REGULAR POWER-LIFTING COMPETITION, THIS MEET WAS ACTUALLY A BATTLE OF THE REGIONS.
LIFTERS WERE GROUPED ACCORDING TO PLACE OF ORIGIN, TOTALS COMBINED TO MAKE ONE SUPERTOTAL.
SLAM!
WE WEREN'T REALLY SURE ON PRIZES, JUST FOCUSED ON WHAT WE COULD CONTROL.
WHICH REGION IS HE?
NOT OURS, SADLY.

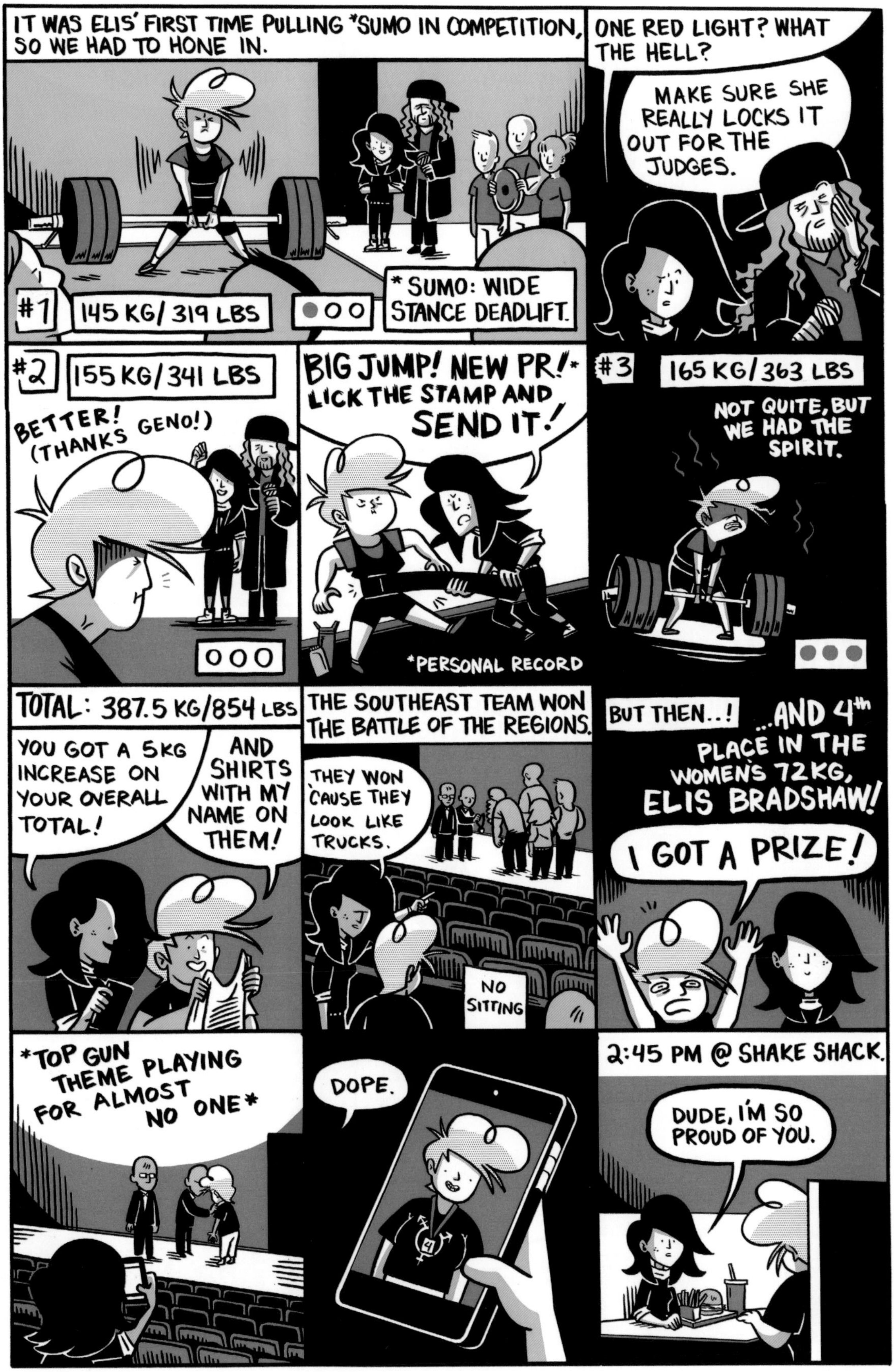
IT WAS ELIS' FIRST TIME PULLING *SUMO IN COMPETITION, SO WE HAD TO HONE IN.
#1
145 KG/ 319 LBS
*SUMO: WIDE STANCE DEADLIFT.
ONE RED LIGHT? WHAT THE HELL?
MAKE SURE SHE REALLY LOCKS IT OUT FOR THE JUDGES.
#2
155 KG/ 341 LBS
BETTER! (THANKS GENO!)
BIG JUMP! NEW PR!* LICK THE STAMP AND SEND IT!
*PERSONAL RECORD
#3
165 KG/ 363 LBS
NOT QUITE, BUT WE HAD THE SPIRIT.
TOTAL: 387.5 KG/854 LBS
YOU GOT A 5KG INCREASE ON YOUR OVERALL TOTAL!
AND SHIRTS WITH MY NAME ON THEM!
THE SOUTHEAST TEAM WON THE BATTLE OF THE REGIONS.
THEY WON 'CAUSE THEY LOOK LIKE TRUCKS.
NO SITTING
BUT THEN..!
...AND 4th PLACE IN THE WOMEN'S 72 KG, ELIS BRADSHAW!
I GOT A PRIZE!
TOP GUN THEME PLAYING FOR ALMOST NO ONE
DOPE.
2:45 PM @ SHAKE SHACK.
DUDE, I'M SO PROUD OF YOU.

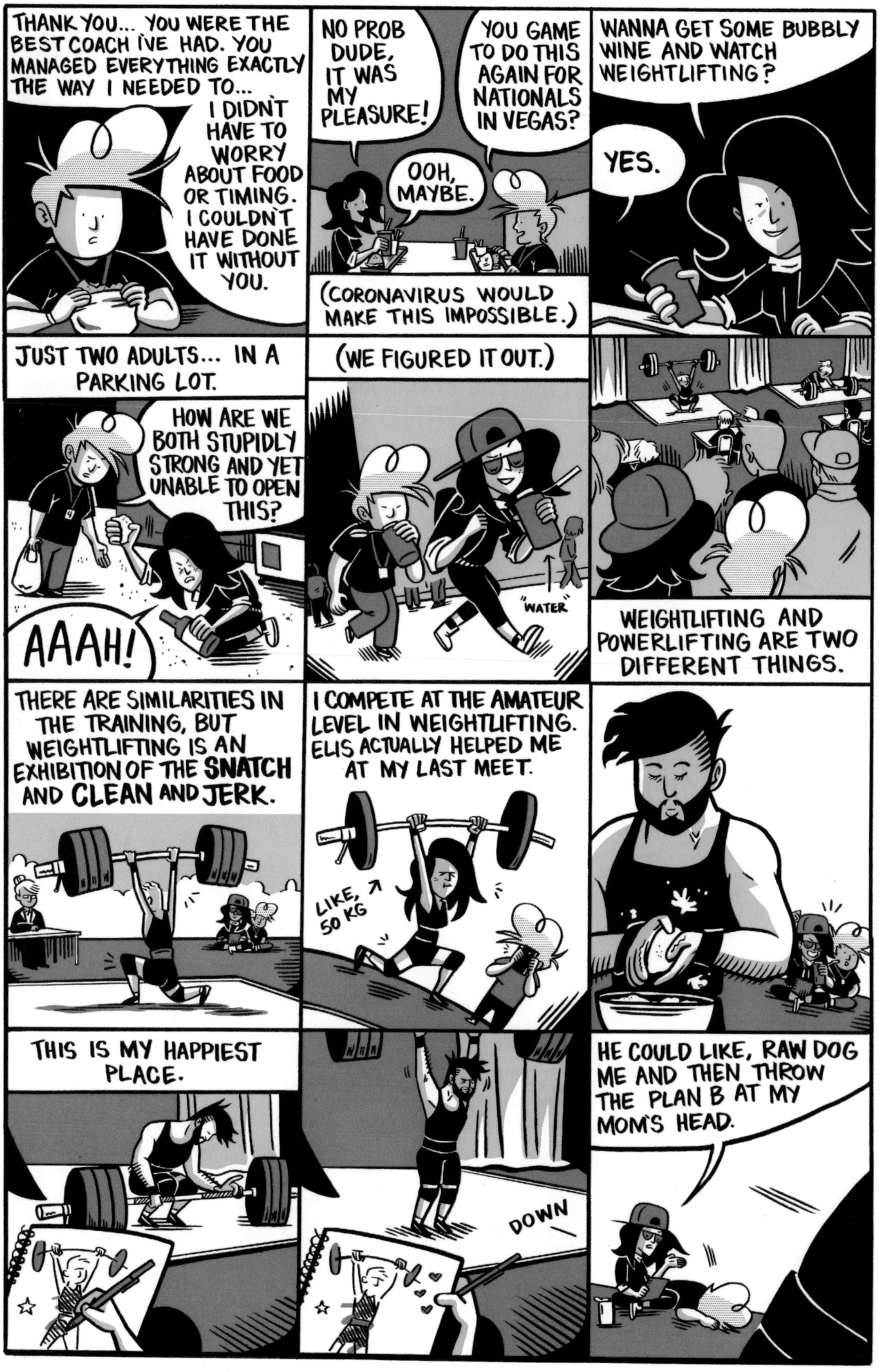
THANK YOU... YOU WERE THE BEST COACH I'VE HAD. YOU MANAGED EVERYTHING EXACTLY THE WAY I NEEDED TO...
I DIDN'T HAVE TO WORRY ABOUT FOOD OR TIMING. I COULDN'T HAVE DONE IT WITHOUT YOU.
NO PROB DUDE, IT WAS MY PLEASURE!
YOU GAME TO DO THIS AGAIN FOR NATIONALS IN VEGAS?
OOH, MAYBE.
(CORONAVIRUS WOULD MAKE THIS IMPOSSIBLE.)
WANNA GET SOME BUBBLY WINE AND WATCH WEIGHTLIFTING?
YES.
JUST TWO ADULTS... IN A PARKING LOT.
HOW ARE WE BOTH STUPIDLY STRONG AND YET UNABLE TO OPEN THIS?
AAAH!
(WE FIGURED IT OUT.)
"WATER"
WEIGHTLIFTING AND POWERLIFTING ARE TWO DIFFERENT THINGS.
THERE ARE SIMILARITIES IN THE TRAINING, BUT WEIGHTLIFTING IS AN EXHIBITION OF THE **SNATCH** AND **CLEAN** AND **JERK**.
I COMPETE AT THE AMATEUR LEVEL IN WEIGHTLIFTING. ELIS ACTUALLY HELPED ME AT MY LAST MEET.
LIKE, 50 KG
THIS IS MY HAPPIEST PLACE.
DOWN
HE COULD LIKE, RAW DOG ME AND THEN THROW THE PLAN B AT MY MOM'S HEAD.

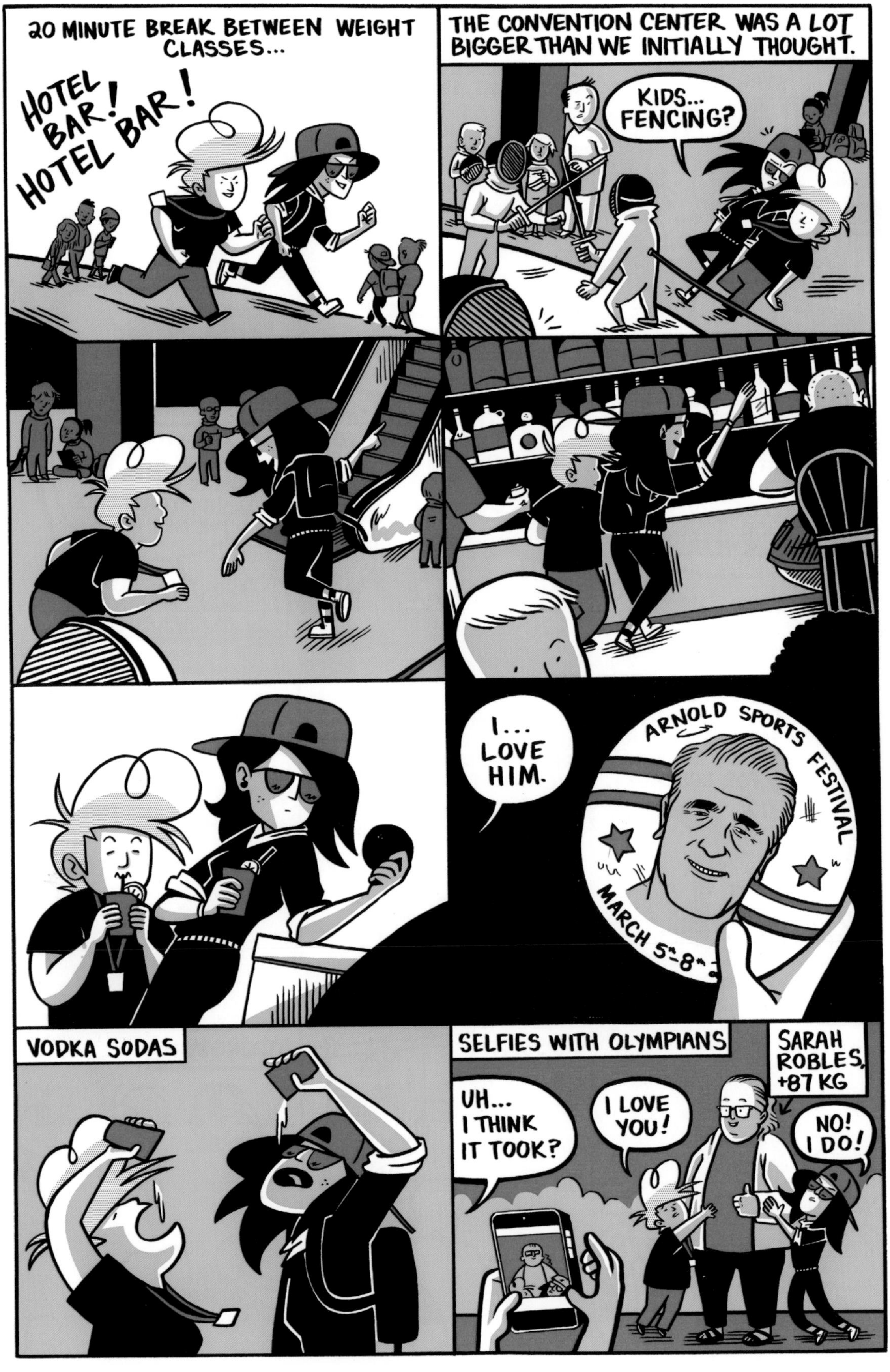

20 MINUTE BREAK BETWEEN WEIGHT CLASSES...
HOTEL BAR! HOTEL BAR!
THE CONVENTION CENTER WAS A LOT BIGGER THAN WE INITIALLY THOUGHT.
KIDS... FENCING?
I... LOVE HIM.
ARNOLD SPORTS FESTIVAL
MARCH 5th-8th
VODKA SODAS
SELFIES WITH OLYMPIANS
SARAH ROBLES, +87 KG
UH... I THINK IT TOOK?
I LOVE YOU!
NO! I DO!

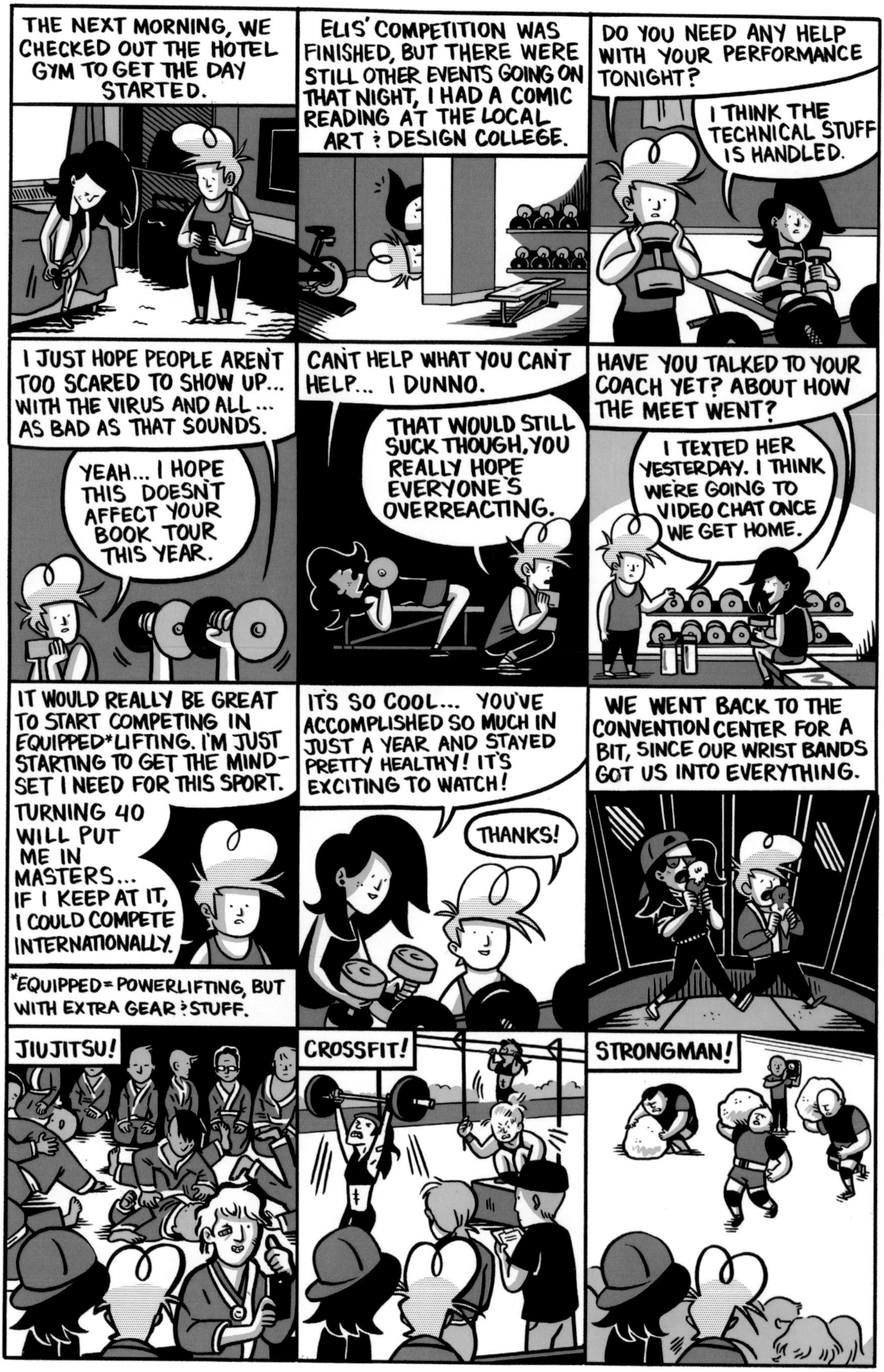
THE NEXT MORNING, WE CHECKED OUT THE HOTEL GYM TO GET THE DAY STARTED.
ELIS' COMPETITION WAS FINISHED, BUT THERE WERE STILL OTHER EVENTS GOING ON THAT NIGHT, I HAD A COMIC READING AT THE LOCAL ART & DESIGN COLLEGE.
DO YOU NEED ANY HELP WITH YOUR PERFORMANCE TONIGHT?
I THINK THE TECHNICAL STUFF IS HANDLED.
I JUST HOPE PEOPLE AREN'T TOO SCARED TO SHOW UP... WITH THE VIRUS AND ALL... AS BAD AS THAT SOUNDS.
YEAH... I HOPE THIS DOESN'T AFFECT YOUR BOOK TOUR THIS YEAR.
CAN'T HELP WHAT YOU CAN'T HELP... I DUNNO.
THAT WOULD STILL SUCK THOUGH, YOU REALLY HOPE EVERYONE'S OVERREACTING.
HAVE YOU TALKED TO YOUR COACH YET? ABOUT HOW THE MEET WENT?
I TEXTED HER YESTERDAY. I THINK WE'RE GOING TO VIDEO CHAT ONCE WE GET HOME.
IT WOULD REALLY BE GREAT TO START COMPETING IN EQUIPPED*LIFTING. I'M JUST STARTING TO GET THE MIND-SET I NEED FOR THIS SPORT.
TURNING 40 WILL PUT ME IN MASTERS... IF I KEEP AT IT, I COULD COMPETE INTERNATIONALLY.
*EQUIPPED = POWERLIFTING, BUT WITH EXTRA GEAR & STUFF.
IT'S SO COOL... YOU'VE ACCOMPLISHED SO MUCH IN JUST A YEAR AND STAYED PRETTY HEALTHY! IT'S EXCITING TO WATCH!
THANKS!
WE WENT BACK TO THE CONVENTION CENTER FOR A BIT, SINCE OUR WRIST BANDS GOT US INTO EVERYTHING.
JIUJITSU!
CROSSFIT!
STRONGMAN!

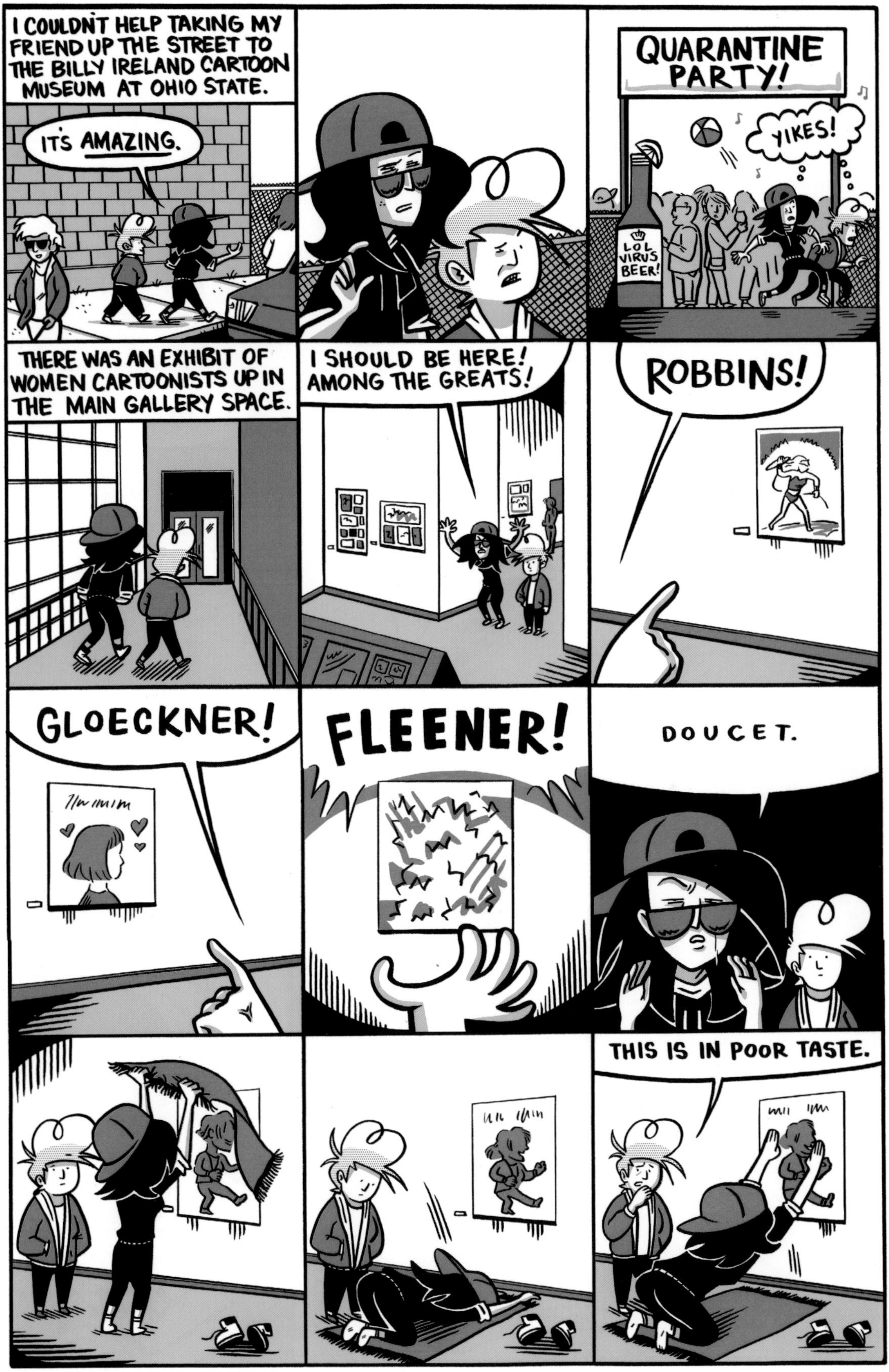
I COULDN'T HELP TAKING MY FRIEND UP THE STREET TO THE BILLY IRELAND CARTOON MUSEUM AT OHIO STATE.
IT'S AMAZING.
QUARANTINE PARTY!
YIKES!
LOL VIRUS BEER!
THERE WAS AN EXHIBIT OF WOMEN CARTOONISTS UP IN THE MAIN GALLERY SPACE.
I SHOULD BE HERE! AMONG THE GREATS!
ROBBINS!
GLOECKNER!
FLEENER!
DOUCET.
THIS IS IN POOR TASTE.

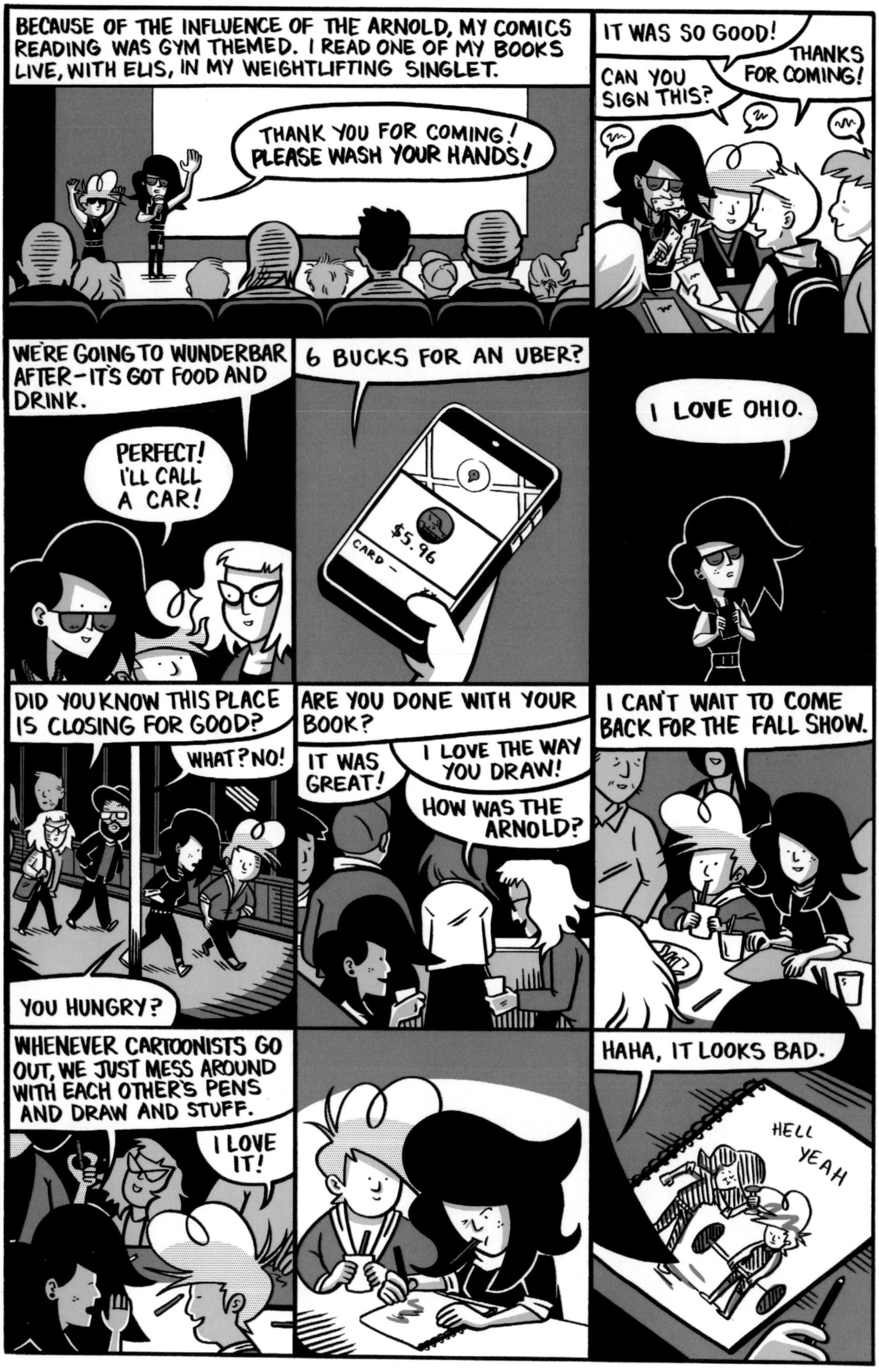
BECAUSE OF THE INFLUENCE OF THE ARNOLD, MY COMICS READING WAS GYM THEMED. I READ ONE OF MY BOOKS LIVE, WITH ELIS, IN MY WEIGHTLIFTING SINGLET.
THANK YOU FOR COMING! PLEASE WASH YOUR HANDS!
IT WAS SO GOOD!
CAN YOU SIGN THIS?
THANKS FOR COMING!
WE'RE GOING TO WUNDERBAR AFTER—IT'S GOT FOOD AND DRINK.
PERFECT! I'LL CALL A CAR!
6 BUCKS FOR AN UBER?
$5.96
CARD —
I LOVE OHIO.
DID YOU KNOW THIS PLACE IS CLOSING FOR GOOD?
WHAT? NO!
YOU HUNGRY?
ARE YOU DONE WITH YOUR BOOK?
IT WAS GREAT!
I LOVE THE WAY YOU DRAW!
HOW WAS THE ARNOLD?
I CAN'T WAIT TO COME BACK FOR THE FALL SHOW.
WHENEVER CARTOONISTS GO OUT, WE JUST MESS AROUND WITH EACH OTHER'S PENS AND DRAW AND STUFF.
I LOVE IT!
HAHA, IT LOOKS BAD.
HELL YEAH

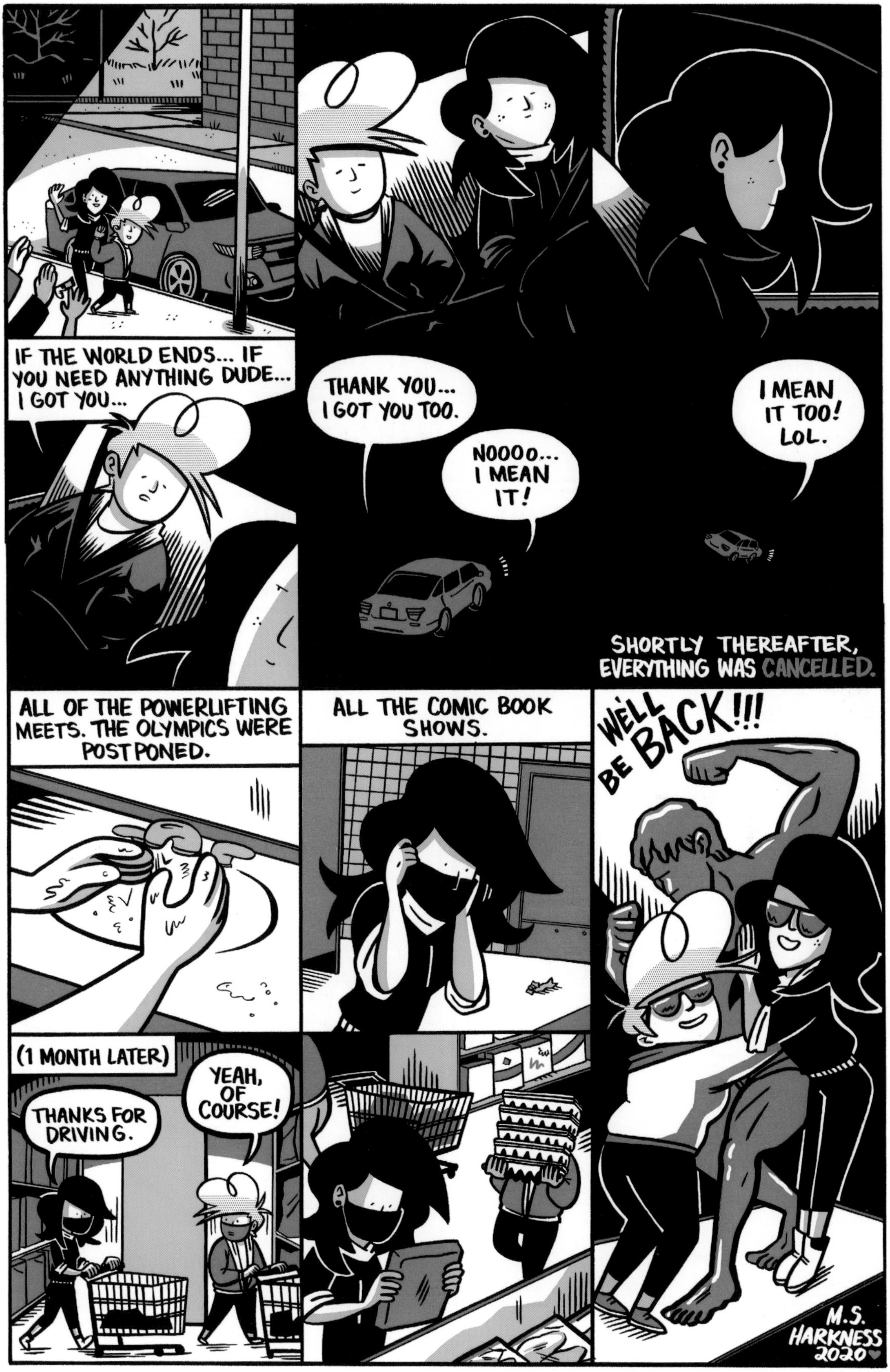
IF THE WORLD ENDS... IF YOU NEED ANYTHING DUDE... I GOT YOU...
THANK YOU... I GOT YOU TOO.
NOOOO... I MEAN IT!
I MEAN IT TOO! LOL.
SHORTLY THEREAFTER, EVERYTHING WAS CANCELLED.
ALL OF THE POWERLIFTING MEETS. THE OLYMPICS WERE POSTPONED.
ALL THE COMIC BOOK SHOWS.
WE'LL BE BACK!!!
(1 MONTH LATER)
THANKS FOR DRIVING.
YEAH, OF COURSE!
M.S. HARKNESS 2020

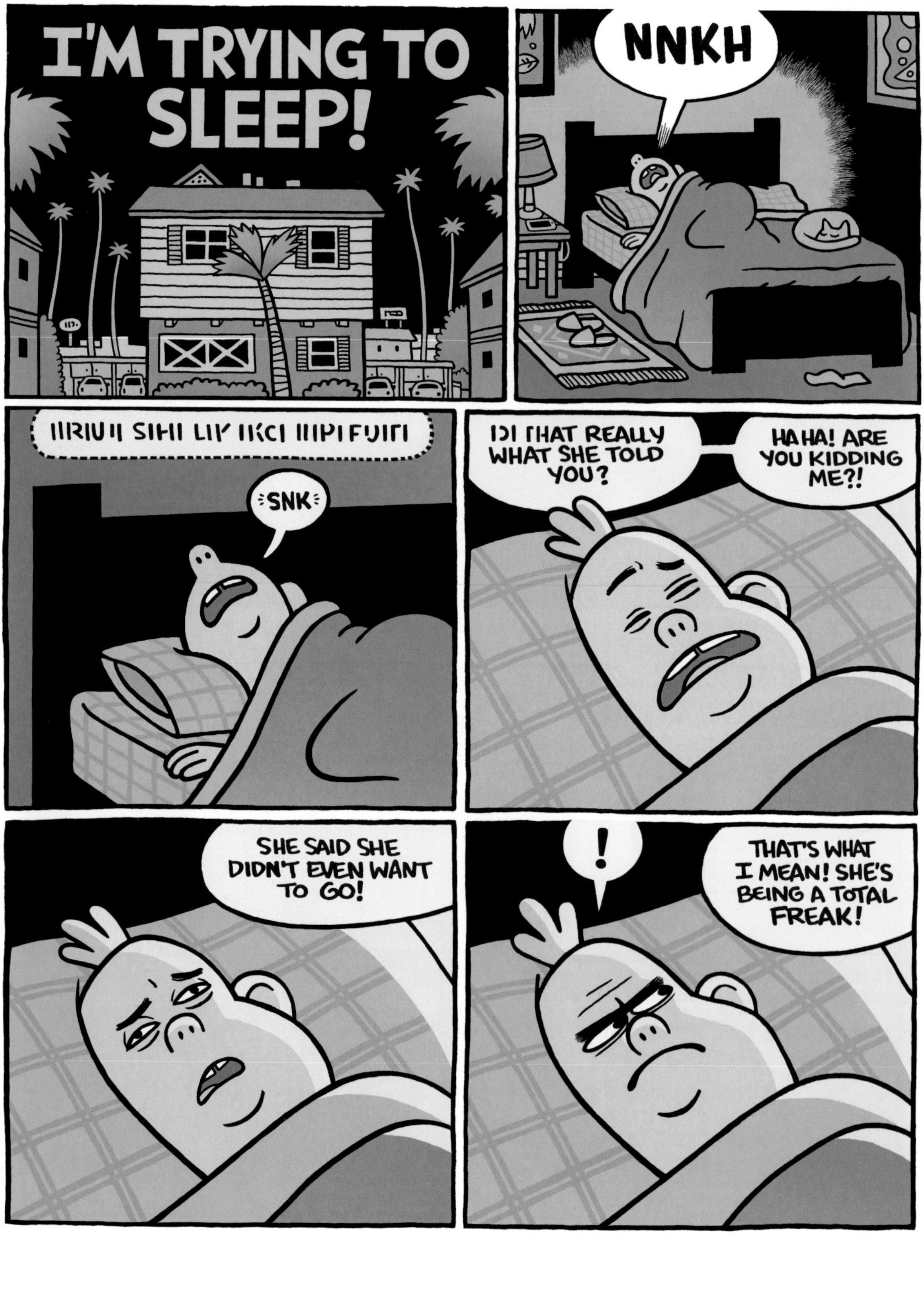

I'M TRYING TO SLEEP!
NNKH
SNK
IS THAT REALLY WHAT SHE TOLD YOU?
HA HA! ARE YOU KIDDING ME?!
SHE SAID SHE DIDN'T EVEN WANT TO GO!
!
THAT'S WHAT I MEAN! SHE'S BEING A TOTAL FREAK!

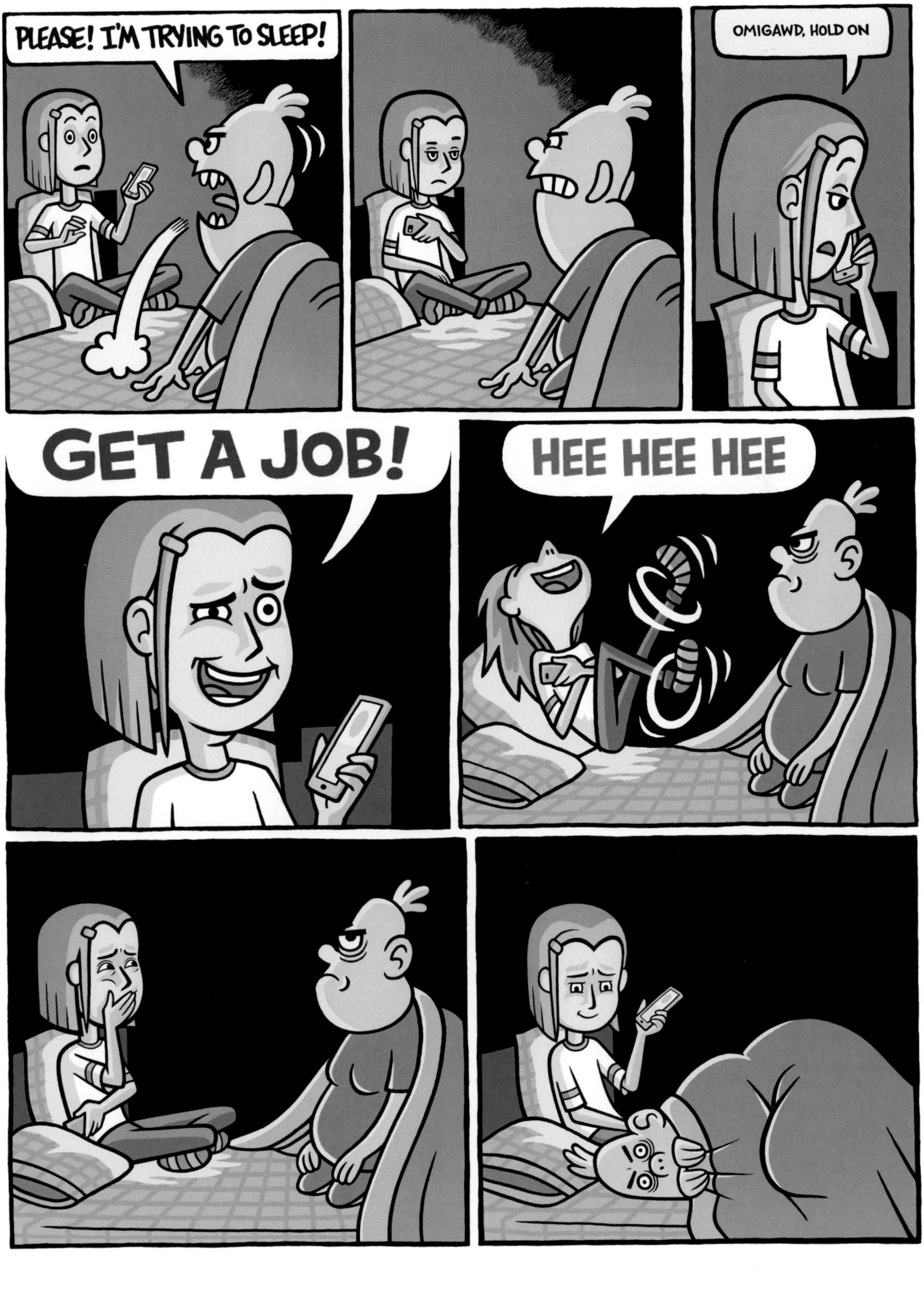
PLEASE! I'M TRYING TO SLEEP!
OMIGAWD, HOLD ON
GET A JOB!
HEE HEE HEE

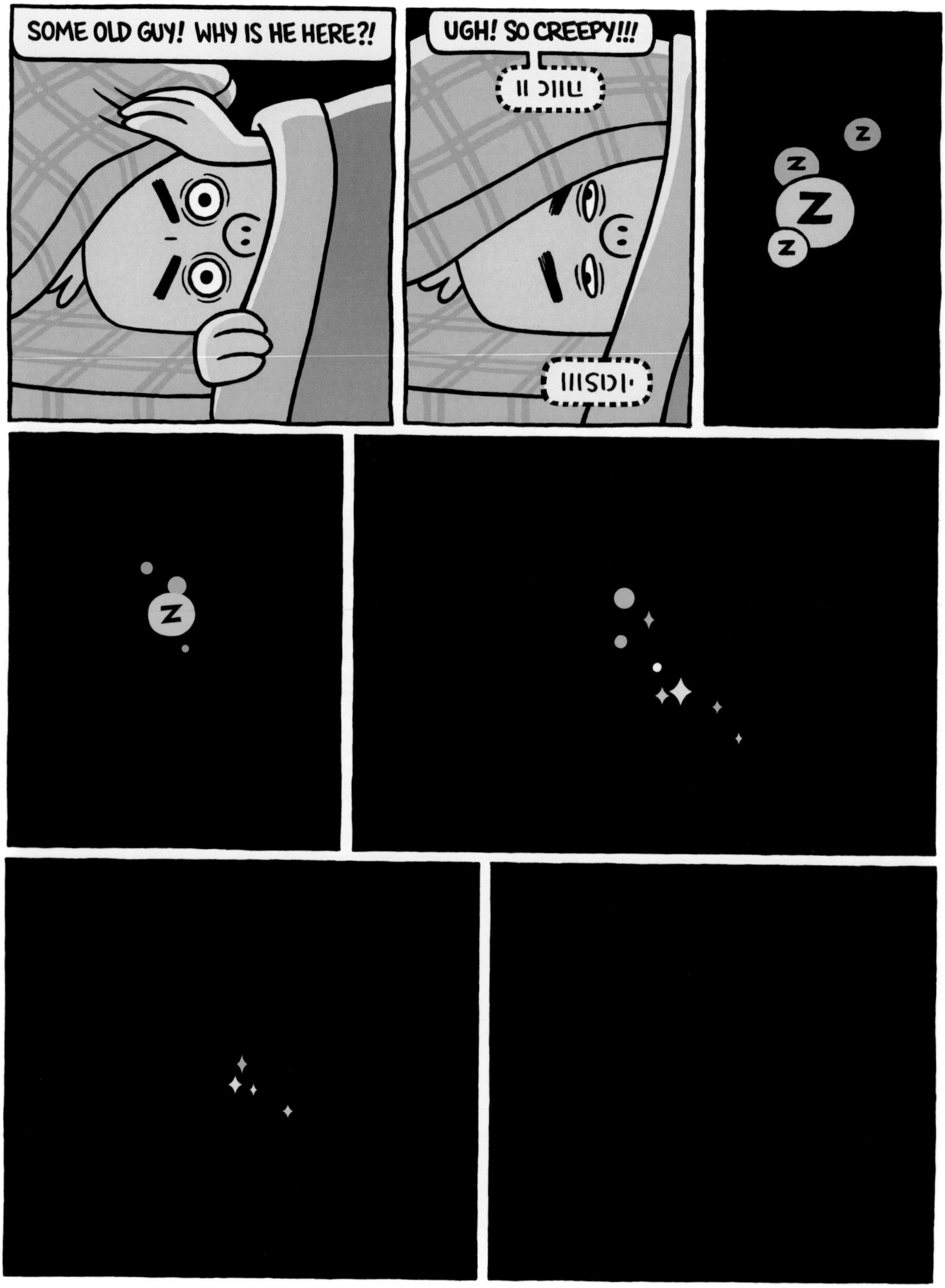
SOME OLD GUY! WHY IS HE HERE?!
UGH! SO CREEPY!!!

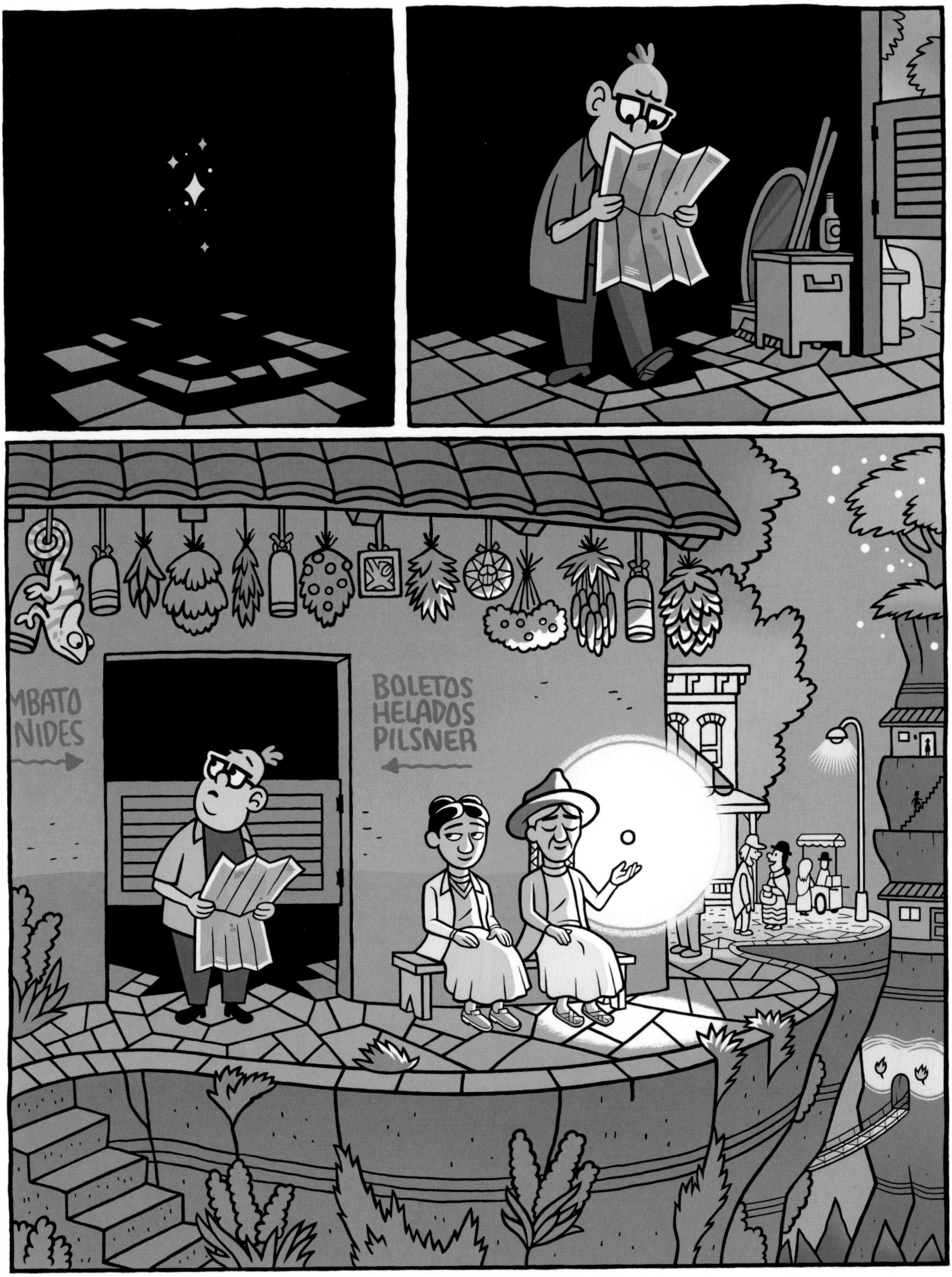
MBATO
NIDES
BOLETOS
HELADOS
PILSNER

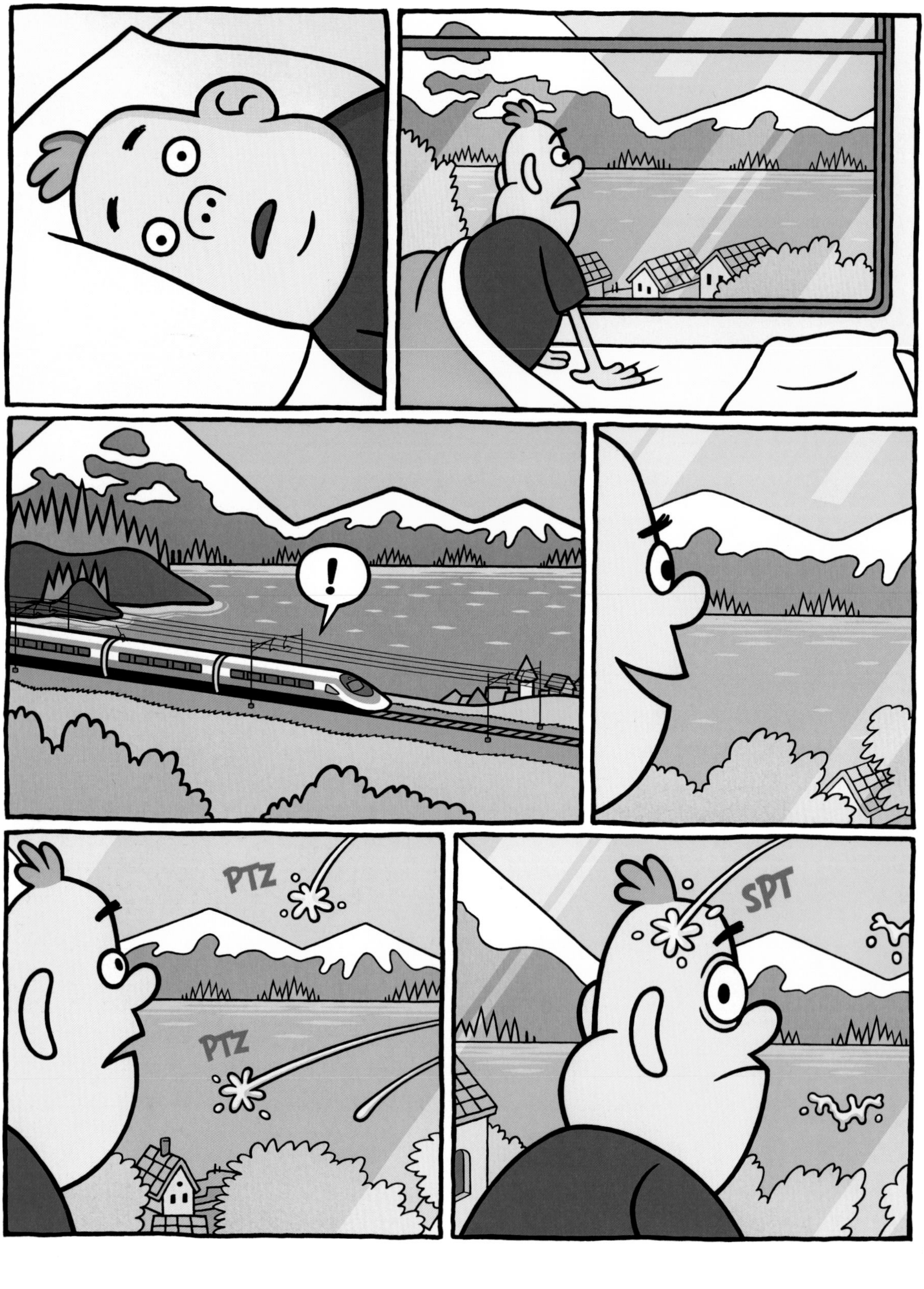
!
PTZ
PTZ
SPT

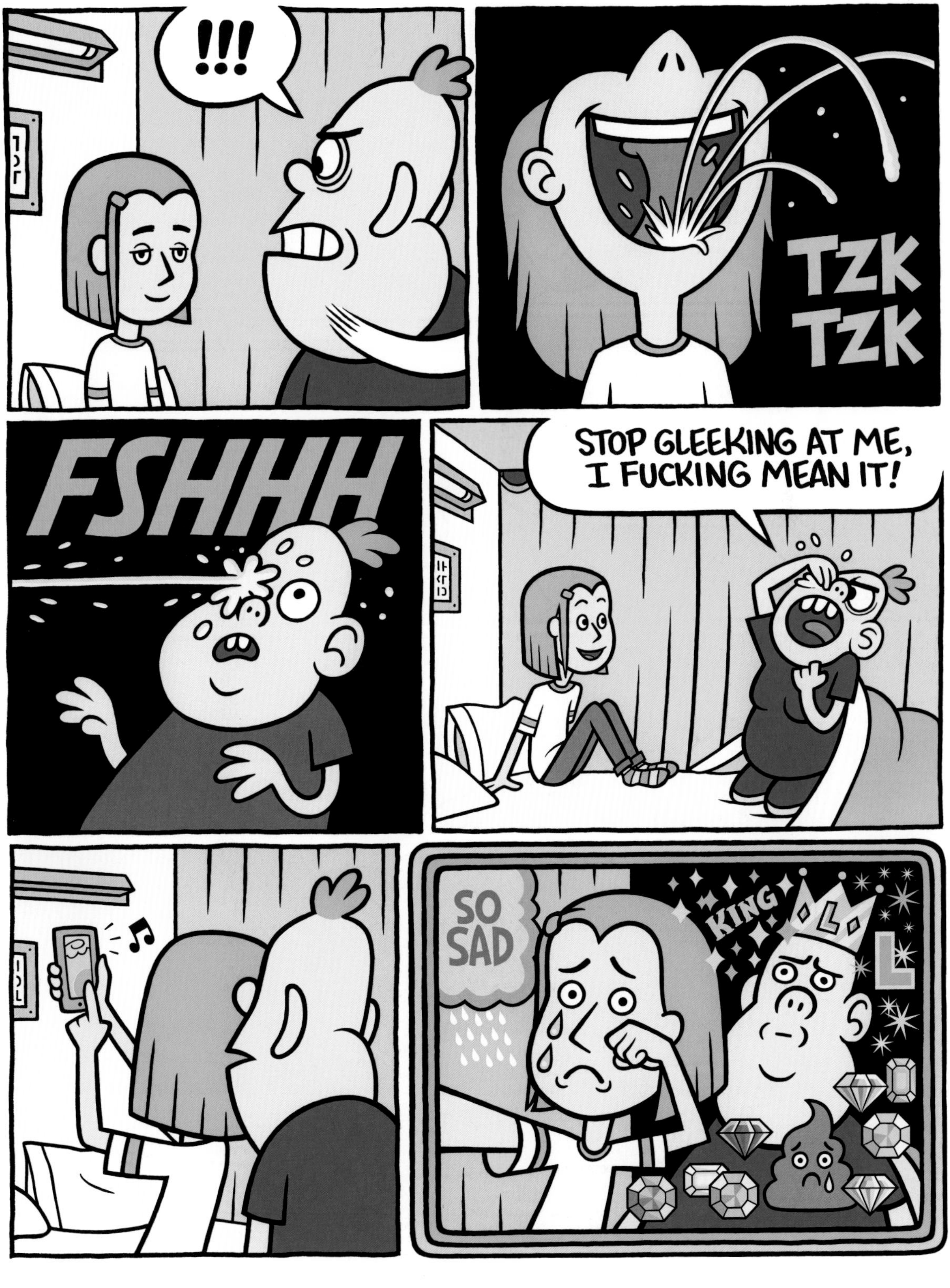
!!!
TZK
TZK
FSHHH
STOP GLEEKING AT ME, I FUCKING MEAN IT!
SO SAD
KING

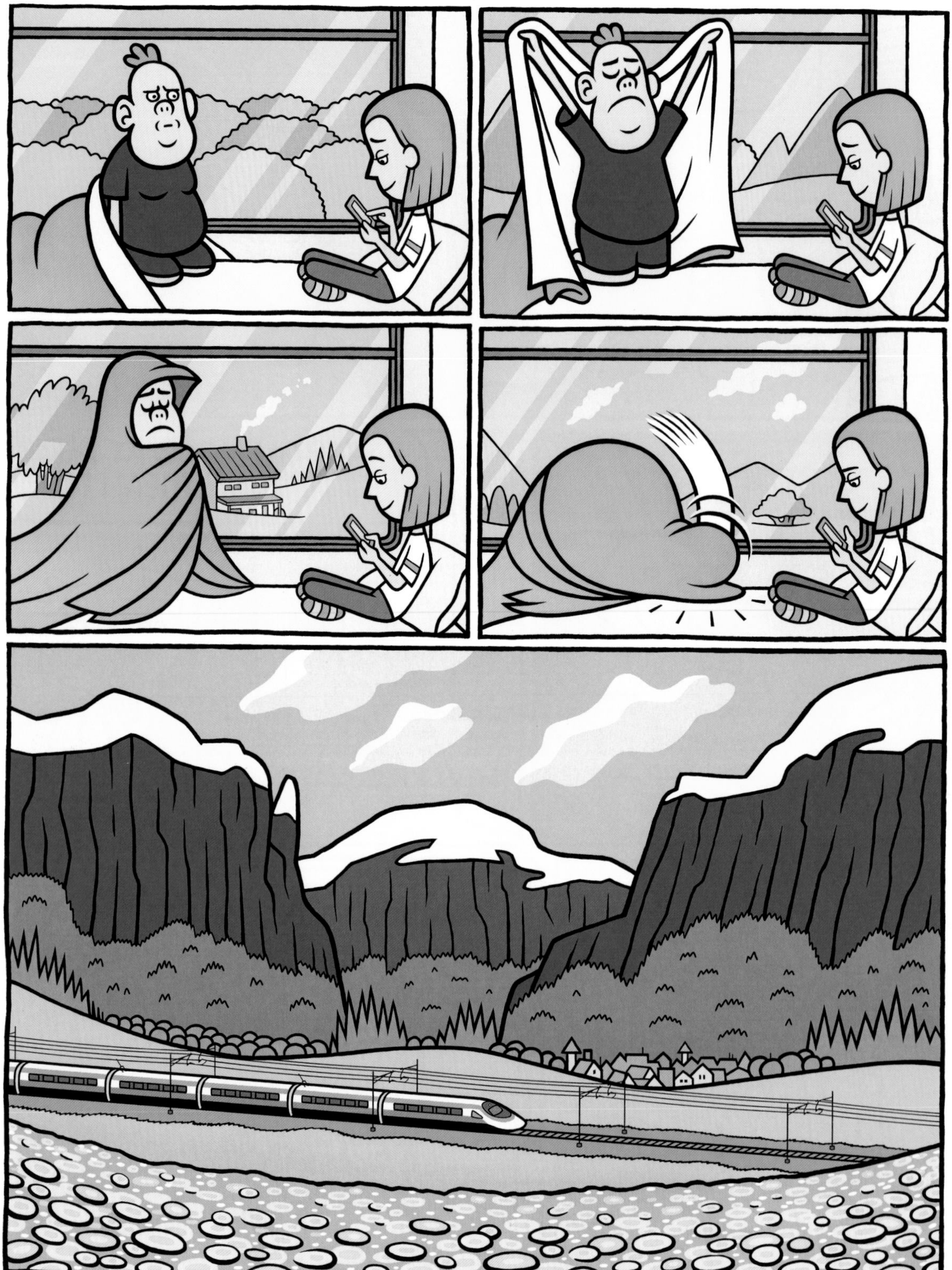

Walt 2019

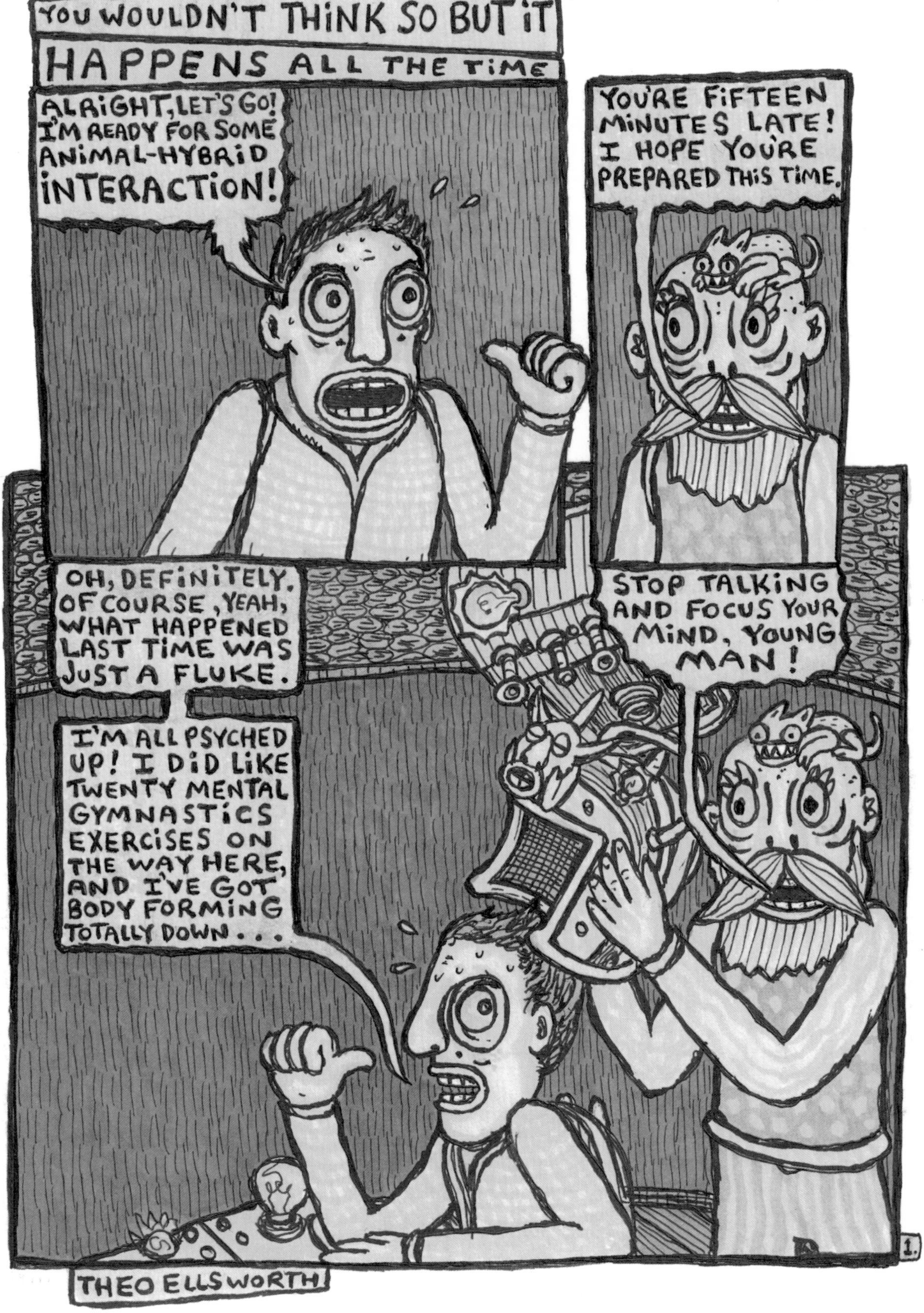
YOU WOULDN'T THINK SO BUT IT HAPPENS ALL THE TIME
ALRIGHT, LET'S GO! I'M READY FOR SOME ANIMAL-HYBRID INTERACTION!
YOU'RE FIFTEEN MINUTES LATE! I HOPE YOU'RE PREPARED THIS TIME.
OH, DEFINITELY. OF COURSE, YEAH, WHAT HAPPENED LAST TIME WAS JUST A FLUKE.
I'M ALL PSYCHED UP! I DID LIKE TWENTY MENTAL GYMNASTICS EXERCISES ON THE WAY HERE, AND I'VE GOT BODY FORMING TOTALLY DOWN . . .
STOP TALKING AND FOCUS YOUR MIND, YOUNG MAN!
1.
THEO ELLSWORTH

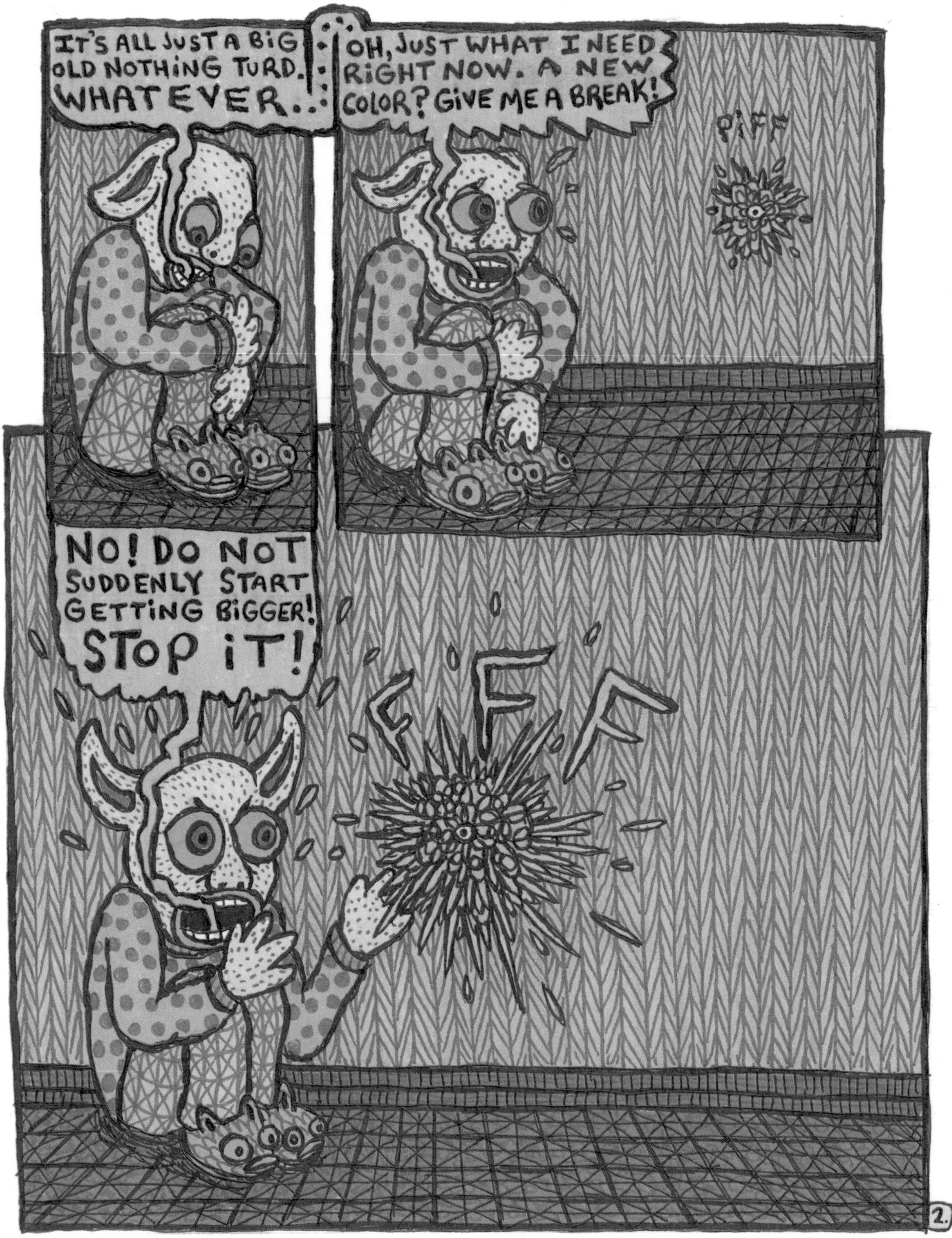
IT'S ALL JUST A BIG OLD NOTHING TURD. WHATEVER..
OH, JUST WHAT I NEED RIGHT NOW. A NEW COLOR? GIVE ME A BREAK!
PIFF
NO! DO NOT SUDDENLY START GETTING BIGGER! STOP IT!
FFF
2.

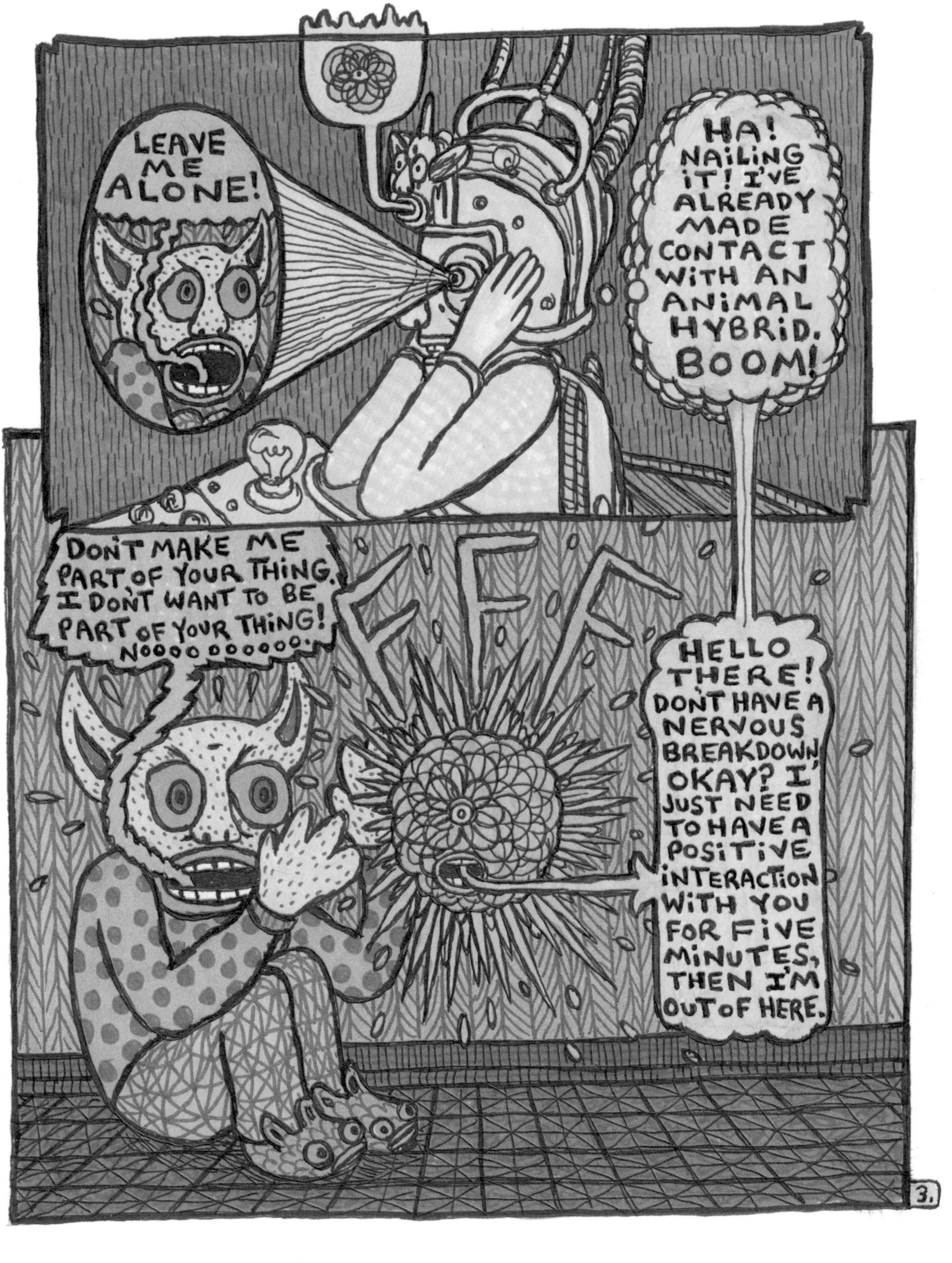
LEAVE ME ALONE!
HA! NAILING IT! I'VE ALREADY MADE CONTACT WITH AN ANIMAL HYBRID. BOOM!
DON'T MAKE ME PART OF YOUR THING. I DON'T WANT TO BE PART OF YOUR THING! NOOOOOOOOOOO.
FFF
HELLO THERE! DON'T HAVE A NERVOUS BREAKDOWN, OKAY? I JUST NEED TO HAVE A POSITIVE INTERACTION WITH YOU FOR FIVE MINUTES, THEN I'M OUT OF HERE.
3.

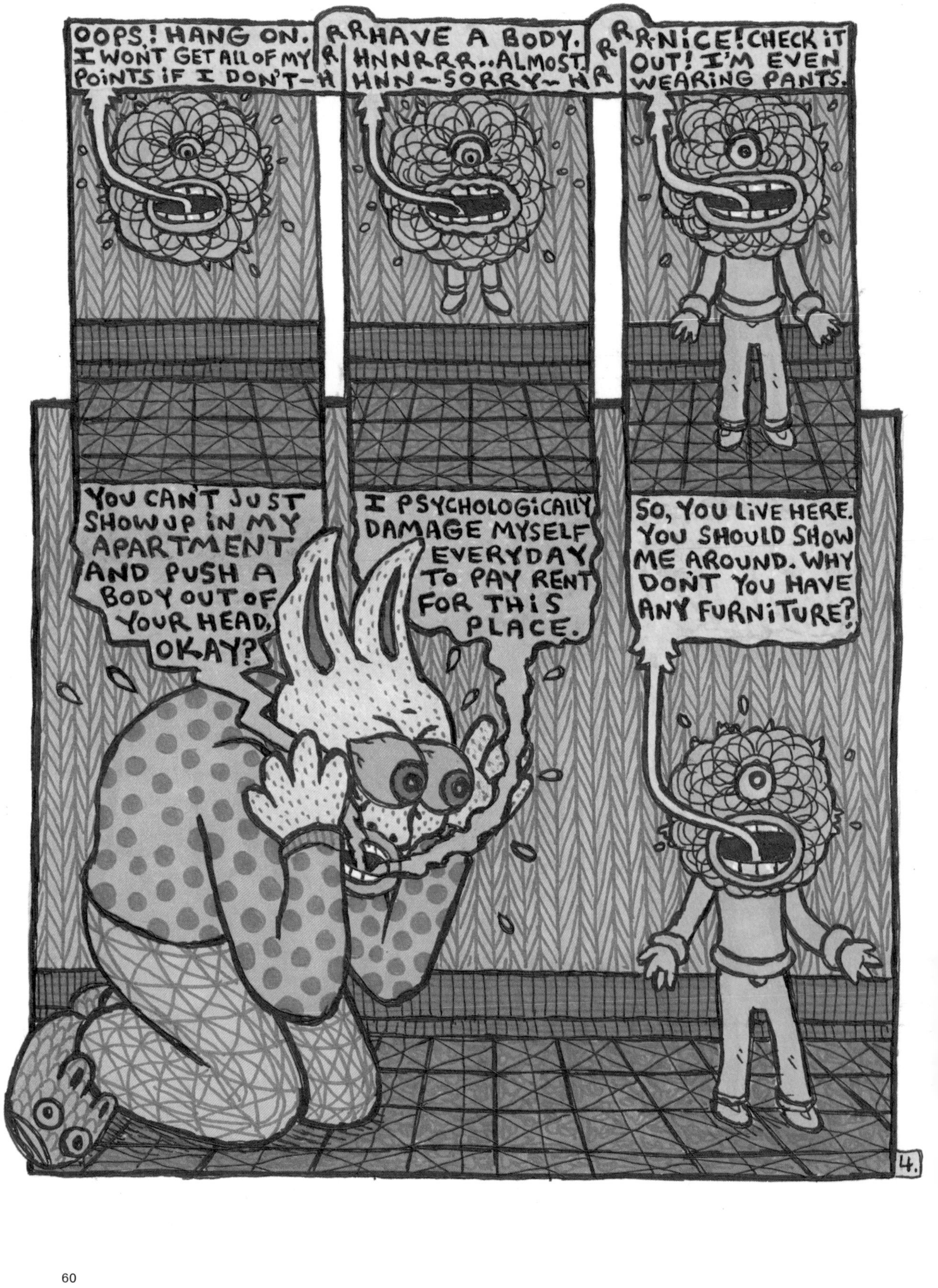

OOPS! HANG ON. I WON'T GET ALL OF MY POINTS IF I DON'T-H
RRRHAVE A BODY. HNNRRR..ALMOST. HNN~SORRY~HR
RRR NICE! CHECK IT OUT! I'M EVEN WEARING PANTS.
YOU CAN'T JUST SHOW UP IN MY APARTMENT AND PUSH A BODY OUT OF YOUR HEAD, OKAY?
I PSYCHOLOGICALLY DAMAGE MYSELF EVERYDAY TO PAY RENT FOR THIS PLACE.
SO, YOU LIVE HERE. YOU SHOULD SHOW ME AROUND. WHY DON'T YOU HAVE ANY FURNITURE?
4.

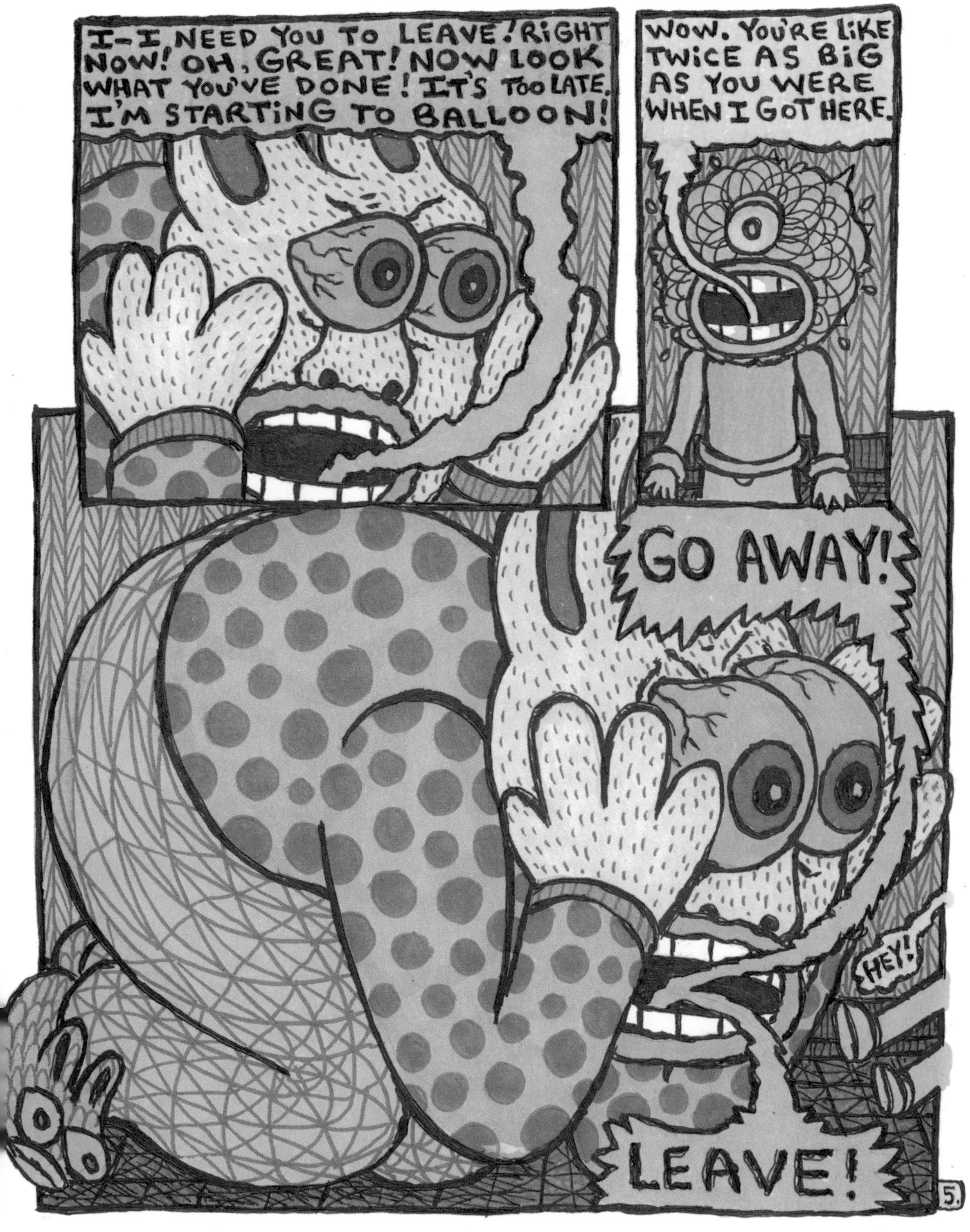

I-I NEED YOU TO LEAVE! RIGHT NOW! OH, GREAT! NOW LOOK WHAT YOU'VE DONE! IT'S TOO LATE, I'M STARTING TO BALLOON!
WOW. YOU'RE LIKE TWICE AS BIG AS YOU WERE WHEN I GOT HERE.
GO AWAY!
HEY!
LEAVE!
5.

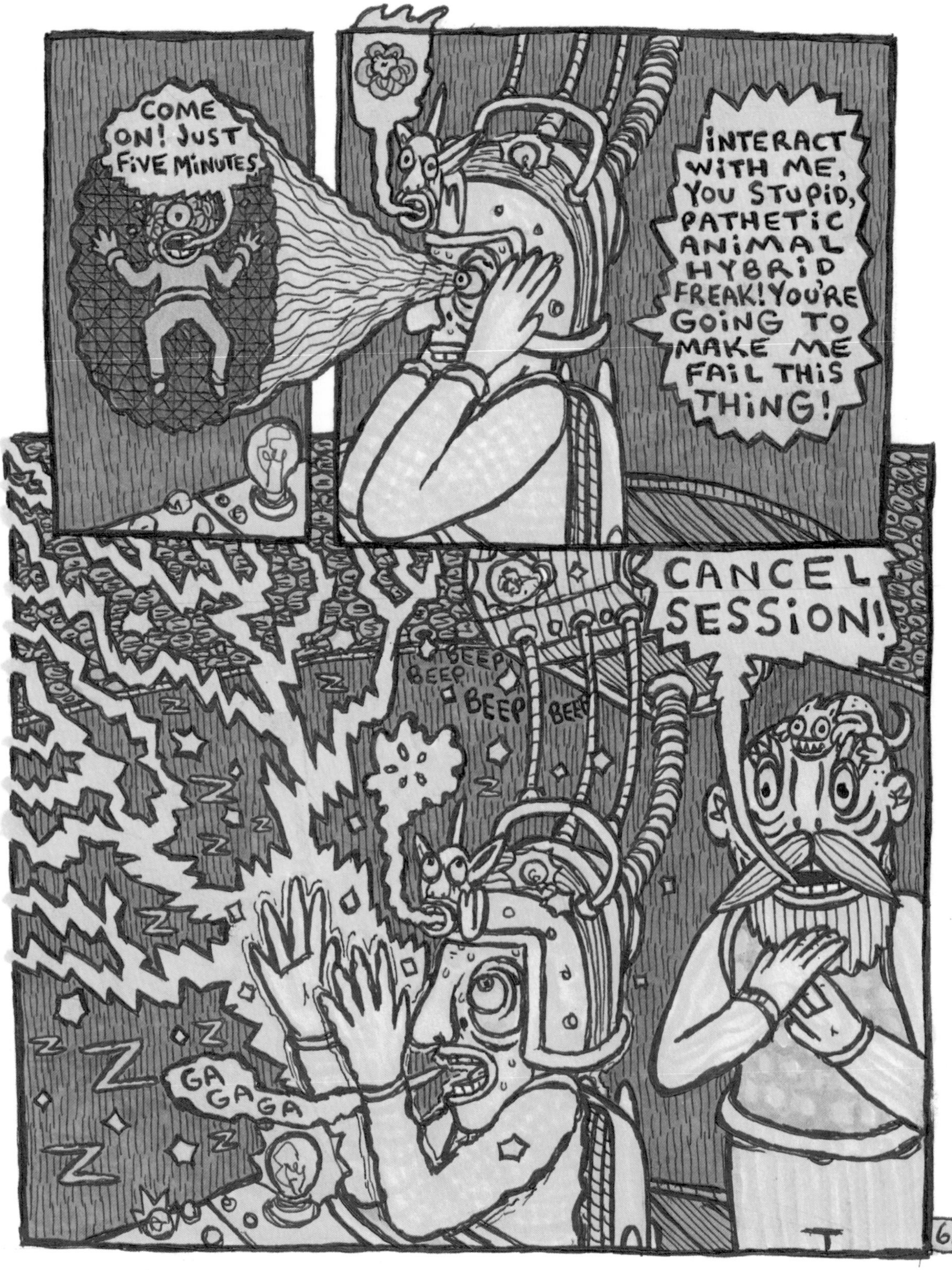
COME ON! JUST FIVE MINUTES
INTERACT WITH ME, YOU STUPID, PATHETIC ANIMAL HYBRID FREAK! YOU'RE GOING TO MAKE ME FAIL THIS THING!
CANCEL SESSION!
BEEP BEEP BEEP
GA GAGA
6.

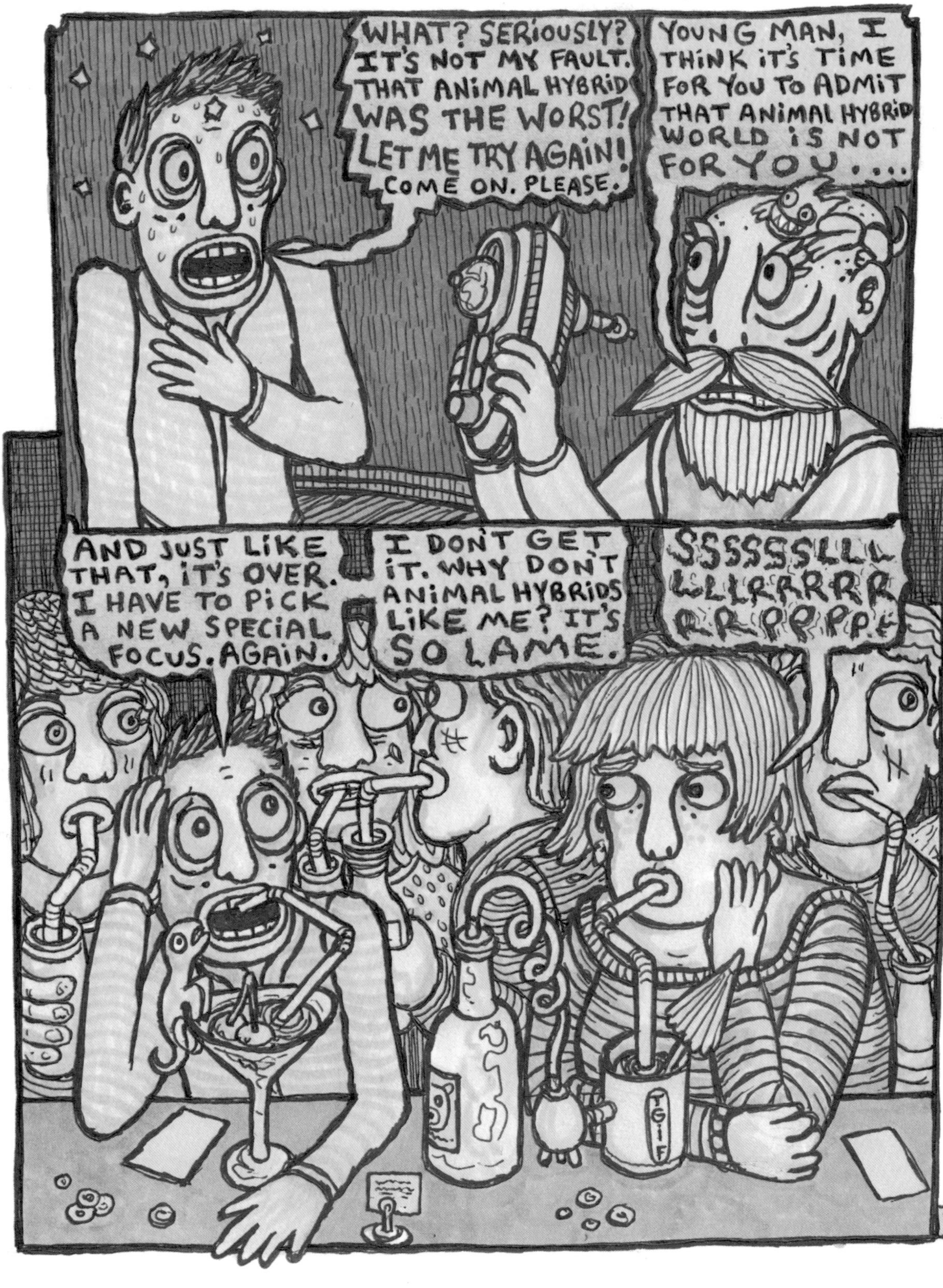
WHAT? SERIOUSLY? IT'S NOT MY FAULT. THAT ANIMAL HYBRID WAS THE WORST! LET ME TRY AGAIN! COME ON. PLEASE.
YOUNG MAN, I THINK IT'S TIME FOR YOU TO ADMIT THAT ANIMAL HYBRID WORLD IS NOT FOR YOU....
AND JUST LIKE THAT, IT'S OVER. I HAVE TO PICK A NEW SPECIAL FOCUS. AGAIN.
I DON'T GET IT. WHY DON'T ANIMAL HYBRIDS LIKE ME? IT'S SO LAME.
SSSSSSLLLLLLRRRRRRRRPPPPP.
TGIF
7.

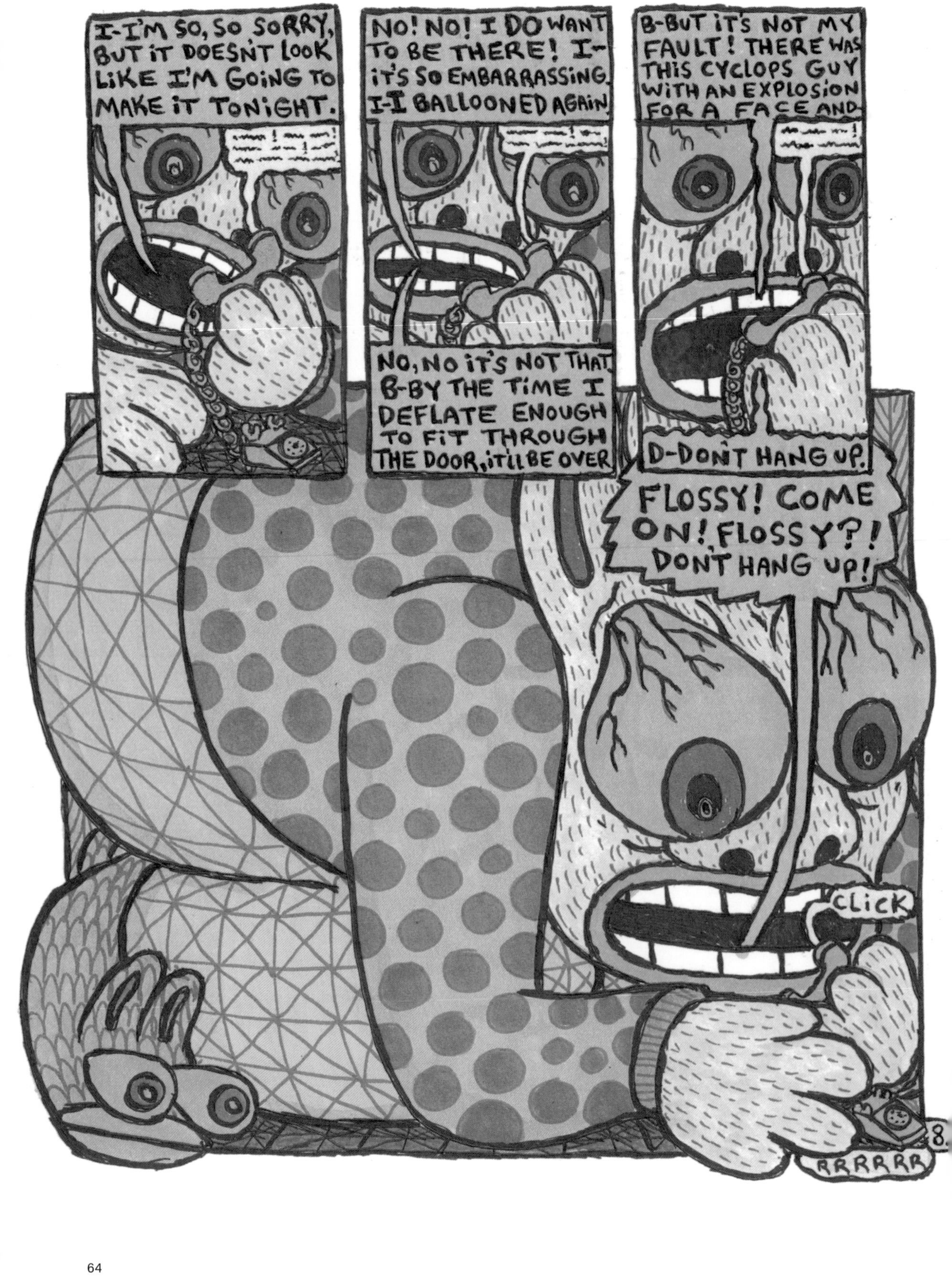
I-I'M SO, SO SORRY, BUT IT DOESN'T LOOK LIKE I'M GOING TO MAKE IT TONIGHT.
NO! NO! I DO WANT TO BE THERE! I- IT'S SO EMBARRASSING. I-I BALLOONED AGAIN.
NO, NO IT'S NOT THAT. B-BY THE TIME I DEFLATE ENOUGH TO FIT THROUGH THE DOOR, IT'LL BE OVER
B-BUT IT'S NOT MY FAULT! THERE WAS THIS CYCLOPS GUY WITH AN EXPLOSION FOR A FACE AND-
D-DON'T HANG UP.
FLOSSY! COME ON! FLOSSY?! DON'T HANG UP!
CLICK
RRRRRR
8.

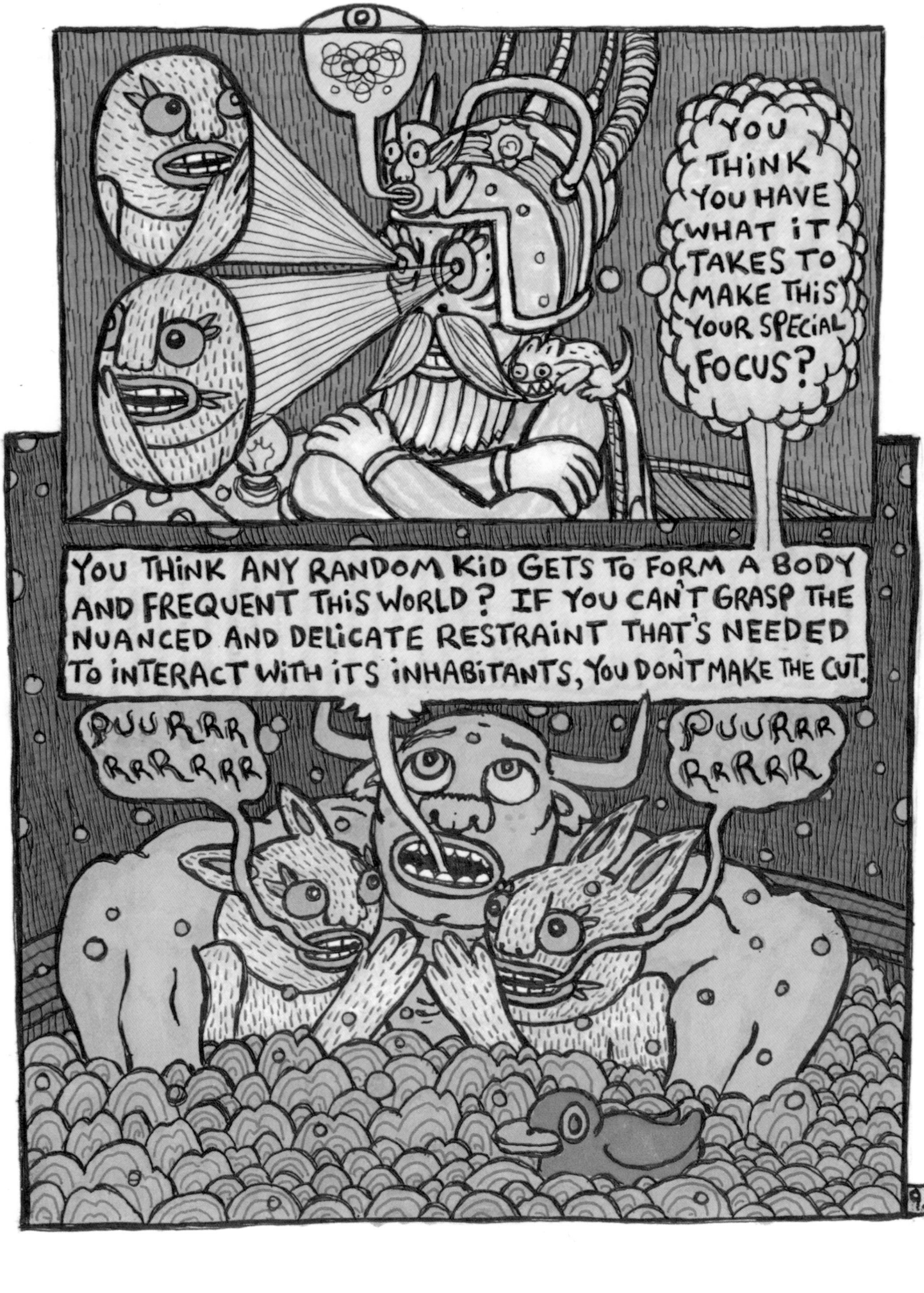
YOU THINK YOU HAVE WHAT IT TAKES TO MAKE THIS YOUR SPECIAL FOCUS?
YOU THINK ANY RANDOM KID GETS TO FORM A BODY AND FREQUENT THIS WORLD? IF YOU CAN'T GRASP THE NUANCED AND DELICATE RESTRAINT THAT'S NEEDED TO INTERACT WITH ITS INHABITANTS, YOU DON'T MAKE THE CUT.
PUURRR RRRRRR
PUURRR RRRRR
9.

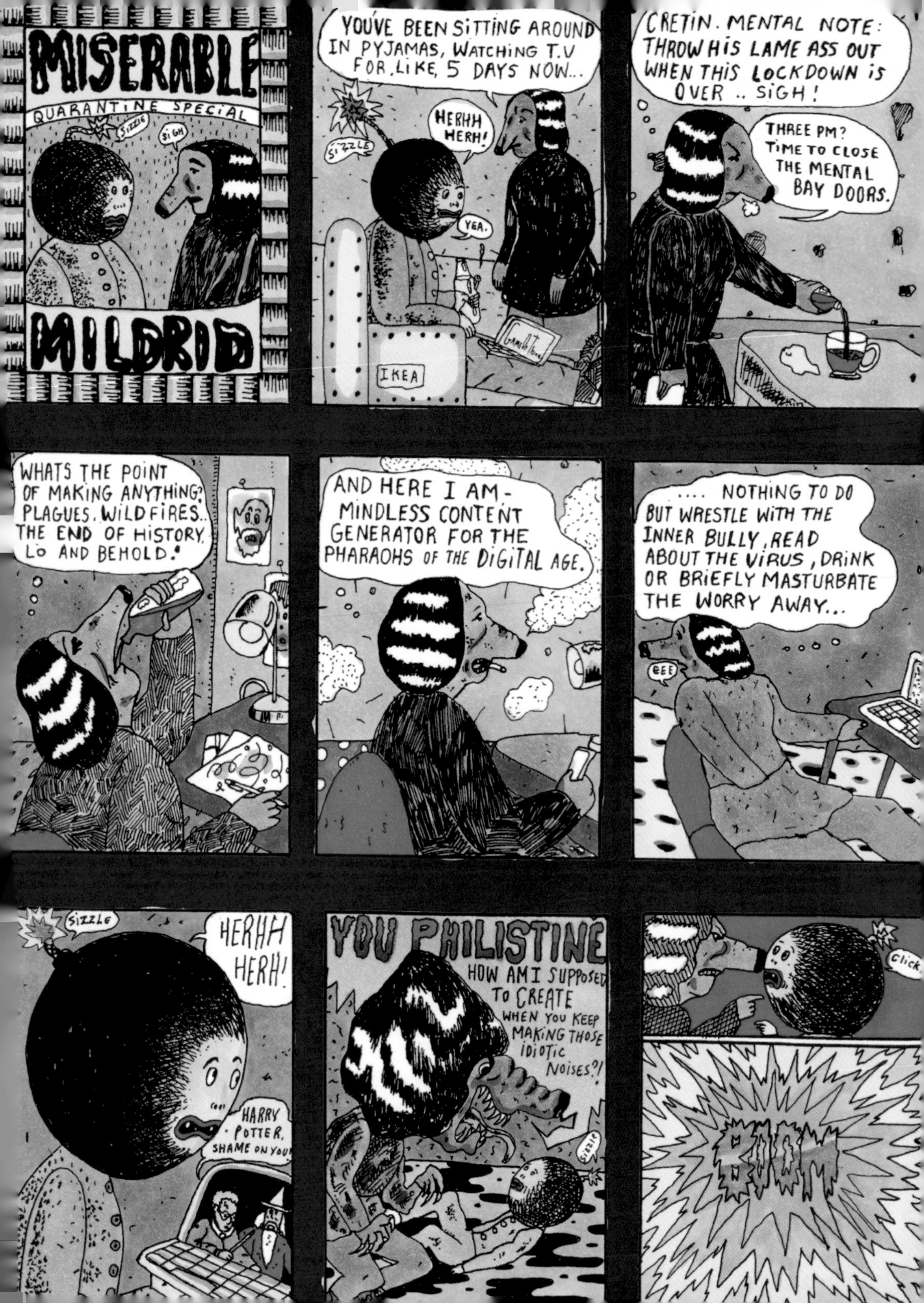
MISERABLE
QUARANTINE SPECIAL
SIZZLE
SIGH
MILDRID
YOU'VE BEEN SITTING AROUND IN PYJAMAS, WATCHING T.V FOR, LIKE, 5 DAYS NOW...
SIZZLE
HERHH HERH!
YEA.
IKEA
CRETIN. MENTAL NOTE: THROW HIS LAME ASS OUT WHEN THIS LOCKDOWN IS OVER .. SIGH!
THREE PM? TIME TO CLOSE THE MENTAL BAY DOORS.
WHATS THE POINT OF MAKING ANYTHING? PLAGUES. WILDFIRES. THE END OF HISTORY. LO AND BEHOLD!
AND HERE I AM - MINDLESS CONTENT GENERATOR FOR THE PHARAOHS OF THE DIGITAL AGE.
.... NOTHING TO DO BUT WRESTLE WITH THE INNER BULLY, READ ABOUT THE VIRUS, DRINK OR BRIEFLY MASTURBATE THE WORRY AWAY...
EEE
SIZZLE
HERHH HERH!
HARRY POTTER, SHAME ON YOU!
YOU PHILISTINE
HOW AM I SUPPOSED TO CREATE WHEN YOU KEEP MAKING THOSE IDIOTIC NOISES?!
SIZZLE
CLICK
BOOM

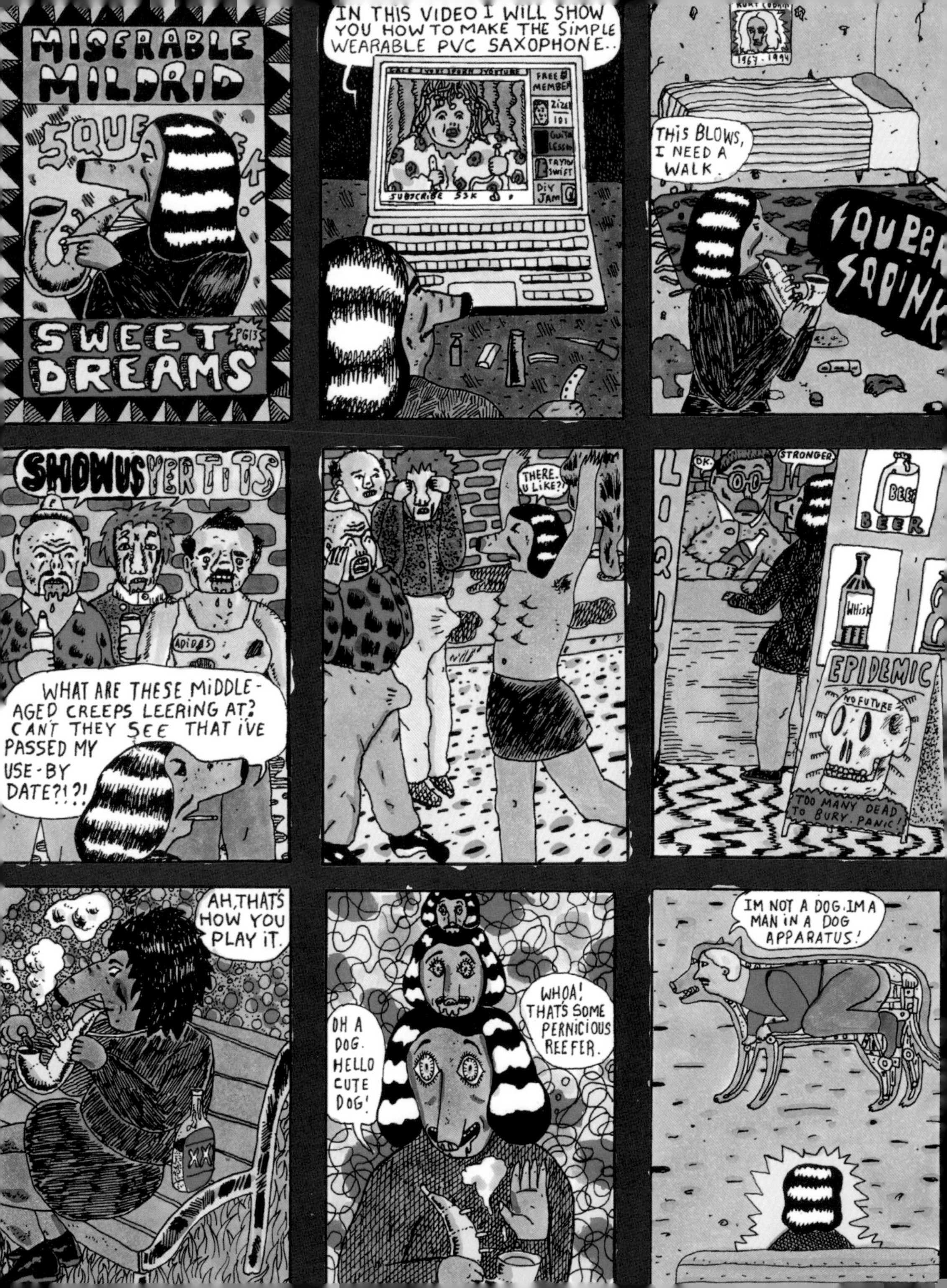
MISERABLE MILDRID
SQUE
SWEET DREAMS
PG13
IN THIS VIDEO I WILL SHOW YOU HOW TO MAKE THE SIMPLE WEARABLE PVC SAXOPHONE..
FREE MEMBER
ZIZEK 101
TAYLOR SWIFT
DIY JAM
SUBSCRIBE 55K
1967 - 1994
THIS BLOWS, I NEED A WALK.
SQUEE
SQOINK
SHOW US YER TITS
ADIDAS
WHAT ARE THESE MIDDLE-AGED CREEPS LEERING AT? CAN'T THEY SEE THAT I'VE PASSED MY USE-BY DATE?!?!
THERE. U LIKE?
OK.
STRONGER
BEER
BEER
WHISK
EPIDEMIC
NO FUTURE
TOO MANY DEAD TO BURY. PANIC!
AH, THAT'S HOW YOU PLAY IT.
XX
WHOA! THAT'S SOME PERNICIOUS REEFER.
OH A DOG. HELLO CUTE DOG!
I'M NOT A DOG. I'M A MAN IN A DOG APPARATUS!

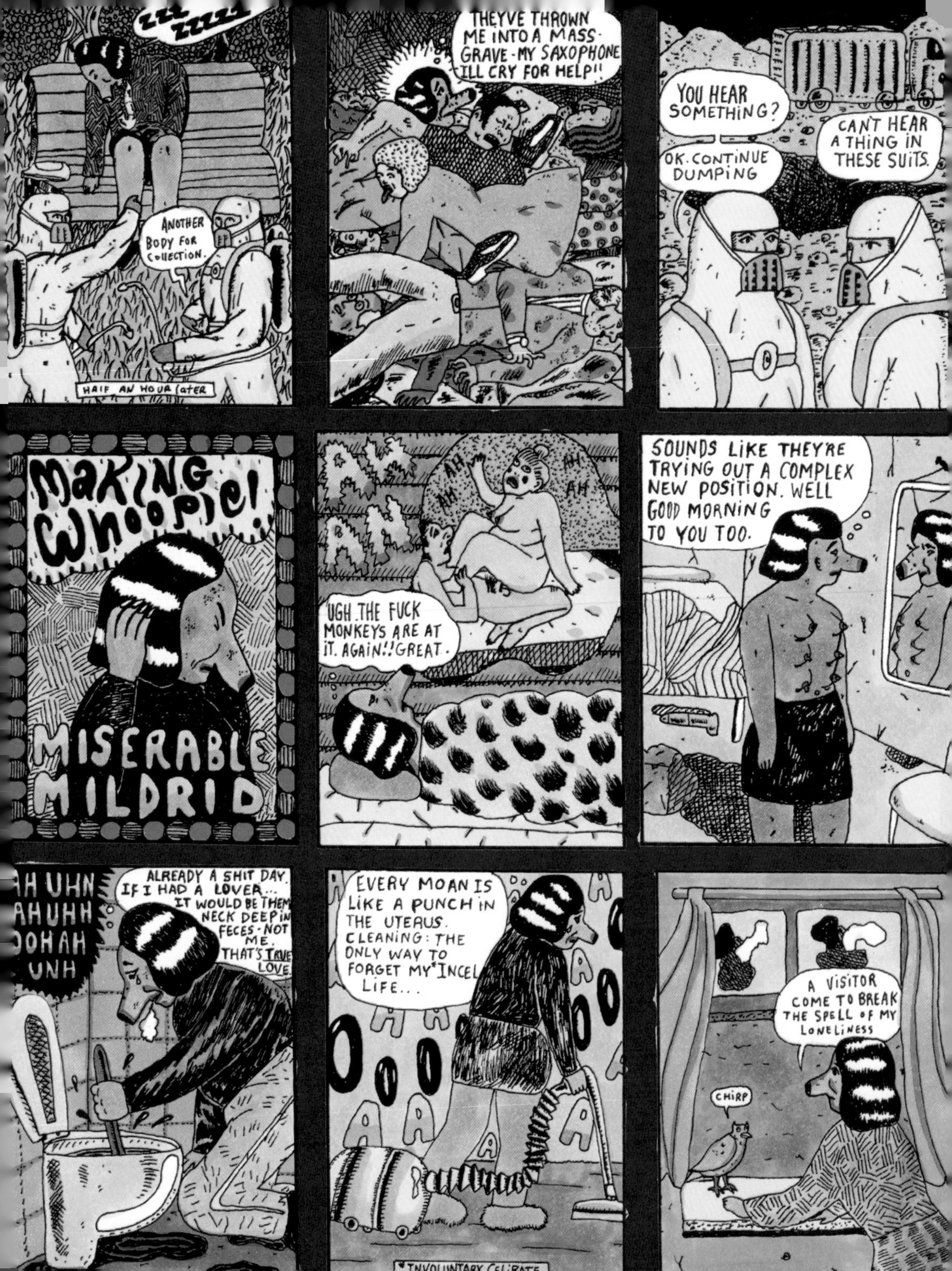

ZZZ ZZZZZ
ANOTHER BODY FOR COLLECTION.
HALF AN HOUR LATER
THEYVE THROWN ME INTO A MASS-GRAVE - MY SAXOPHONE ILL CRY FOR HELP!!
YOU HEAR SOMETHING?
CAN'T HEAR A THING IN THESE SUITS.
OK. CONTINUE DUMPING
MAKING WHOOPIE!
MISERABLE MILDRID
AH AH AH AH AH
UGH THE FUCK MONKEYS ARE AT IT. AGAIN!! GREAT.
SOUNDS LIKE THEY'RE TRYING OUT A COMPLEX NEW POSITION. WELL GOOD MORNING TO YOU TOO.
AH UHN AHUHH OOHAH UNH
ALREADY A SHIT DAY. IF I HAD A LOVER... IT WOULD BE THEM NECK DEEP IN FECES - NOT ME. THAT'S TRUE LOVE.
EVERY MOAN IS LIKE A PUNCH IN THE UTERUS. CLEANING: THE ONLY WAY TO FORGET MY* INCEL LIFE...
*INVOLUNTARY CELIBATE
A VISITOR COME TO BREAK THE SPELL OF MY LONELINESS
CHIRP

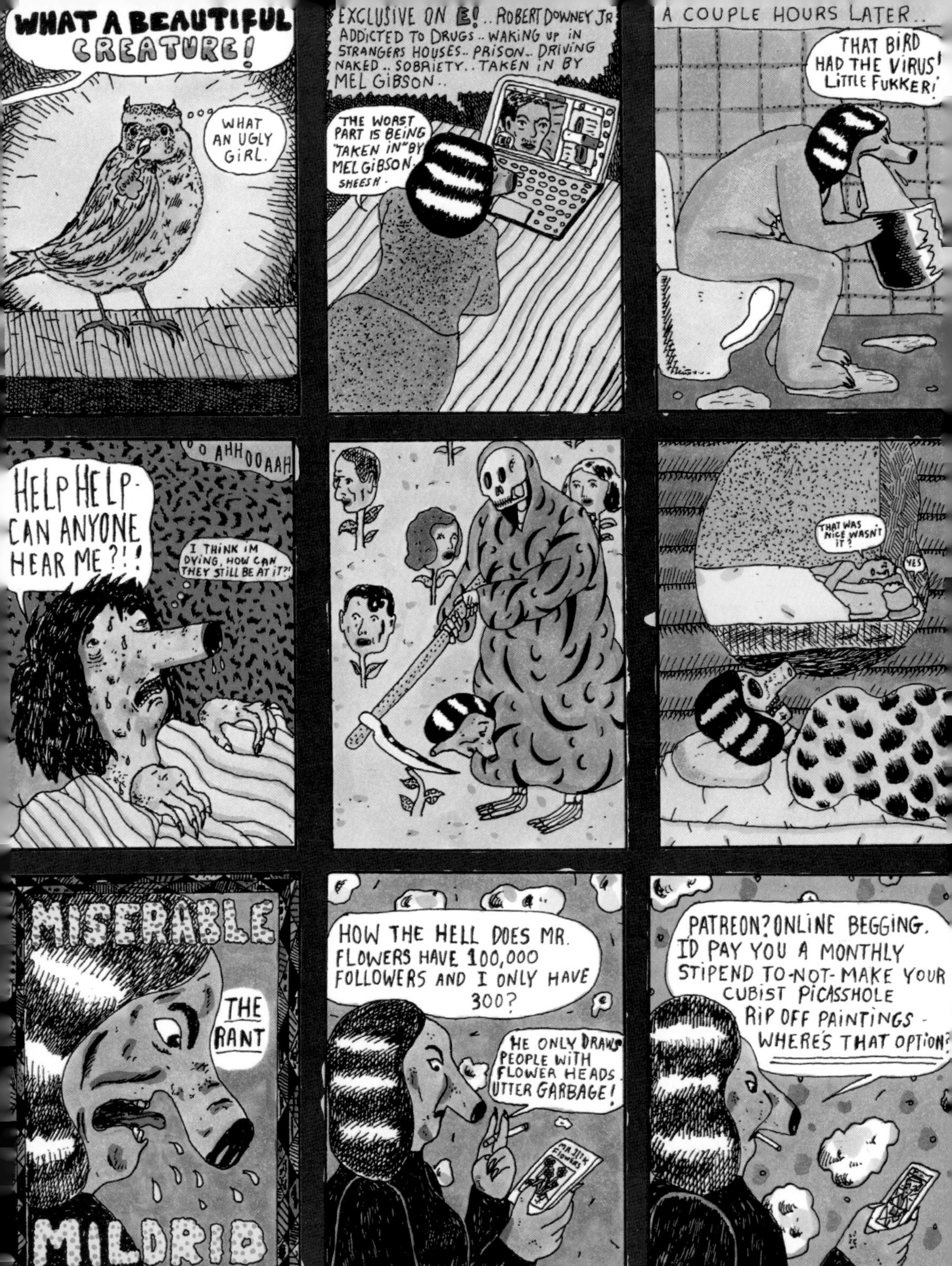
WHAT A BEAUTIFUL CREATURE!
WHAT AN UGLY GIRL.
EXCLUSIVE ON E! .. ROBERT DOWNEY JR ADDICTED TO DRUGS .. WAKING UP IN STRANGERS HOUSES .. PRISON .. DRIVING NAKED .. SOBRIETY .. TAKEN IN BY MEL GIBSON ..
THE WORST PART IS BEING "TAKEN IN" BY MEL GIBSON - SHEESH .
A COUPLE HOURS LATER ..
THAT BIRD HAD THE VIRUS! LITTLE FUKKER!
O AHHOOAAH
HELP HELP - CAN ANYONE HEAR ME ?!!
I THINK IM DYING, HOW CAN THEY STILL BE AT IT?!
THAT WAS NICE WASN'T IT ?
YES
MISERABLE
THE RANT
MILDRID
HOW THE HELL DOES MR. FLOWERS HAVE 100,000 FOLLOWERS AND I ONLY HAVE 300?
HE ONLY DRAWS PEOPLE WITH FLOWER HEADS UTTER GARBAGE!
PATREON? ONLINE BEGGING. ID PAY YOU A MONTHLY STIPEND TO-NOT-MAKE YOUR CUBIST PICASSHOLE RIP OFF PAINTINGS - WHERE'S THAT OPTION?

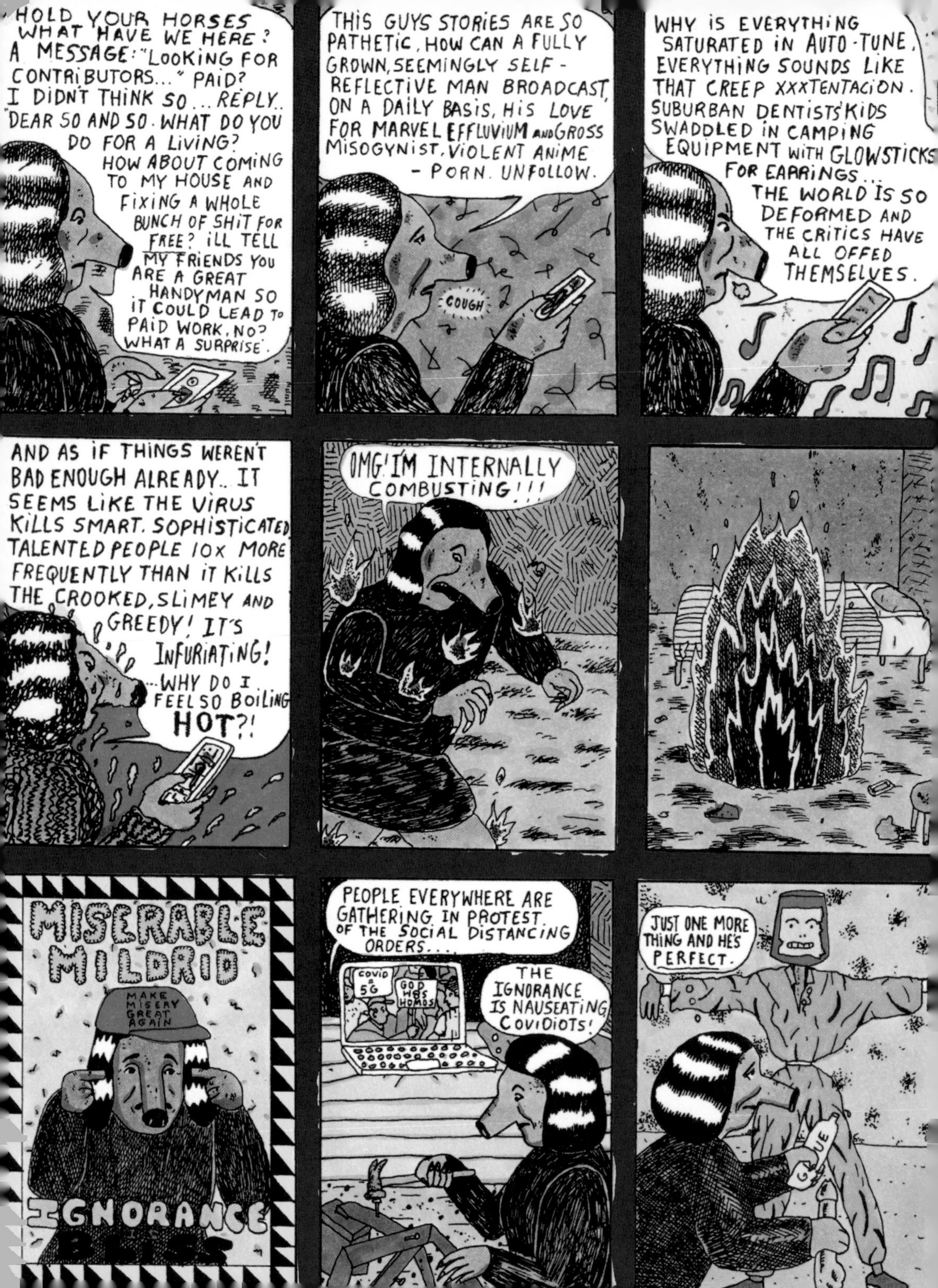
HOLD YOUR HORSES WHAT HAVE WE HERE? A MESSAGE: "LOOKING FOR CONTRIBUTORS..." PAID? I DIDN'T THINK SO... REPLY.. "DEAR SO AND SO. WHAT DO YOU DO FOR A LIVING? HOW ABOUT COMING TO MY HOUSE AND FIXING A WHOLE BUNCH OF SHIT FOR FREE? ILL TELL MY FRIENDS YOU ARE A GREAT HANDYMAN SO IT COULD LEAD TO PAID WORK, NO? WHAT A SURPRISE".
THIS GUYS STORIES ARE SO PATHETIC. HOW CAN A FULLY GROWN, SEEMINGLY SELF-REFLECTIVE MAN BROADCAST, ON A DAILY BASIS, HIS LOVE FOR MARVEL EFFLUVIUM AND GROSS MISOGYNIST, VIOLENT ANIME-PORN. UNFOLLOW.
COUGH
WHY IS EVERYTHING SATURATED IN AUTO-TUNE, EVERYTHING SOUNDS LIKE THAT CREEP XXXTENTACION. SUBURBAN DENTISTS' KIDS SWADDLED IN CAMPING EQUIPMENT WITH GLOWSTICKS FOR EARRINGS... THE WORLD IS SO DEFORMED AND THE CRITICS HAVE ALL OFFED THEMSELVES.
AND AS IF THINGS WEREN'T BAD ENOUGH ALREADY.. IT SEEMS LIKE THE VIRUS KILLS SMART, SOPHISTICATED, TALENTED PEOPLE 10X MORE FREQUENTLY THAN IT KILLS THE CROOKED, SLIMEY AND GREEDY! IT'S INFURIATING! ...WHY DO I FEEL SO BOILING HOT?!
OMG! I'M INTERNALLY COMBUSTING!!!
MISERABLE MILDRID
MAKE MISERY GREAT AGAIN
IGNORANCE
PEOPLE EVERYWHERE ARE GATHERING IN PROTEST OF THE SOCIAL DISTANCING ORDERS...
COVID = 5G
GOD H8S HOMOS
THE IGNORANCE IS NAUSEATING COVIDIOTS!
JUST ONE MORE THING AND HE'S PERFECT.
GLUE

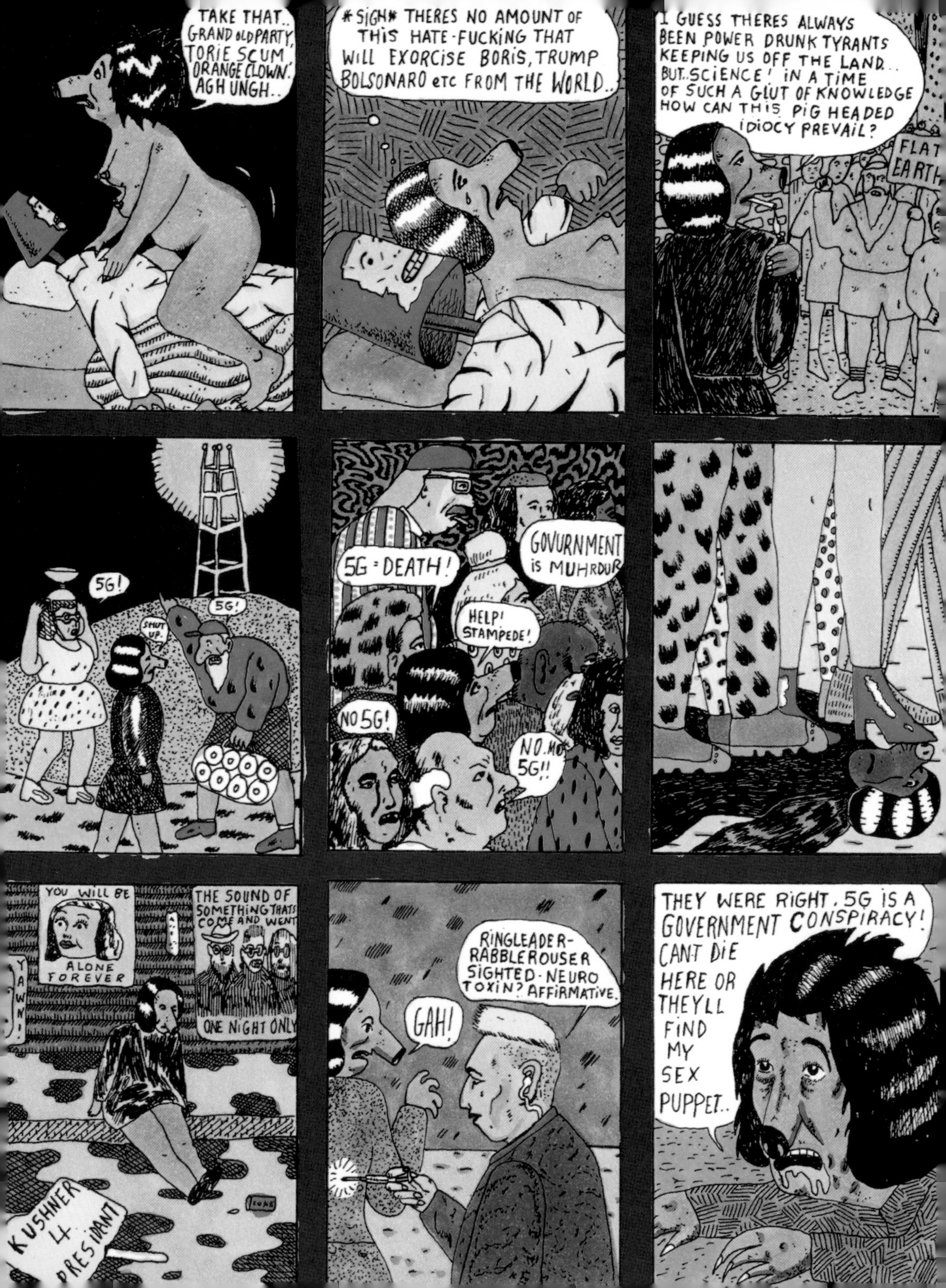
TAKE THAT.. GRAND OLD PARTY, TORIE SCUM, ORANGE CLOWN! AGH UNGH..
SIGH THERES NO AMOUNT OF THIS HATE-FUCKING THAT WILL EXORCISE BORIS, TRUMP BOLSONARO etc FROM THE WORLD..
I GUESS THERES ALWAYS BEEN POWER DRUNK TYRANTS KEEPING US OFF THE LAND.. BUT..SCIENCE! IN A TIME OF SUCH A GLUT OF KNOWLEDGE HOW CAN THIS PIG HEADED IDIOCY PREVAIL?
FLAT EARTH
5G!
5G!
SHUT UP.
5G = DEATH!
GOVURNMENT IS MUHRDUR
HELP! STAMPEDE!
NO 5G!
NO MO 5G!!
YOU WILL BE ALONE FOREVER
THE SOUND OF SOMETHING THATS COME AND WENT
ONE NIGHT ONLY
YAWN!
KUSHNER 4 PRESIDANT
RINGLEADER-RABBLEROUSER SIGHTED. NEURO TOXIN? AFFIRMATIVE.
GAH!
THEY WERE RIGHT. 5G IS A GOVERNMENT CONSPIRACY! CAN'T DIE HERE OR THEY'LL FIND MY SEX PUPPET..

- I HATE PARTIES -

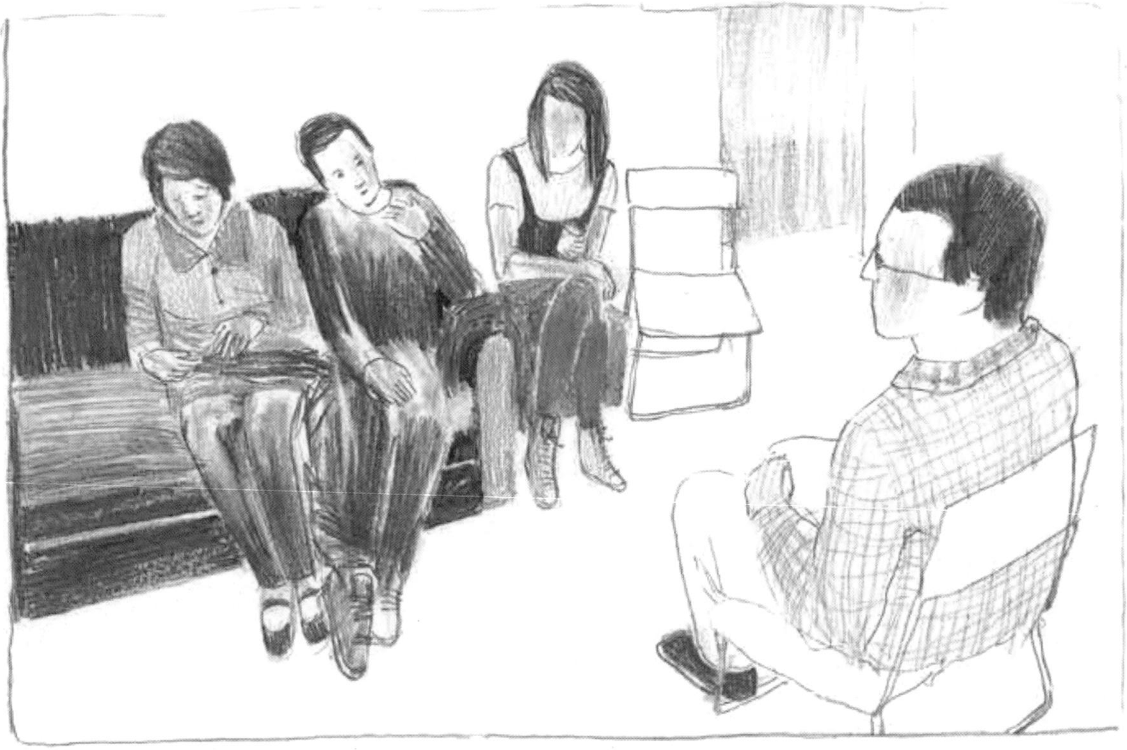

I'M FINE AT PARTIES, BUT WHEN SOMEONE DOESN'T UNDERSTAND ME, I LOSE THE DESIRE TO LISTEN.

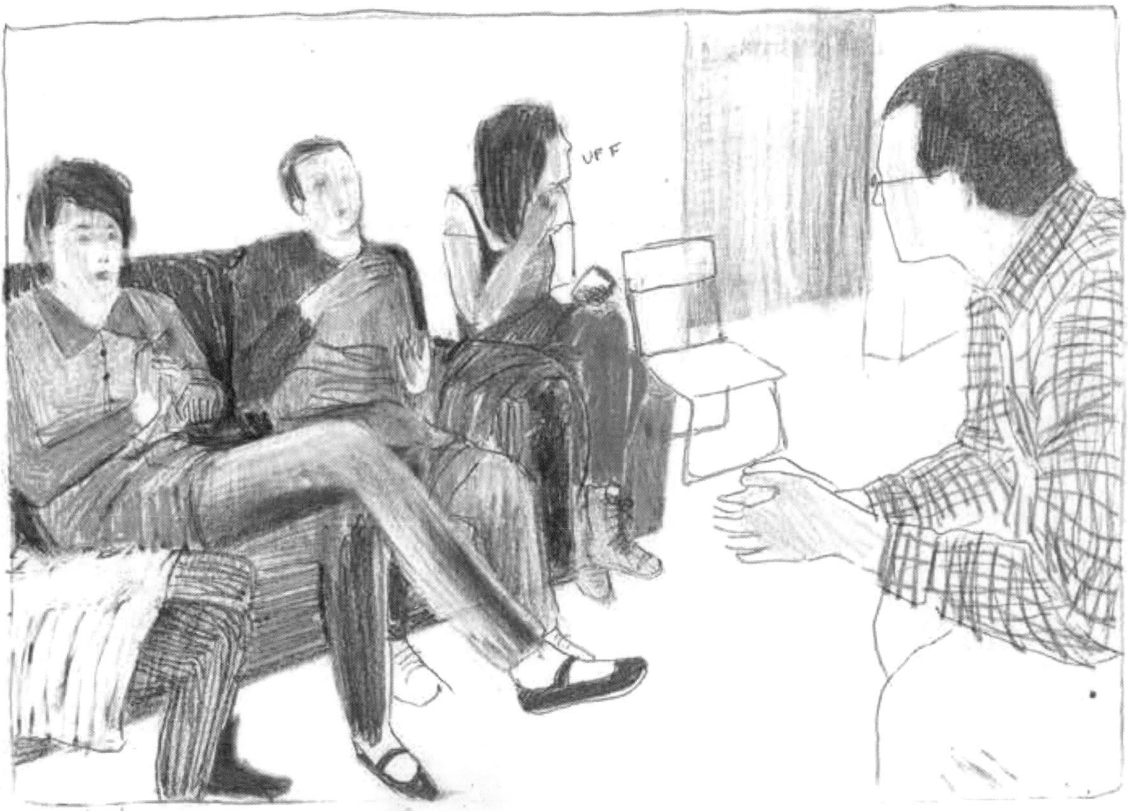
UFF

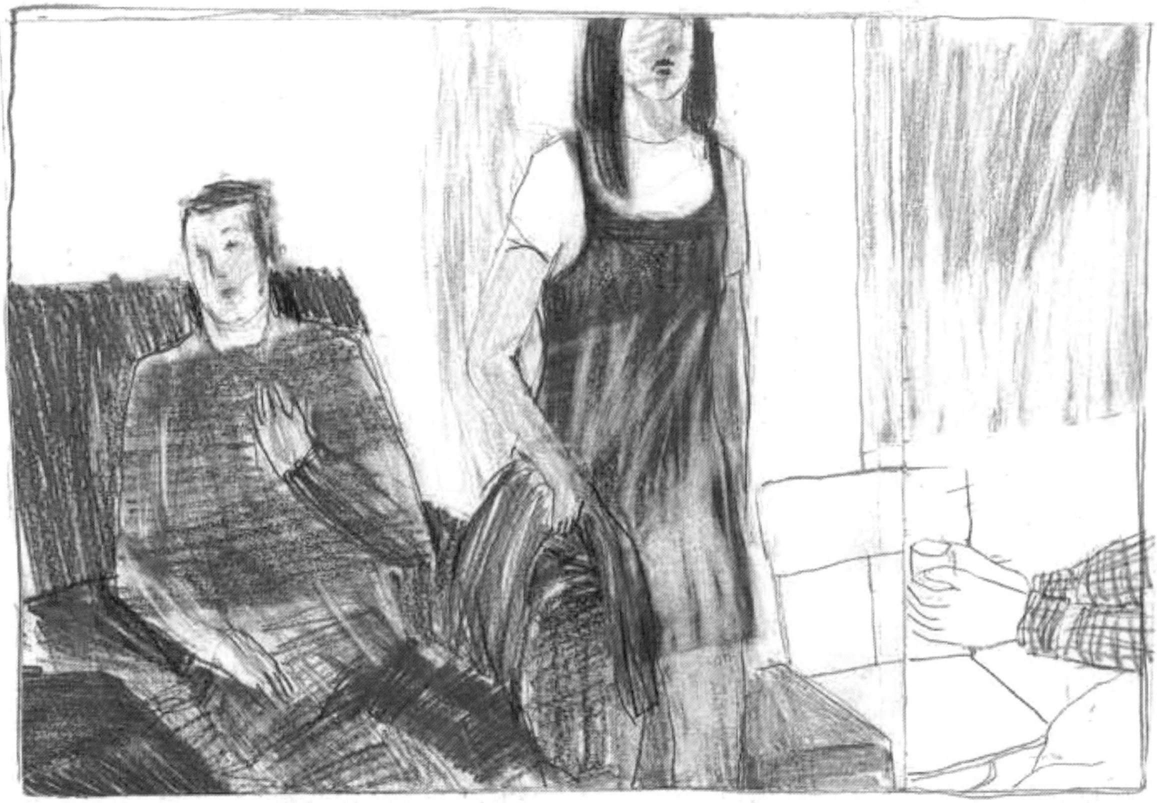

I TRY AND BE CLEAR AND LIVE WITHOUT MISUNDERSTANDING PEOPLE.

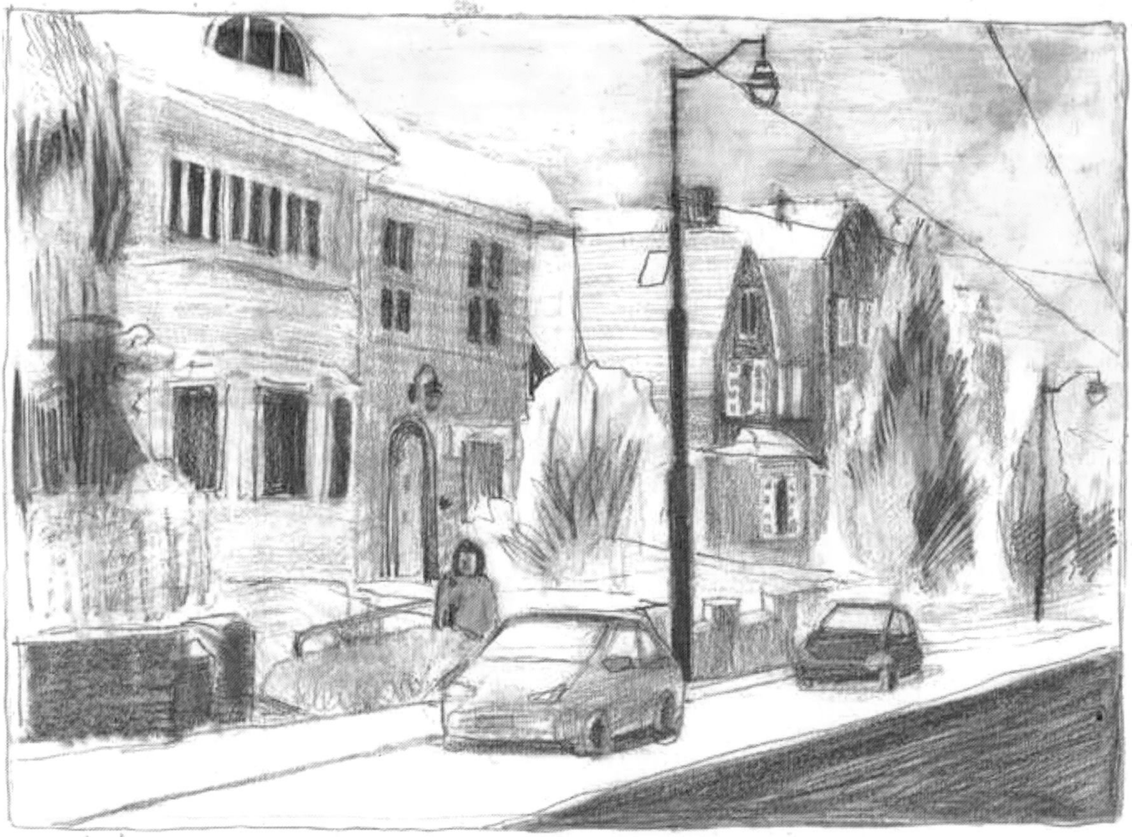

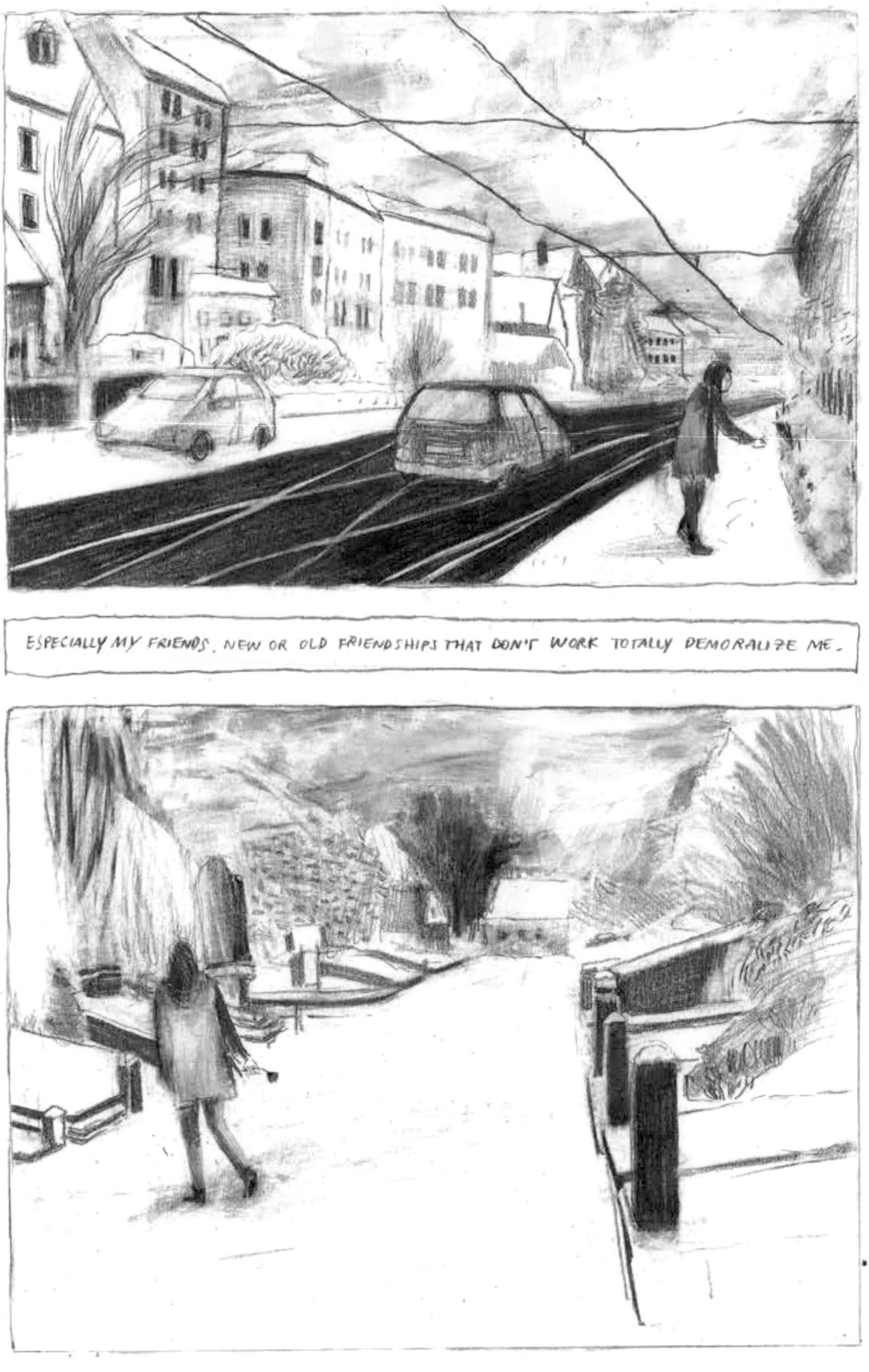
ESPECIALLY MY FRIENDS. NEW OR OLD FRIENDSHIPS THAT DON'T WORK TOTALLY DEMORALIZE ME.

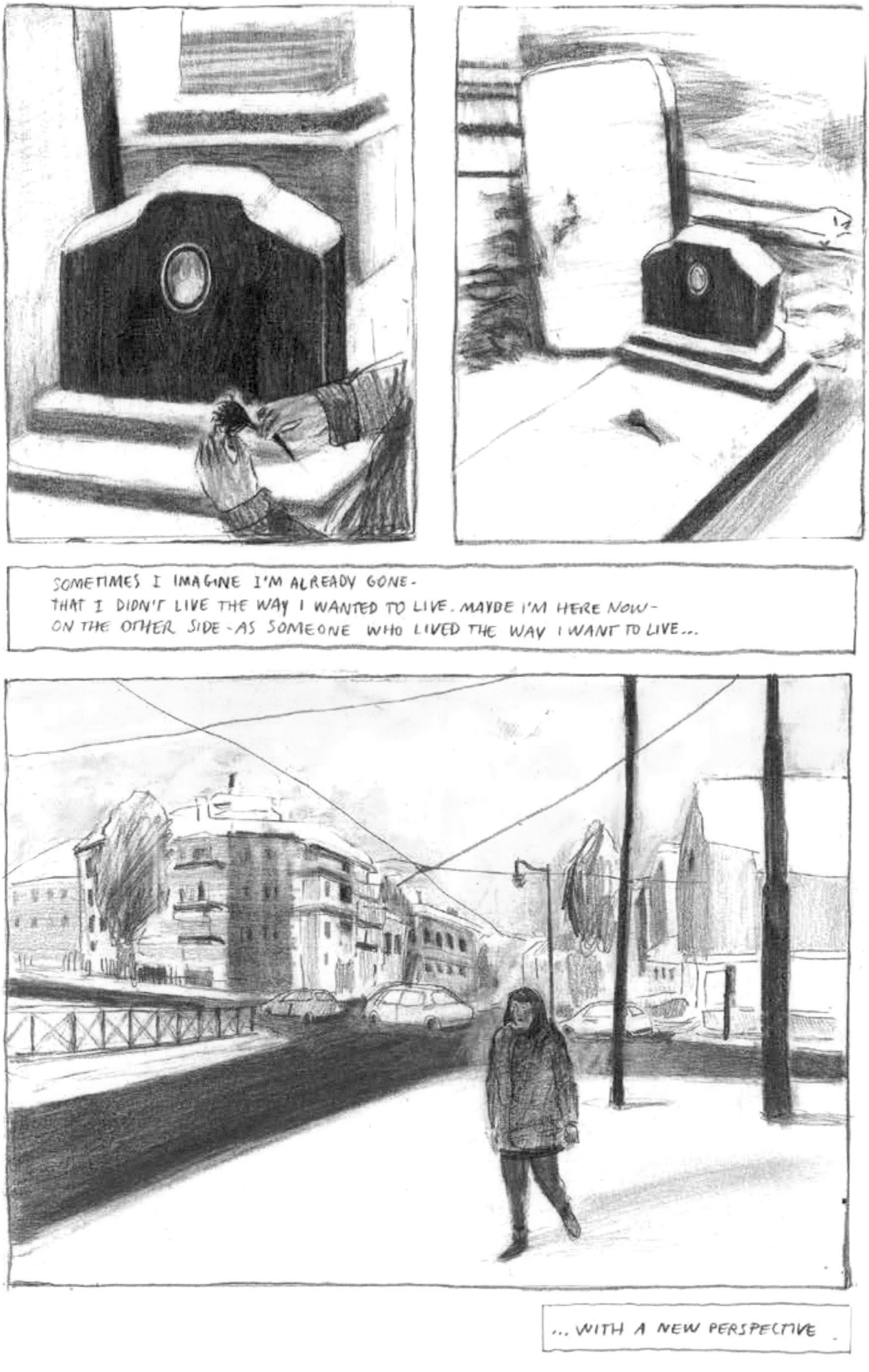
SOMETIMES I IMAGINE I'M ALREADY GONE-
THAT I DIDN'T LIVE THE WAY I WANTED TO LIVE. MAYBE I'M HERE NOW-
ON THE OTHER SIDE-AS SOMEONE WHO LIVED THE WAY I WANT TO LIVE...
...WITH A NEW PERSPECTIVE

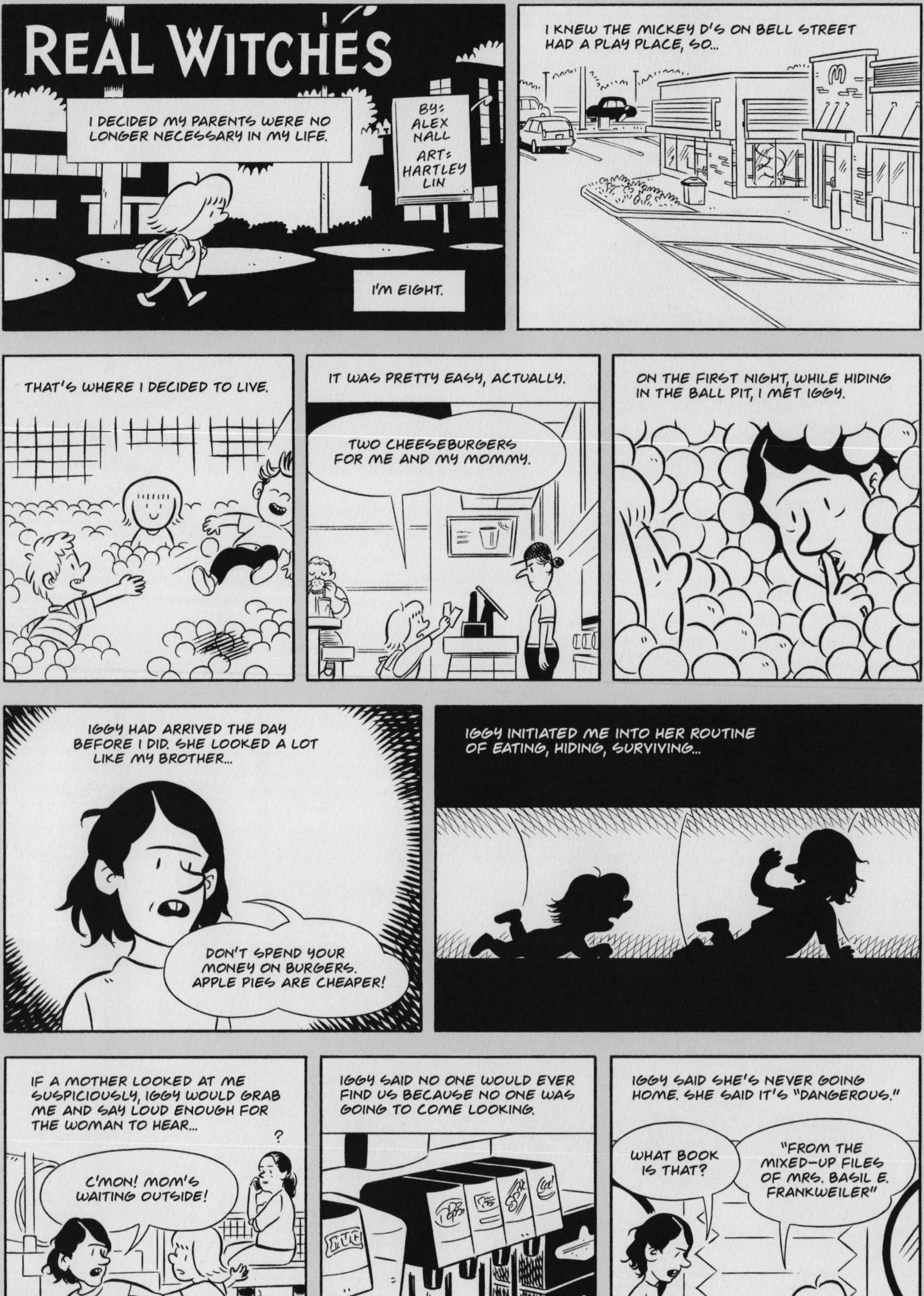
REAL WITCHES
I DECIDED MY PARENTS WERE NO LONGER NECESSARY IN MY LIFE.
BY: ALEX NALL
ART: HARTLEY LIN
I'M EIGHT.
I KNEW THE MICKEY D'S ON BELL STREET HAD A PLAY PLACE, SO...
THAT'S WHERE I DECIDED TO LIVE.
IT WAS PRETTY EASY, ACTUALLY.
TWO CHEESEBURGERS FOR ME AND MY MOMMY.
ON THE FIRST NIGHT, WHILE HIDING IN THE BALL PIT, I MET IGGY.
IGGY HAD ARRIVED THE DAY BEFORE I DID. SHE LOOKED A LOT LIKE MY BROTHER...
DON'T SPEND YOUR MONEY ON BURGERS. APPLE PIES ARE CHEAPER!
IGGY INITIATED ME INTO HER ROUTINE OF EATING, HIDING, SURVIVING...
IF A MOTHER LOOKED AT ME SUSPICIOUSLY, IGGY WOULD GRAB ME AND SAY LOUD ENOUGH FOR THE WOMAN TO HEAR...
?
C'MON! MOM'S WAITING OUTSIDE!
IGGY SAID NO ONE WOULD EVER FIND US BECAUSE NO ONE WAS GOING TO COME LOOKING.
IGGY SAID SHE'S NEVER GOING HOME. SHE SAID IT'S "DANGEROUS."
WHAT BOOK IS THAT?
"FROM THE MIXED-UP FILES OF MRS. BASIL E. FRANKWEILER"

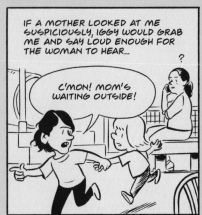

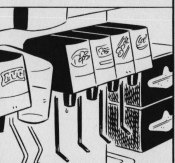

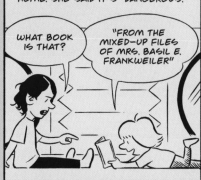

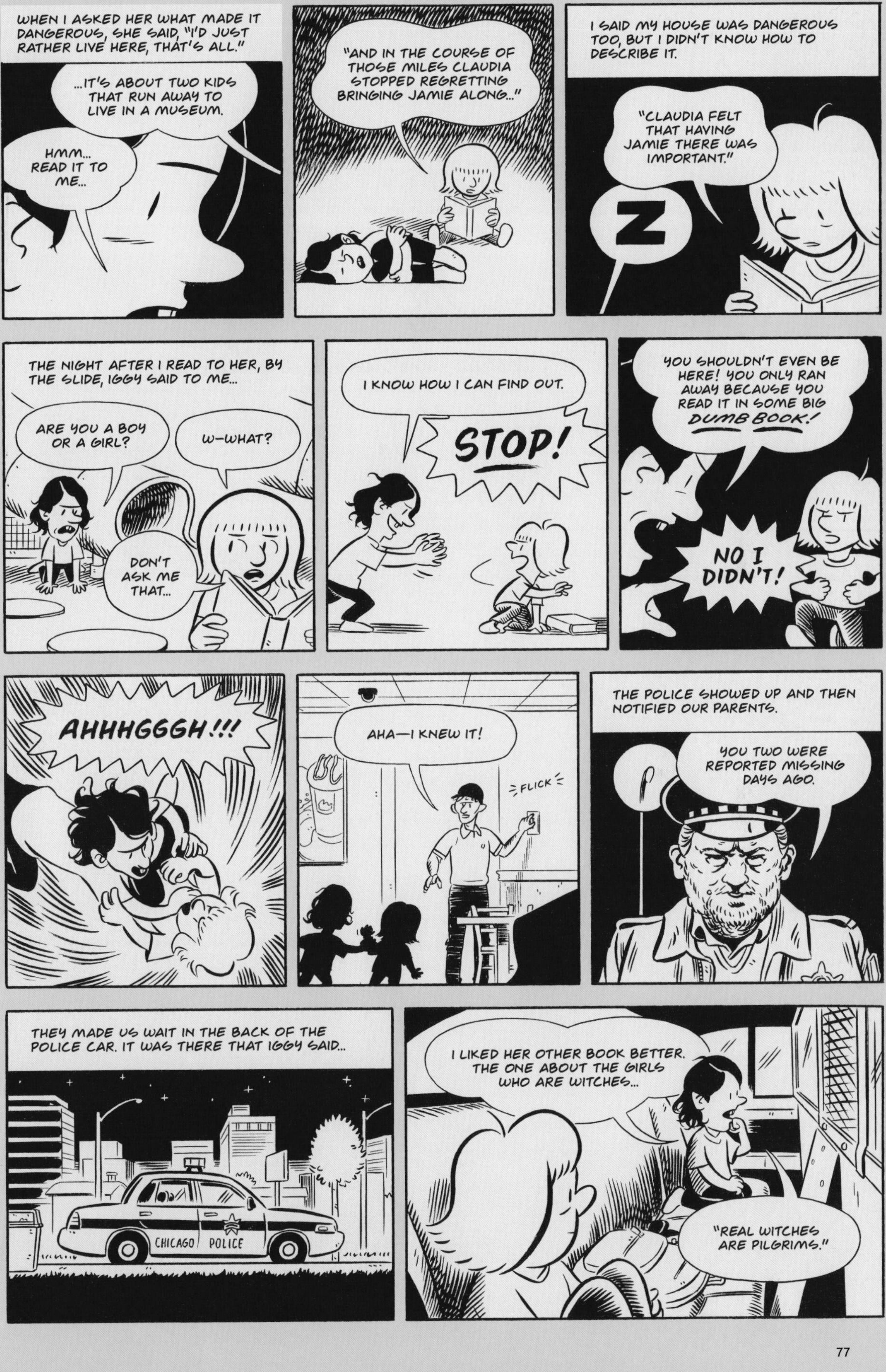
WHEN I ASKED HER WHAT MADE IT DANGEROUS, SHE SAID, "I'D JUST RATHER LIVE HERE, THAT'S ALL."
...IT'S ABOUT TWO KIDS THAT RUN AWAY TO LIVE IN A MUSEUM.
HMM... READ IT TO ME...
"AND IN THE COURSE OF THOSE MILES CLAUDIA STOPPED REGRETTING BRINGING JAMIE ALONG..."
I SAID MY HOUSE WAS DANGEROUS TOO, BUT I DIDN'T KNOW HOW TO DESCRIBE IT.
"CLAUDIA FELT THAT HAVING JAMIE THERE WAS IMPORTANT."
Z
THE NIGHT AFTER I READ TO HER, BY THE SLIDE, IGGY SAID TO ME...
ARE YOU A BOY OR A GIRL?
W-WHAT?
DON'T ASK ME THAT...
I KNOW HOW I CAN FIND OUT.
STOP!
YOU SHOULDN'T EVEN BE HERE! YOU ONLY RAN AWAY BECAUSE YOU READ IT IN SOME BIG DUMB BOOK!
NO I DIDN'T!
AHHHGGGH!!!
AHA—I KNEW IT!
FLICK
THE POLICE SHOWED UP AND THEN NOTIFIED OUR PARENTS.
YOU TWO WERE REPORTED MISSING DAYS AGO.
THEY MADE US WAIT IN THE BACK OF THE POLICE CAR. IT WAS THERE THAT IGGY SAID...
CHICAGO POLICE
I LIKED HER OTHER BOOK BETTER. THE ONE ABOUT THE GIRLS WHO ARE WITCHES...
"REAL WITCHES ARE PILGRIMS."

I went to Taffy's house, Taffy was not in
Taffy came to my house, and stole a silver pin
I went to Taffy's house, Taffy was in bed
I took up a poker, and threw it at his head

- Mother Goose

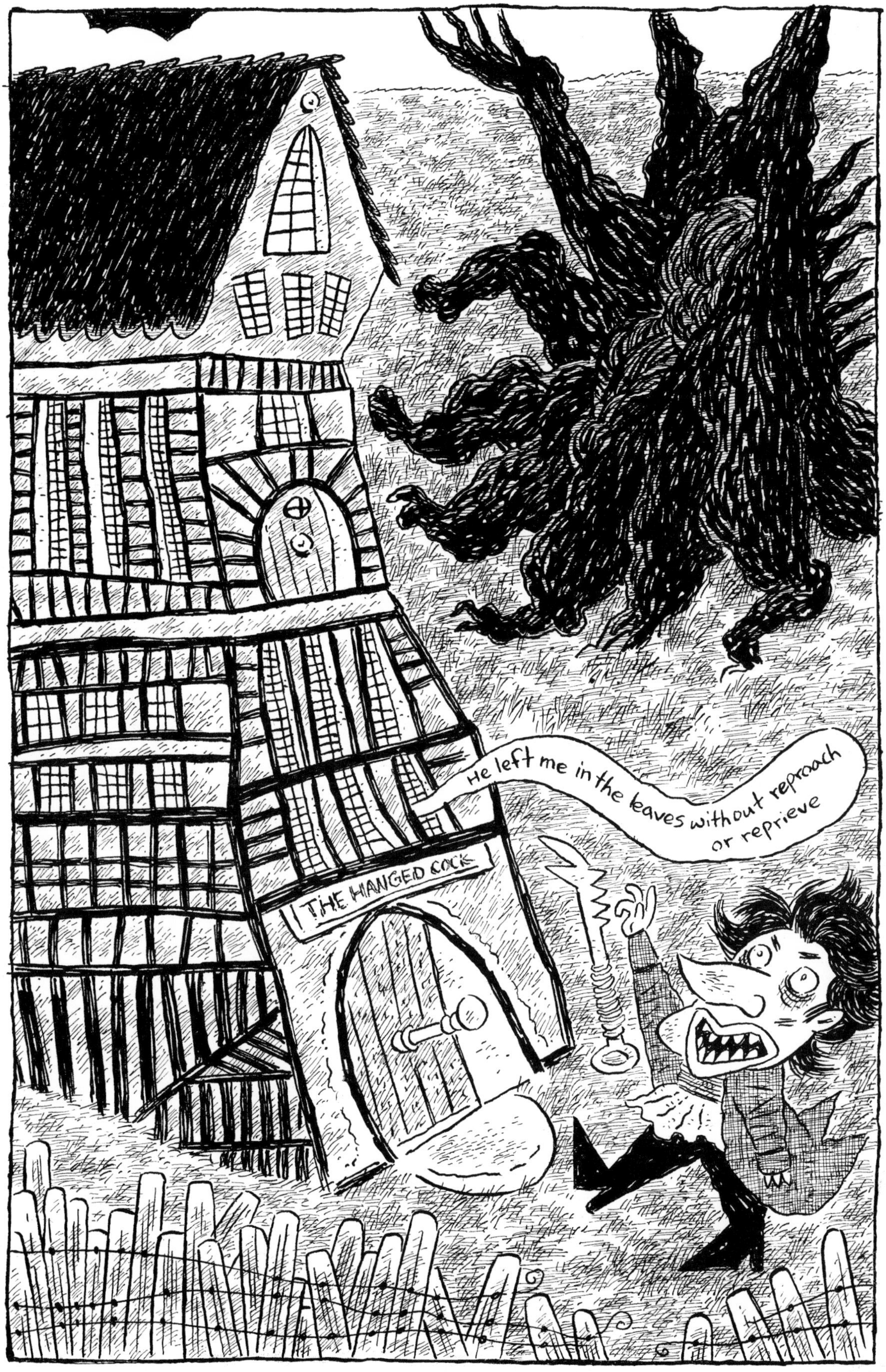
He left me in the leaves without reproach or reprieve
THE HANGED COCK

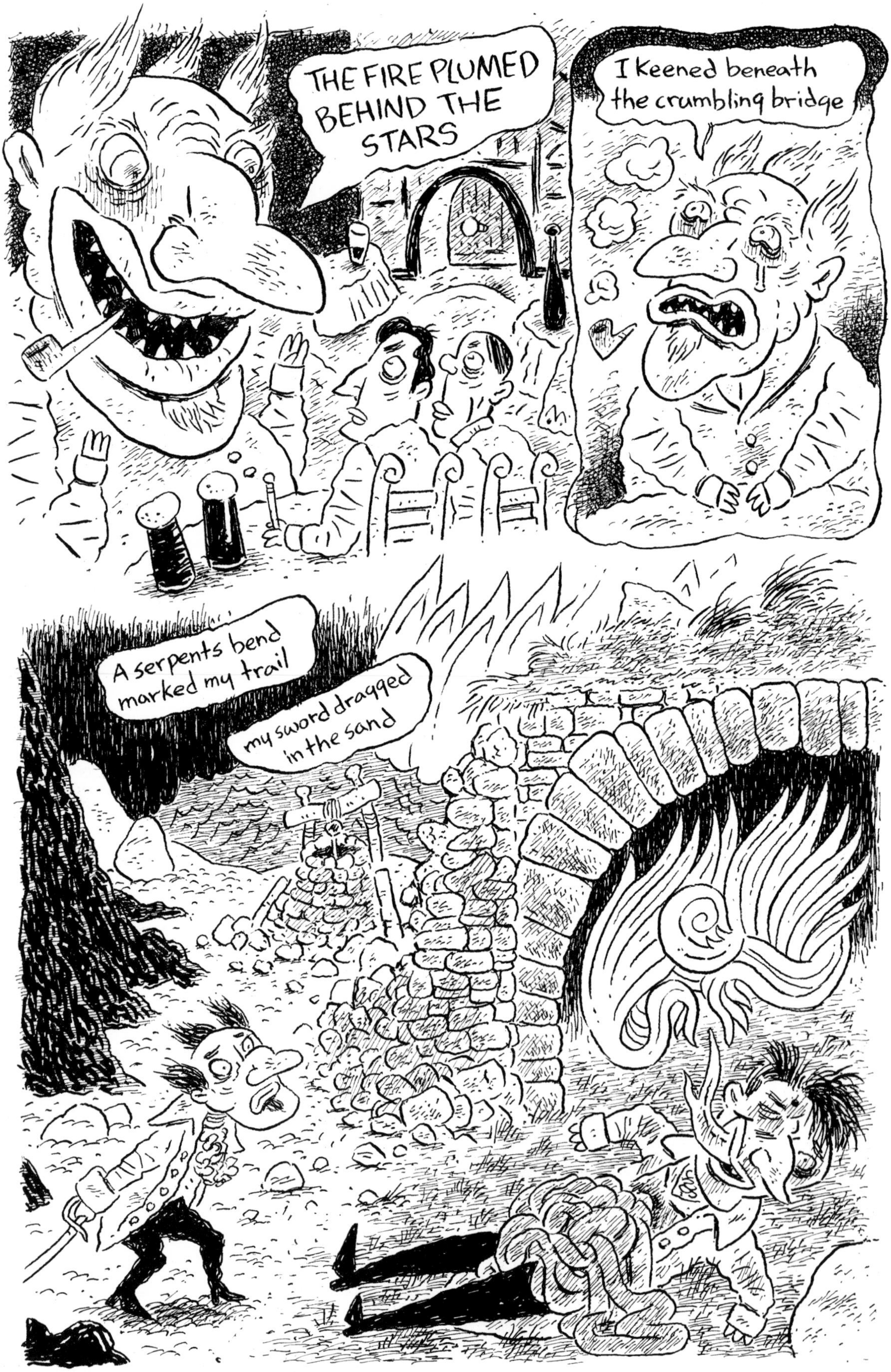
THE FIRE PLUMED BEHIND THE STARS
I keened beneath the crumbling bridge
A serpents bend marked my trail
my sword dragged in the sand

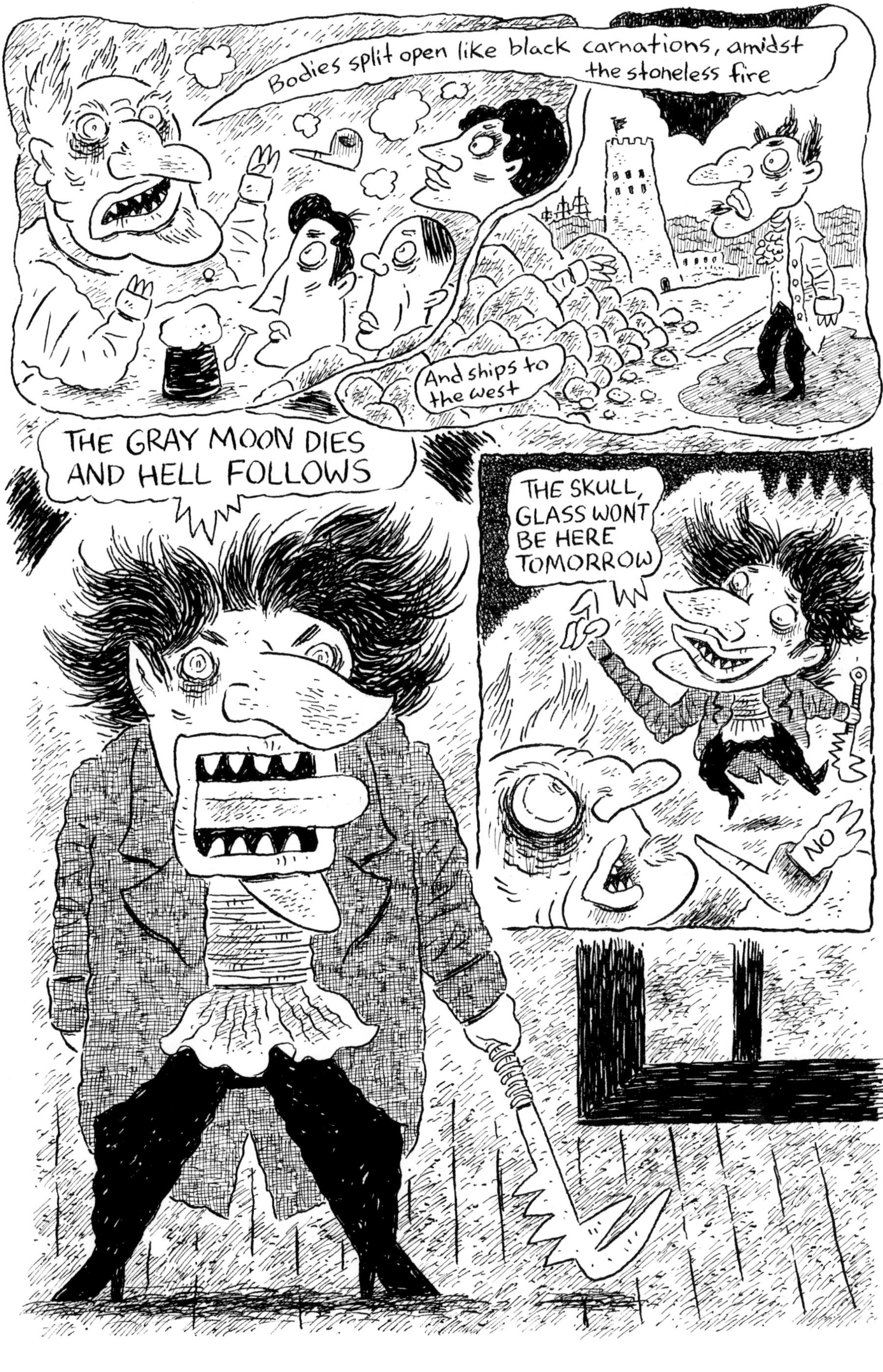
Bodies split open like black carnations, amidst the stoneless fire
And ships to the west
THE GRAY MOON DIES AND HELL FOLLOWS
THE SKULL, GLASS WON'T BE HERE TOMORROW
NO

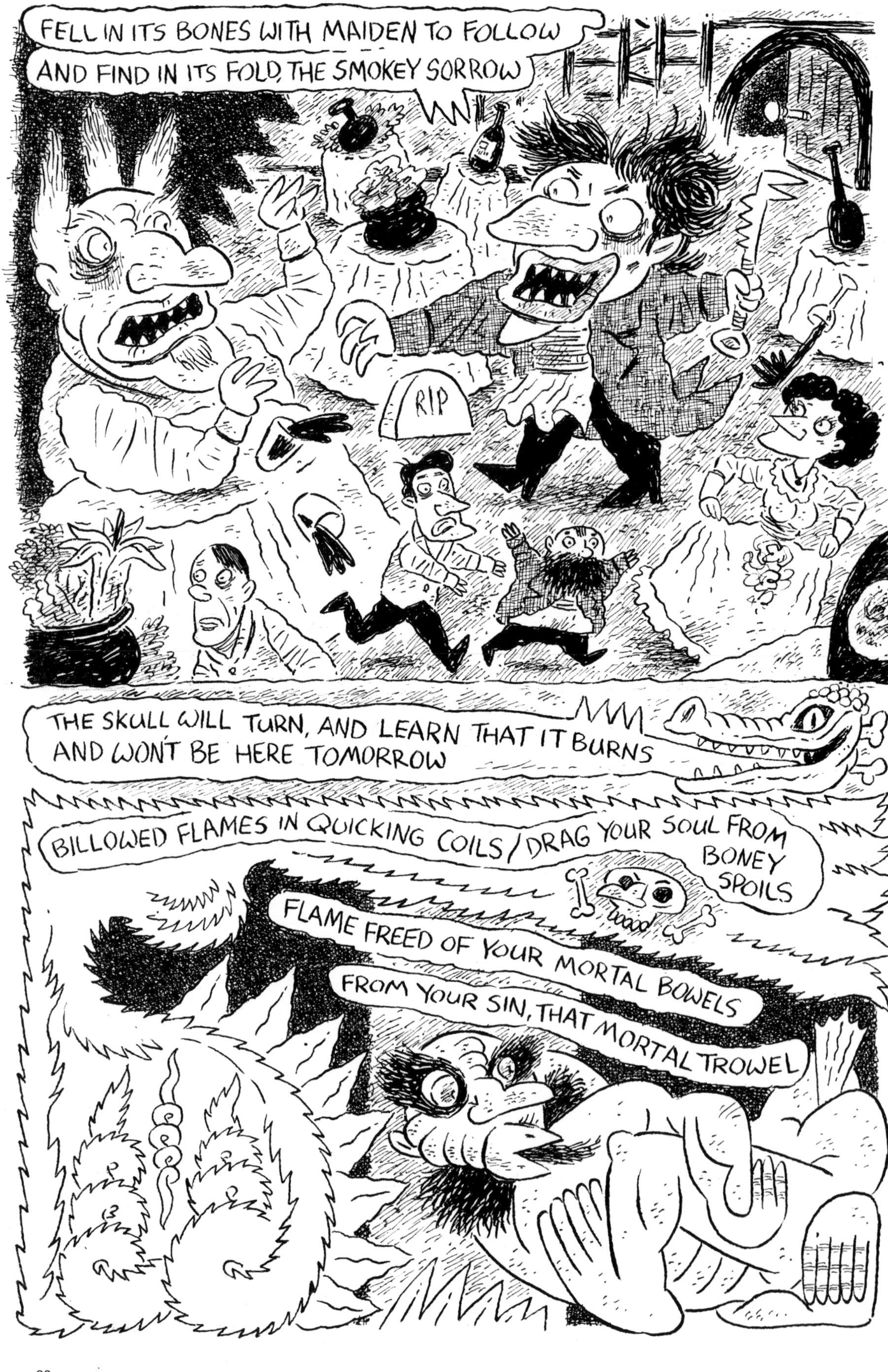
FELL IN ITS BONES WITH MAIDEN TO FOLLOW
AND FIND IN ITS FOLD, THE SMOKEY SORROW
RIP
THE SKULL WILL TURN, AND LEARN THAT IT BURNS
AND WON'T BE HERE TOMORROW
BILLOWED FLAMES IN QUICKING COILS / DRAG YOUR SOUL FROM BONEY SPOILS
FLAME FREED OF YOUR MORTAL BOWELS
FROM YOUR SIN, THAT MORTAL TROWEL

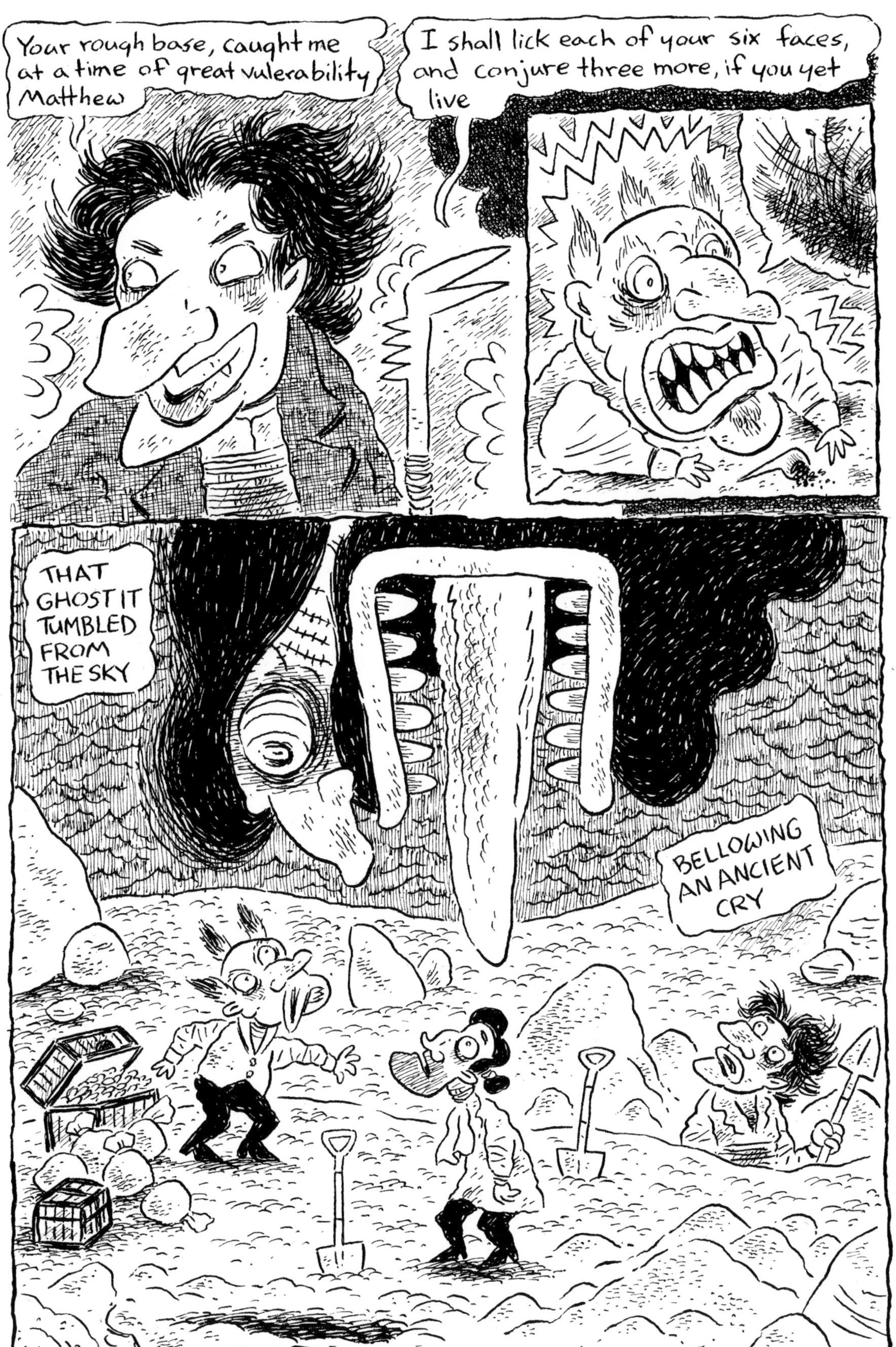

Your rough base, caught me at a time of great vulerability Matthew
I shall lick each of your six faces, and conjure three more, if you yet live
THAT GHOST IT TUMBLED FROM THE SKY
BELLOWING AN ANCIENT CRY

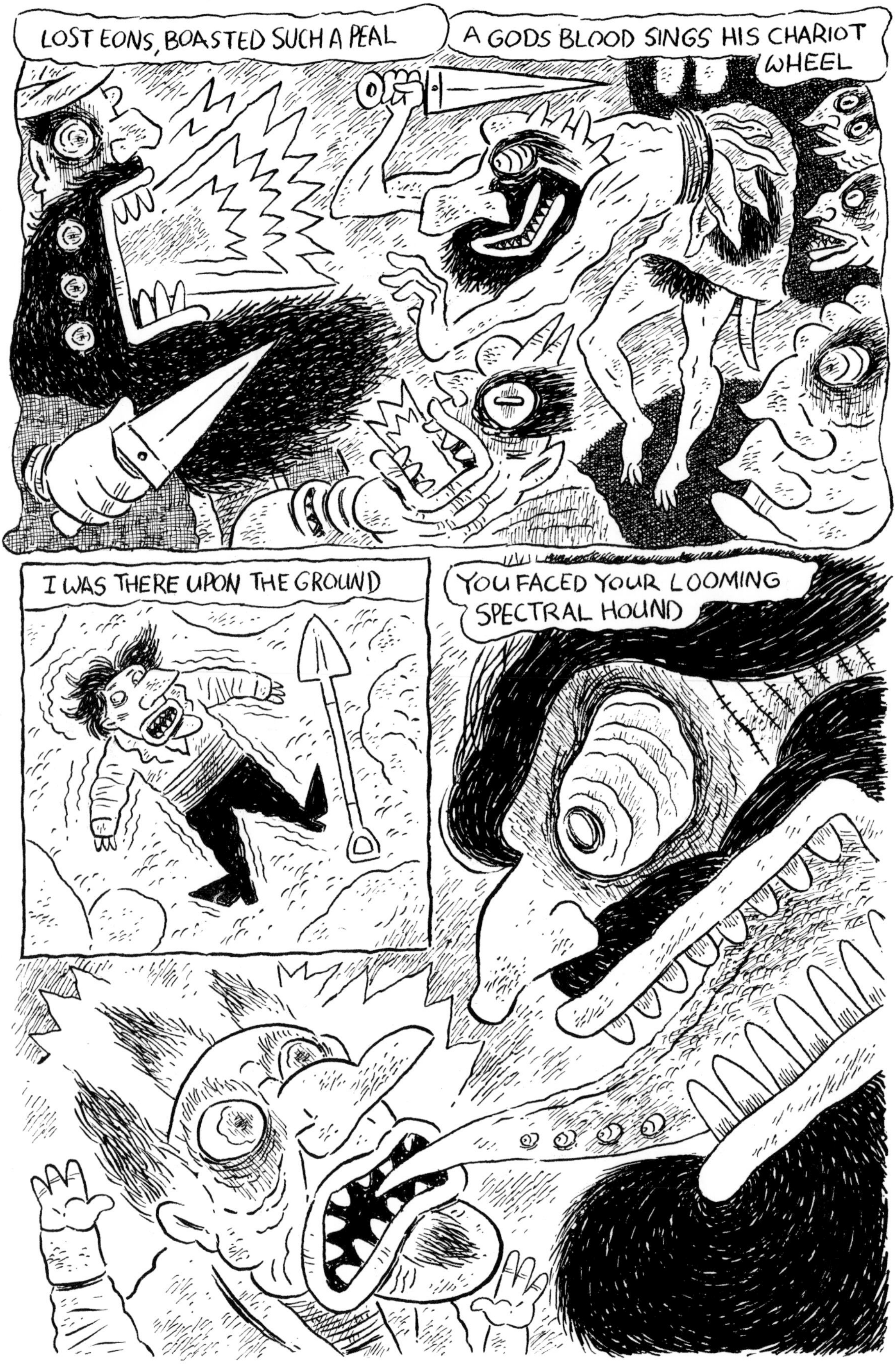
LOST EONS, BOASTED SUCH A PEAL
A GODS BLOOD SINGS HIS CHARIOT WHEEL
I WAS THERE UPON THE GROUND
YOU FACED YOUR LOOMING SPECTRAL HOUND

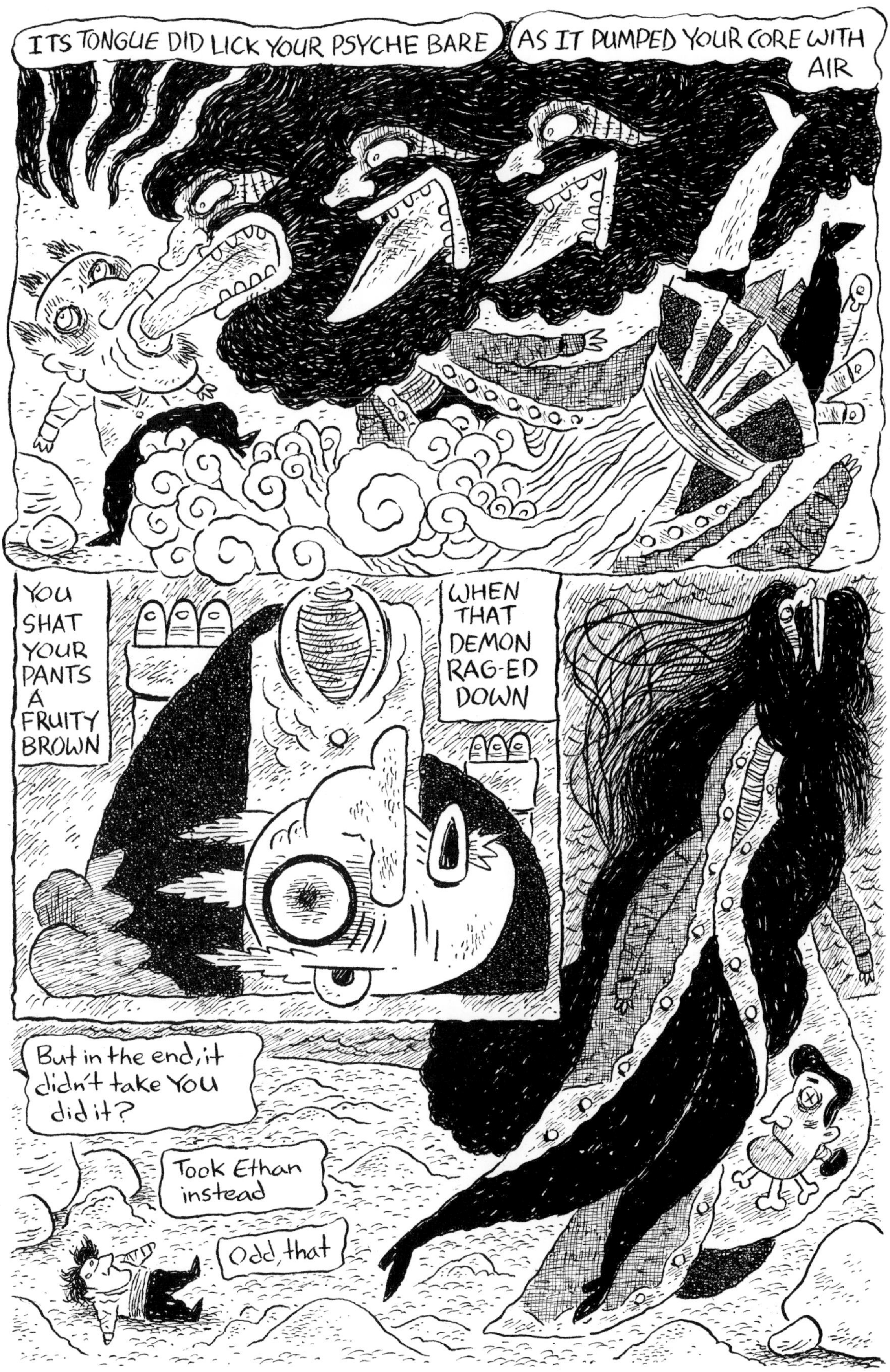
ITS TONGUE DID LICK YOUR PSYCHE BARE
AS IT PUMPED YOUR CORE WITH AIR
YOU SHAT YOUR PANTS A FRUITY BROWN
WHEN THAT DEMON RAG-ED DOWN
But in the end, it didn't take YOU did it?
Took Ethan instead
Odd, that

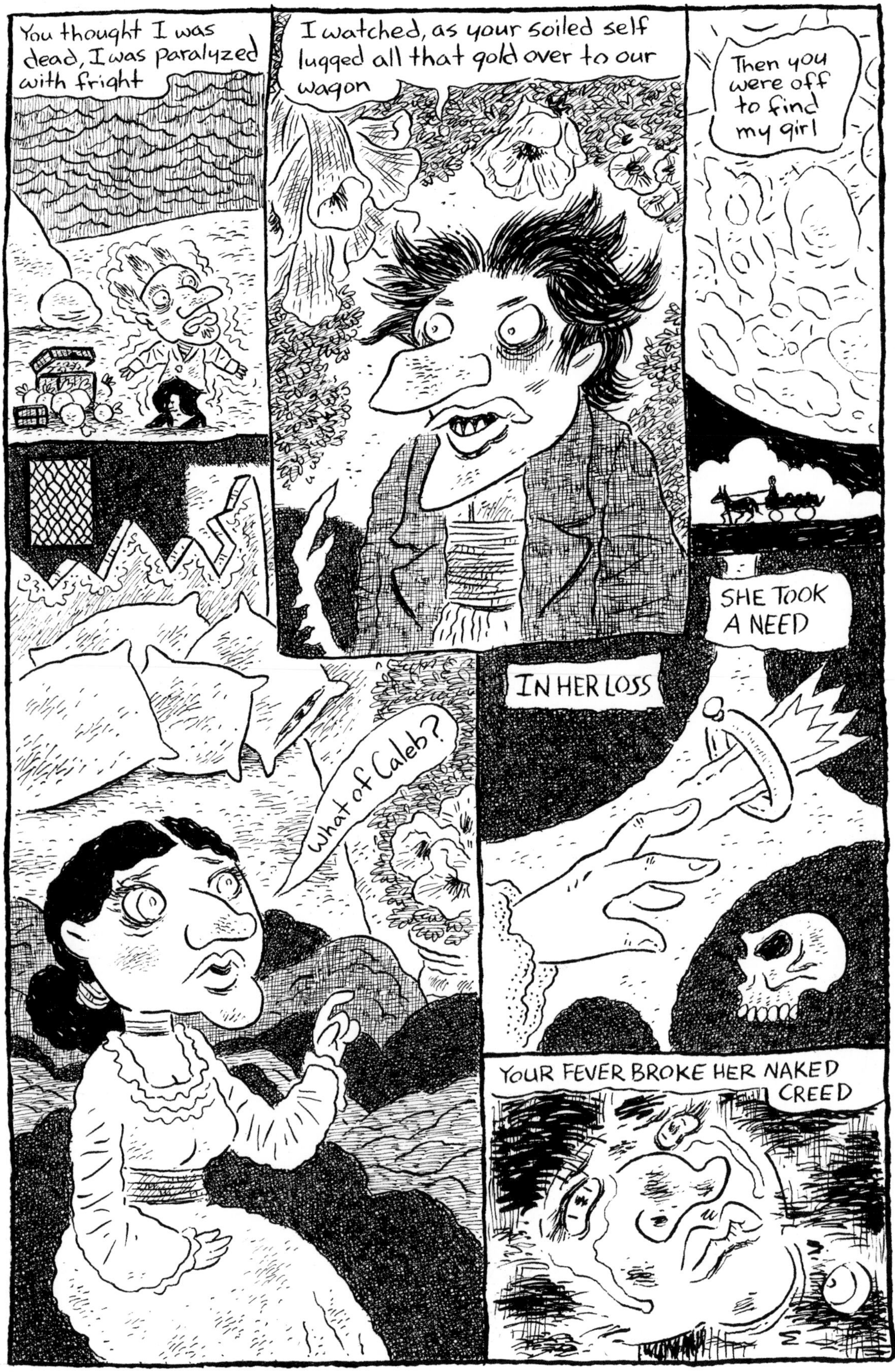
You thought I was dead, I was paralyzed with fright
I watched, as your soiled self lugged all that gold over to our wagon
Then you were off to find my girl
SHE TOOK A NEED
IN HER LOSS
What of Caleb?
YOUR FEVER BROKE HER NAKED CREED

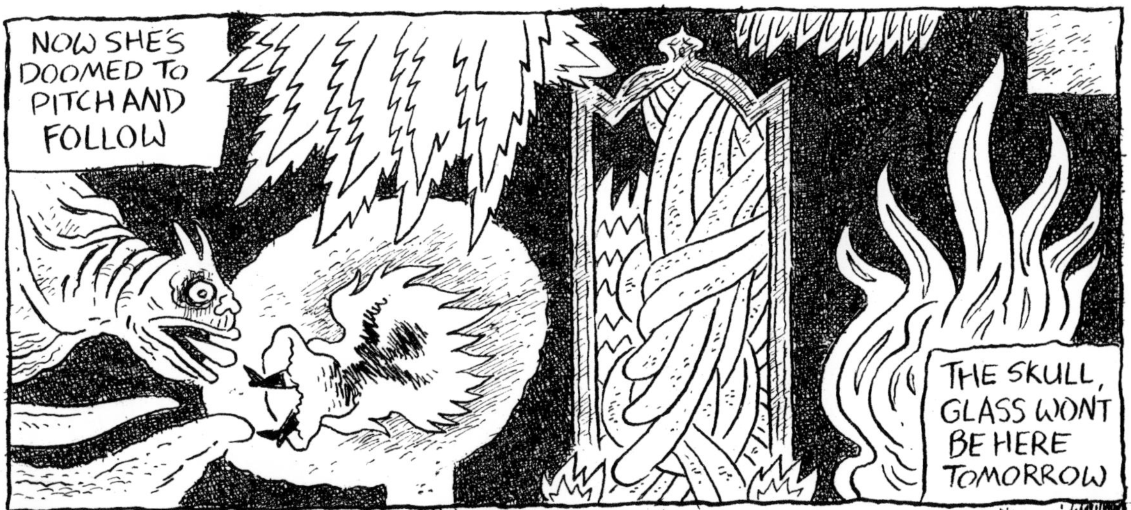
NOW SHE'S DOOMED TO PITCH AND FOLLOW
THE SKULL, GLASS WON'T BE HERE TOMORROW

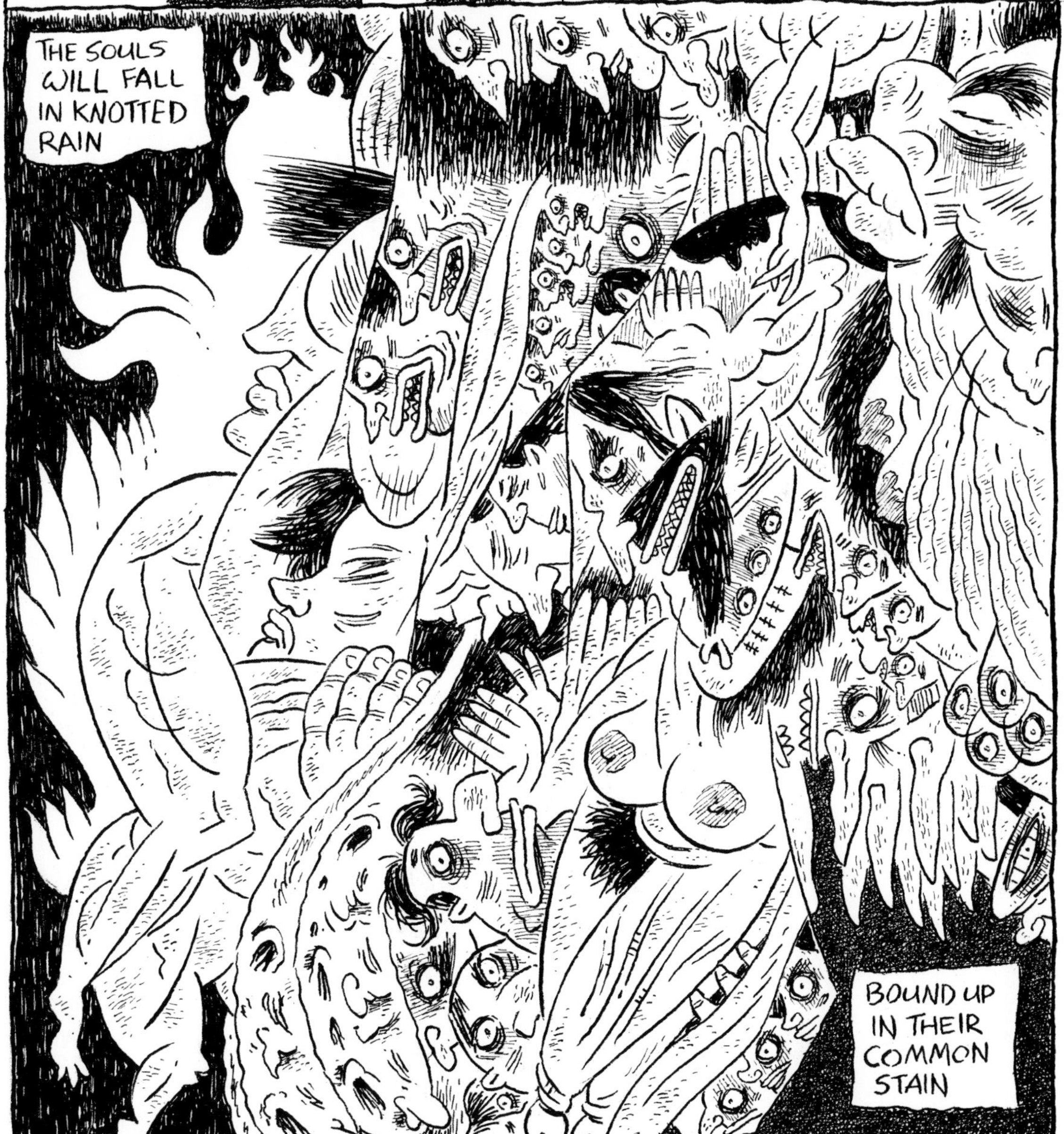
THE SOULS WILL FALL IN KNOTTED RAIN
BOUND UP IN THEIR COMMON STAIN

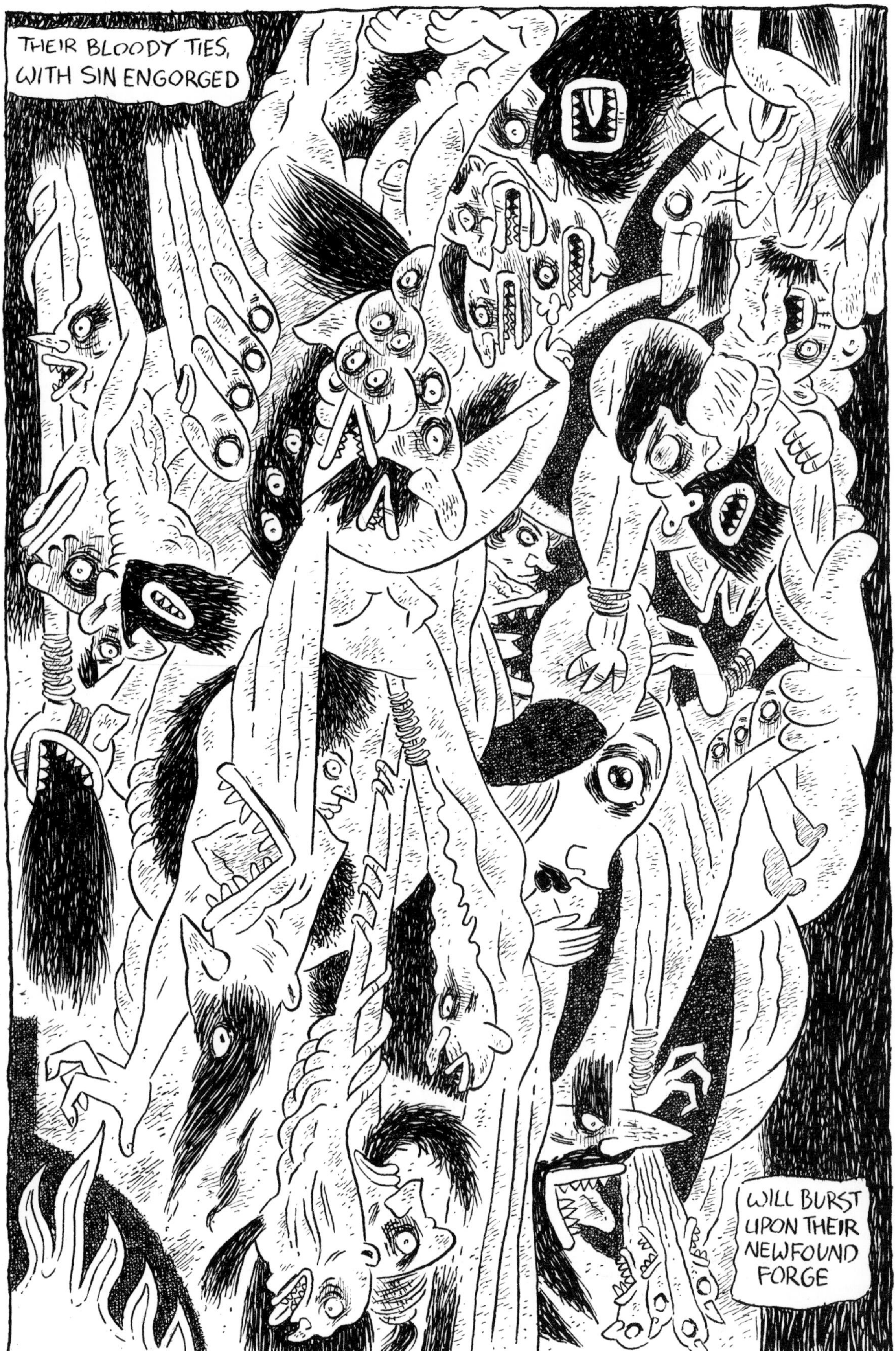
THEIR BLOODY TIES, WITH SIN ENGORGED
WILL BURST UPON THEIR NEWFOUND FORGE

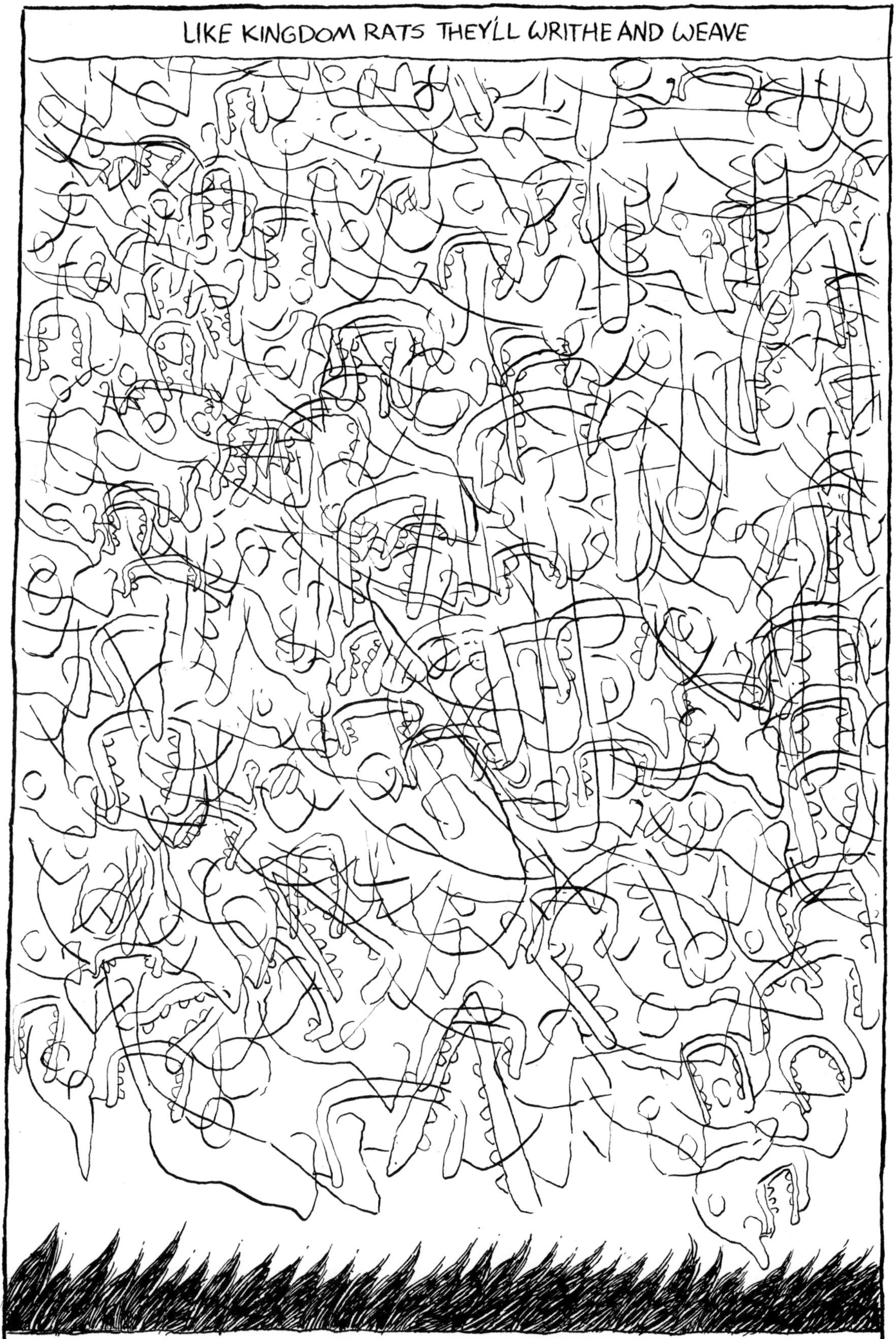
LIKE KINGDOM RATS THEY'LL WRITHE AND WEAVE
IN ENDLESS VATS TO DOLE AND GRIEVE

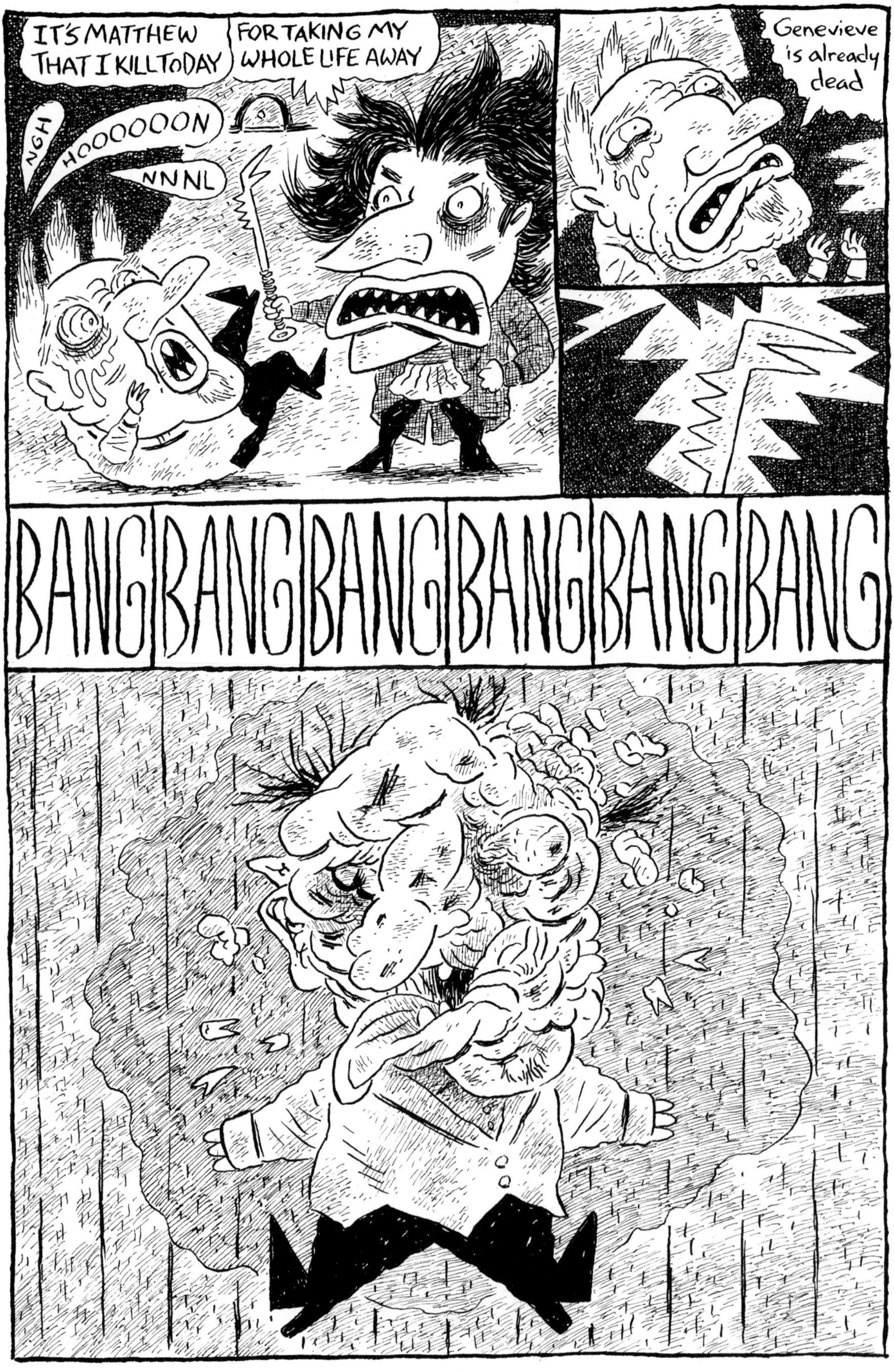
IT'S MATTHEW THAT I KILL TODAY
FOR TAKING MY WHOLE LIFE AWAY
NGH
HOOOOOON
NNNL
Genevieve is already dead
BANG BANG BANG BANG BANG BANG

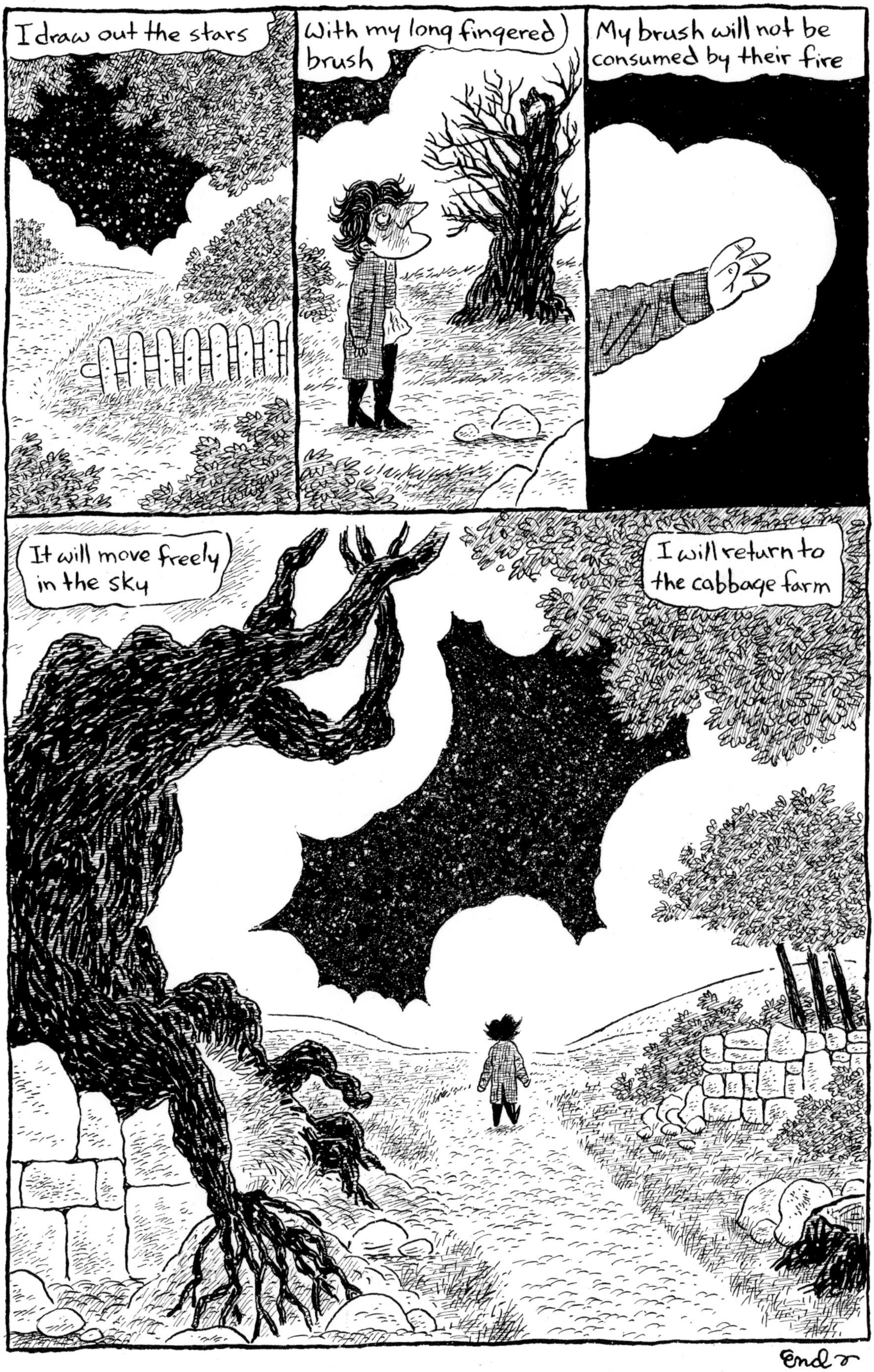
I draw out the stars
With my long fingered brush
My brush will not be consumed by their fire
It will move freely in the sky
I will return to the cabbage farm
End

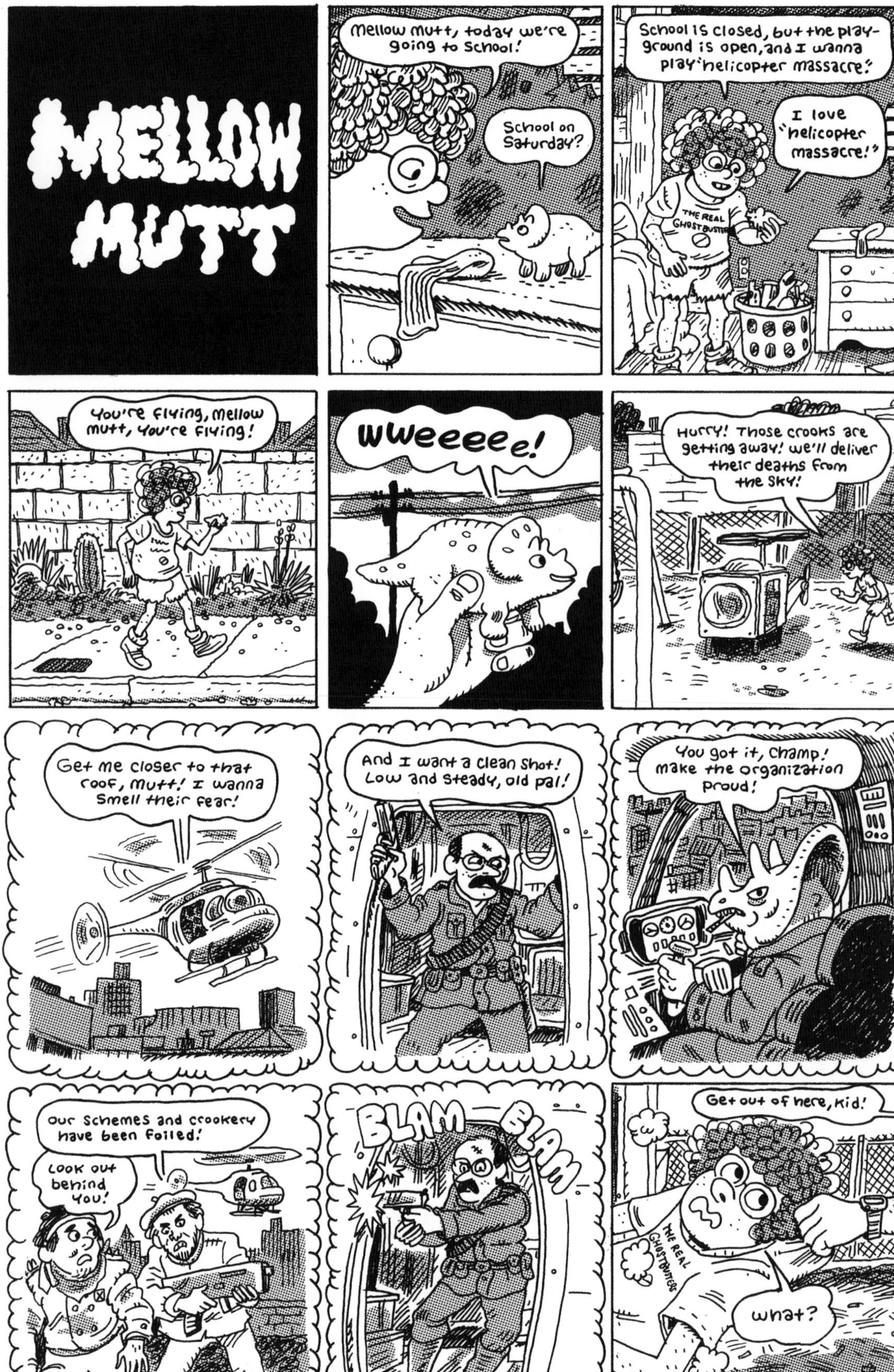
MELLOW MUTT
Mellow mutt, today we're going to school!
School on Saturday?
School is closed, but the playground is open, and I wanna play "helicopter massacre."
I love "helicopter massacre!"
THE REAL GHOSTBUSTERS
You're flying, Mellow mutt, you're flying!
WWeeeee!
Hurry! Those crooks are getting away! We'll deliver their deaths from the sky!
Get me closer to that roof, Mutt! I wanna smell their fear!
And I want a clean shot! Low and steady, old pal!
You got it, champ! Make the organization proud!
Our schemes and crookery have been foiled!
Look out behind you!
BLAM BLAM
Get out of here, kid!
What?
THE REAL GHOSTBUSTERS

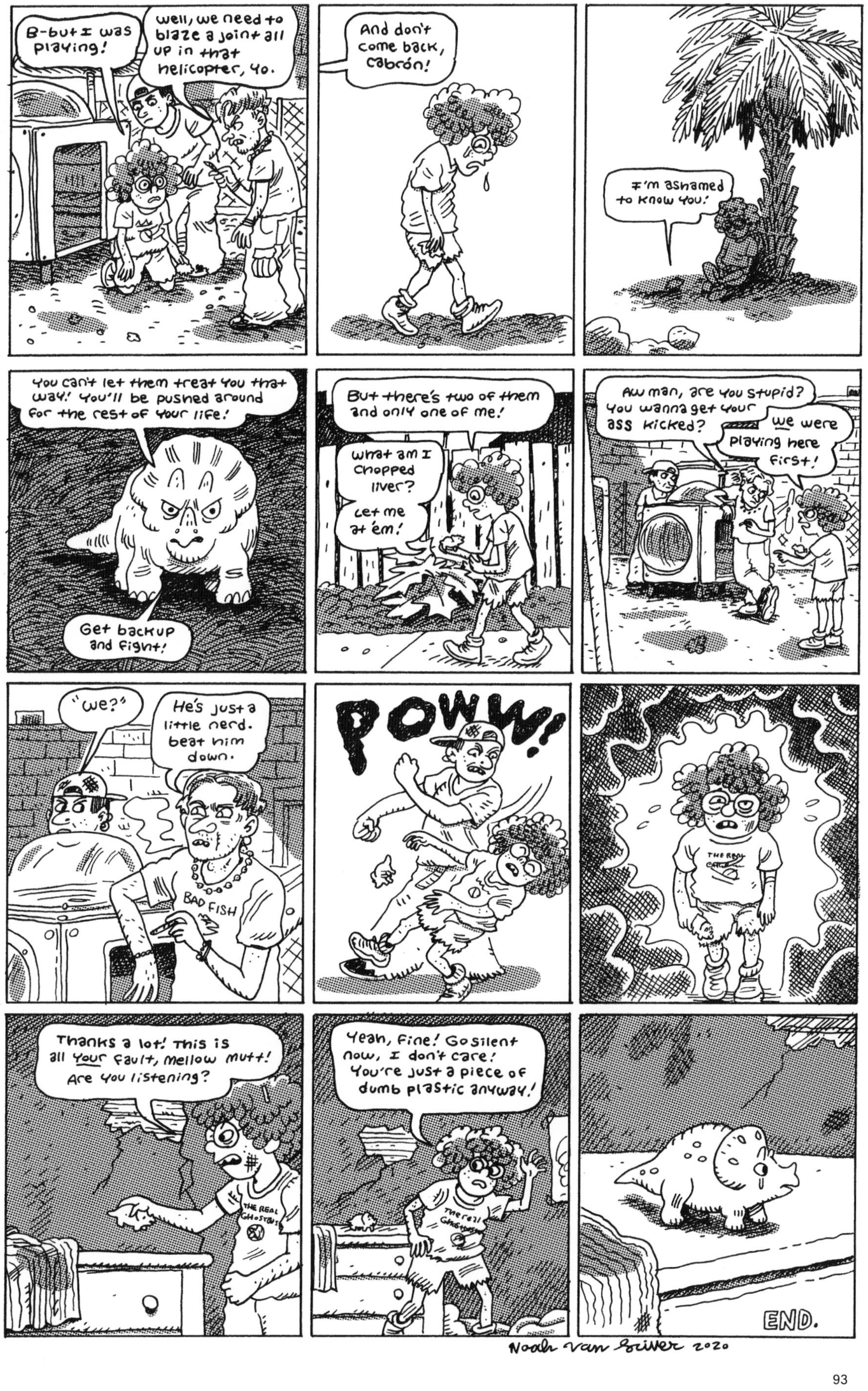
B-but I was playing!
Well, we need to blaze a joint all up in that helicopter, yo.
And don't come back, cabrón!
I'm ashamed to know you!
You can't let them treat you that way! You'll be pushed around for the rest of your life!
Get backup and fight!
But there's two of them and only one of me!
What am I chopped liver?
Let me at 'em!
Aw man, are you stupid? You wanna get your ass kicked?
WE were playing here first!
"We?"
He's just a little nerd. beat him down.
BAD FISH
POW!
Thanks a lot! This is all YOUR fault, Mellow Mutt! Are you listening?
Yeah, fine! Go silent now, I don't care! You're just a piece of dumb plastic anyway!
END.

Noah Van Sciver 2020

SLURP!

TAPTAP

SLURP!

FREE
CONE
DAY!
FREE
CONE
DAY!

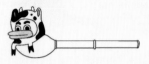

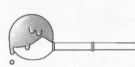

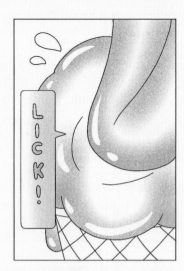

LICK!

SLURP!

TAPTAP

SLURP!

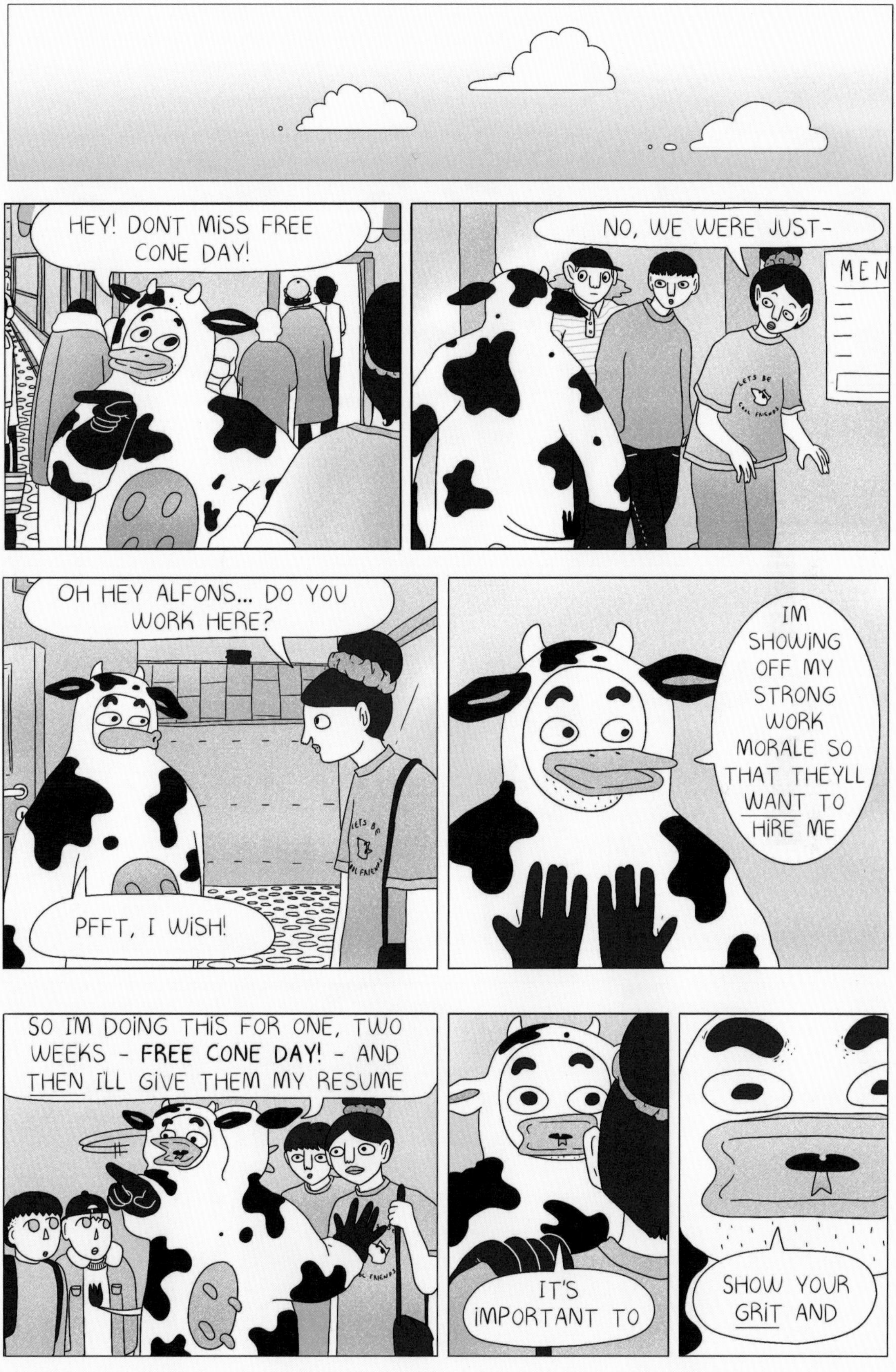
HEY! DON'T MISS FREE CONE DAY!
NO, WE WERE JUST-
MEN
OH HEY ALFONS... DO YOU WORK HERE?
PFFT, I WISH!
I'M SHOWING OFF MY STRONG WORK MORALE SO THAT THEY'LL WANT TO HIRE ME
SO I'M DOING THIS FOR ONE, TWO WEEKS - FREE CONE DAY! - AND THEN I'LL GIVE THEM MY RESUME
IT'S IMPORTANT TO
SHOW YOUR GRIT AND

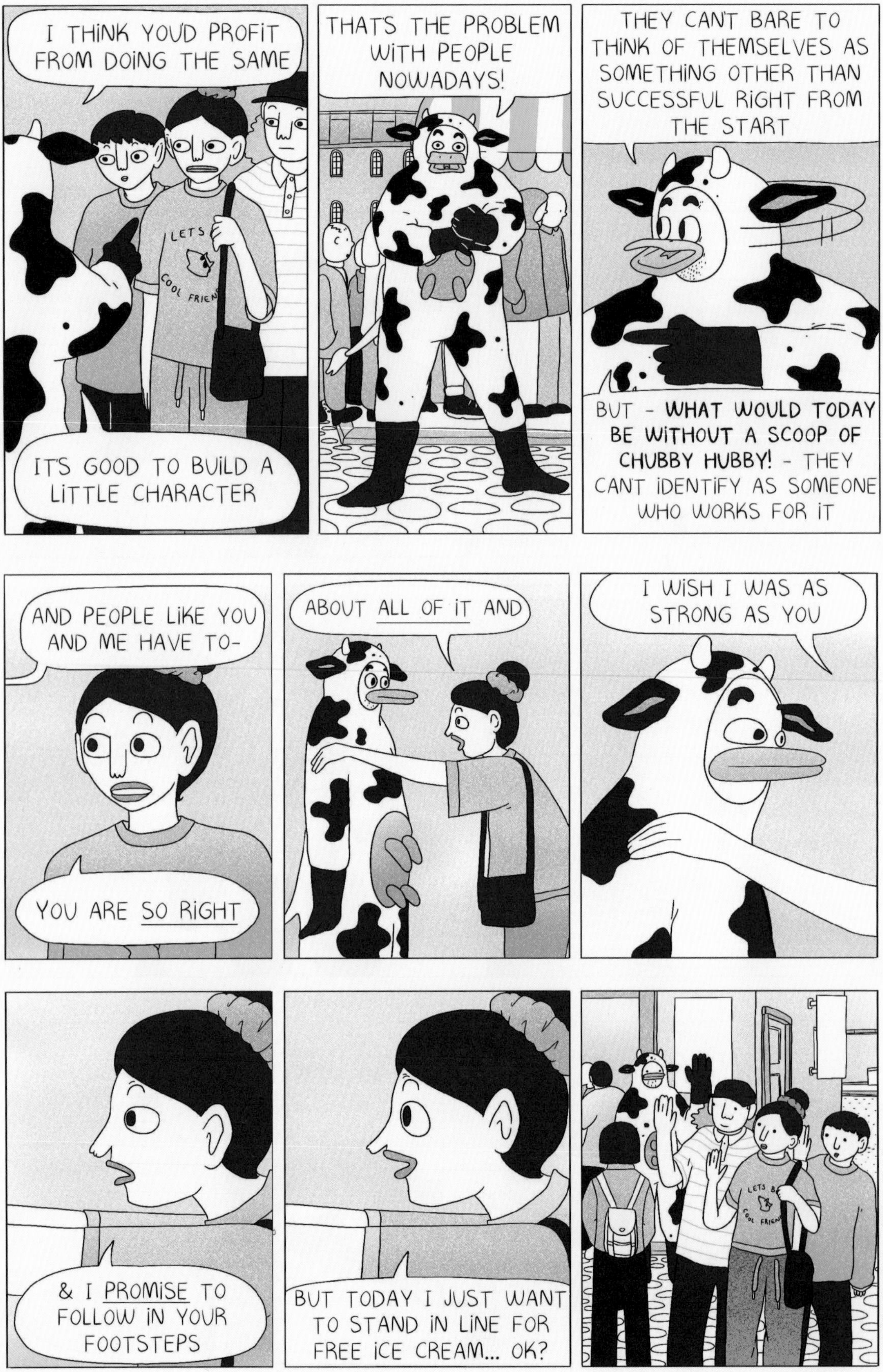
I THINK YOU'D PROFIT FROM DOING THE SAME
IT'S GOOD TO BUILD A LITTLE CHARACTER
THAT'S THE PROBLEM WITH PEOPLE NOWADAYS!
THEY CAN'T BARE TO THINK OF THEMSELVES AS SOMETHING OTHER THAN SUCCESSFUL RIGHT FROM THE START
BUT - **WHAT WOULD TODAY BE WITHOUT A SCOOP OF CHUBBY HUBBY!** - THEY CAN'T IDENTIFY AS SOMEONE WHO WORKS FOR IT
AND PEOPLE LIKE YOU AND ME HAVE TO-
YOU ARE SO RIGHT
ABOUT ALL OF IT AND
I WISH I WAS AS STRONG AS YOU
& I PROMISE TO FOLLOW IN YOUR FOOTSTEPS
BUT TODAY I JUST WANT TO STAND IN LINE FOR FREE ICE CREAM... OK?

CECILIA VARHED - OKEJTJEJGORSINGREJ

Richard Sala
(1955-2020)

In May of 2020, comics lost one of its most uniquely talented creators of the past half-century, the great Richard Sala.

The following nine pages of early comics by Sala have never been published, and their history will remain something of a mystery. They were discovered in Sala's files by his good friend, Daniel Clowes, who was entrusted by Sala's family to help catalog Sala's archives. They almost certainly date between roughly 1979 and 1982, when Richard was between 22 and 25 years old, attending grad school at Mills College in Oakland, CA.

These pages represent a unique, transitional stage in Sala's style and focus. As a child, Sala was obsessed with genre films, pulp fiction, sci fi magazines, and of course comic books. But by the time he entered grad school, he was primarily focused on being a painter and printmaker. These pages seem to wrestle with some of the tension between the "high" art world Sala was immersed in as a painter, while also allowing himself to bring in some of his "low" comics influences as well, from Carl Barks to underground comix to *Heavy Metal*. In many ways, these pages are highly predictive of his later work.

Sala's first comic book, *Night Drive*, would be self-published in 1984, and over the next decade, before going on to author over 20 books, Sala would be a ubiquitous presence on the independent comics scene, experimenting with storytelling and style through dozens of short stories in the pages of virtually every comics anthology on the market: *RAW*, *Prime Cuts*, *Blab!*, *Zero Zero*, *Buzz*, *Deadline USA*, *Drawn & Quarterly*, *Escape*, *Rip Off Comix*, *Street Music*, *Twist*, and *Nickelodeon Magazine*, to name a few. It seems fitting that the following pages see print in a comics anthology, some 40 or so years after their creation and just a few months following the publication of Richard's final book, *Poison Flowers and Pandemonium*, which he completed just weeks before his passing.

There is every reason to believe that Sala would not have wanted these pages to see print. He had never shared them with friends. But we respectfully feel they have value and are pleased to present them to *Now* readers.

ERIC REYNOLDS
January, 2021

BIBLIOGRAPHY

Poison Flowers and Pandemonium
FANTAGRAPHICS, 2021

Phantoms in the Attic
FU PRESS, 2019

The Bloody Cardinal
FANTAGRAPHICS BOOKS, 2017

Violenzia and Other Deadly Amusements
FANTAGRAPHICS, 2015

Violent Girls
FU PRESS, 2015

In a Glass Grotesquely
FANTAGRAPHICS, 2014

Delphine
FANTAGRAPHICS, 2012

The Hidden
FANTAGRAPHICS, 2011

Cat Burglar Black
FIRST SECOND BOOKS, 2009

The Grave Robber's Daughter
FANTAGRAPHICS, 2006

Dracula
IDW, 2005 (IN COLLABORATION WITH STEVE NILES)

Peculia and the Groon Grove Vampires
FANTAGRAPHICS, 2005

Mad Night
FANTAGRAPHICS, 2005

Maniac Killer Strikes Again!
FANTAGRAPHICS, 2003

Peculia
FANTAGRAPHICS, 2002

The Chuckling Whatsit
FANTAGRAPHICS, 1997

The Ghastly Ones and Other Fiendish Frolics
MANIC D PRESS, INC., 1995

Black Cat Crossing
KITCHEN SINK PRESS, 1993

Hypnotic Tales
KITCHEN SINK PRESS, 1992

Night Drive
SELF-PUBLISHED, 1984

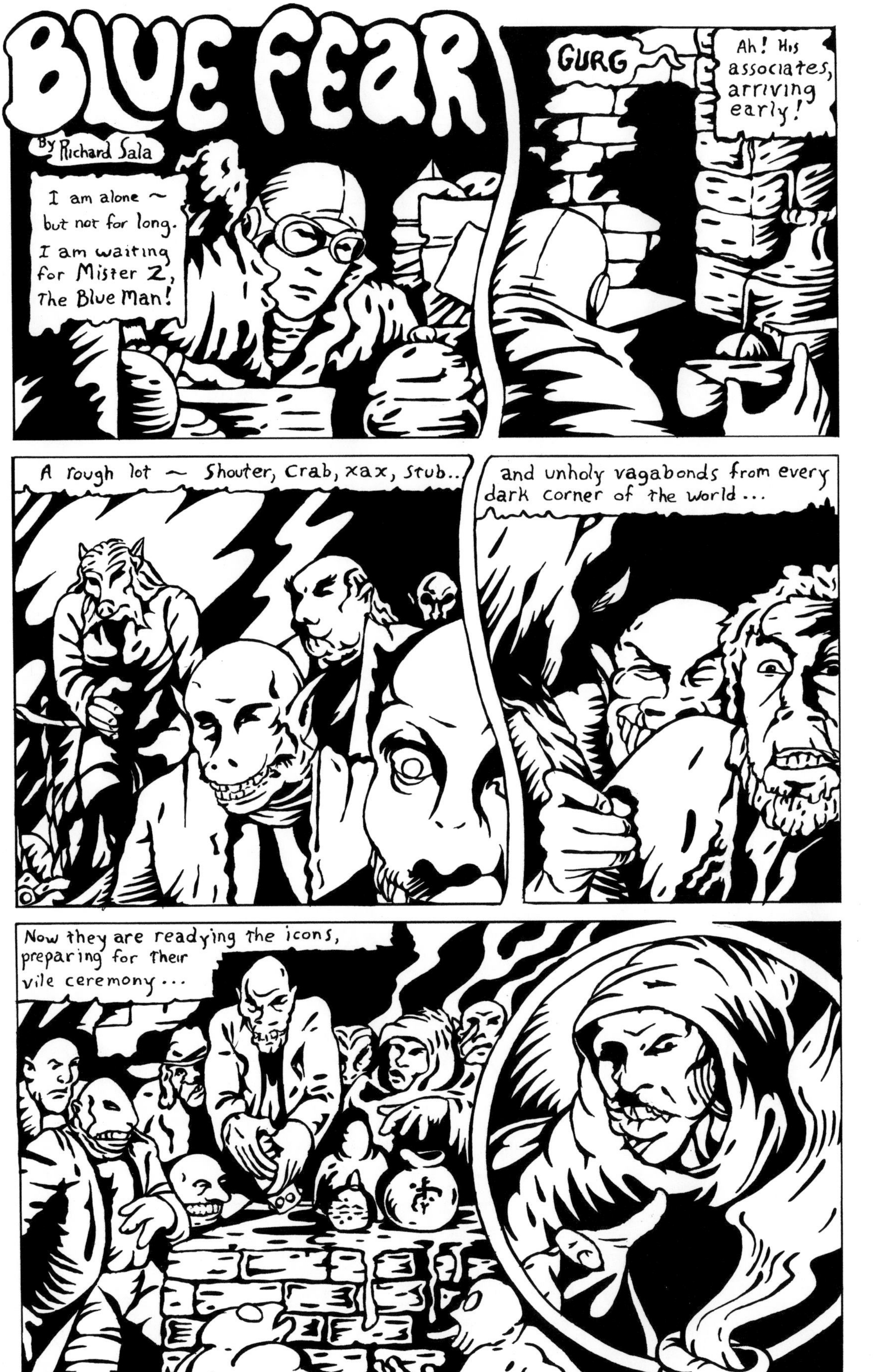
BLUE FEAR
By Richard Sala
I am alone ~ but not for long. I am waiting for Mister Z, The Blue Man!
GURG
Ah! His associates, arriving early!
A rough lot ~ Shouter, Crab, xax, Stub..
and unholy vagabonds from every dark corner of the world...
Now they are readying the icons, preparing for their vile ceremony...

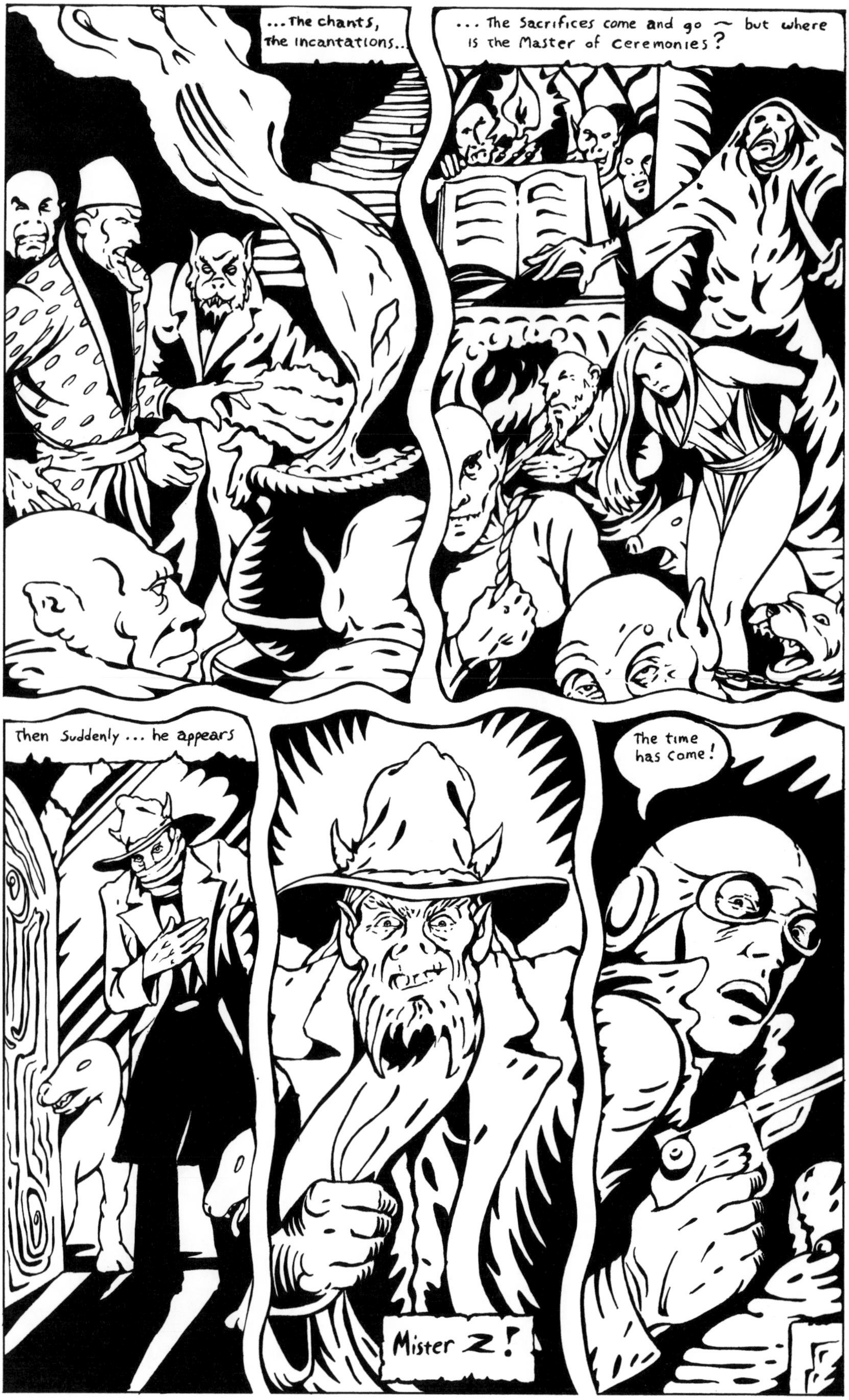
...The chants, the incantations...
...The Sacrifices come and go ~ but where is the Master of Ceremonies?
Then Suddenly ... he appears
Mister Z!
The time has come!

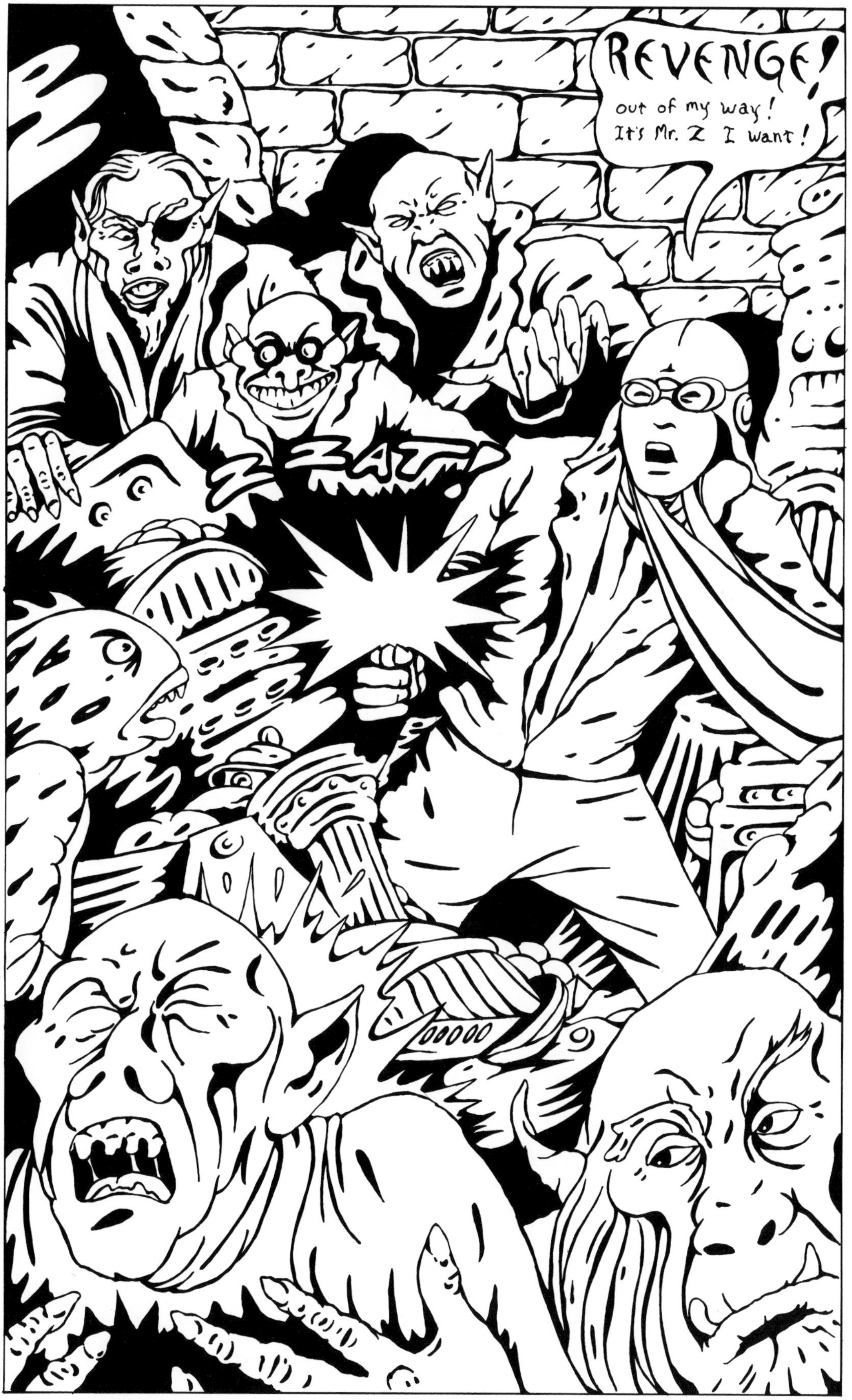
REVENGE!
out of my way! It's Mr. Z I want!
ZZAT!

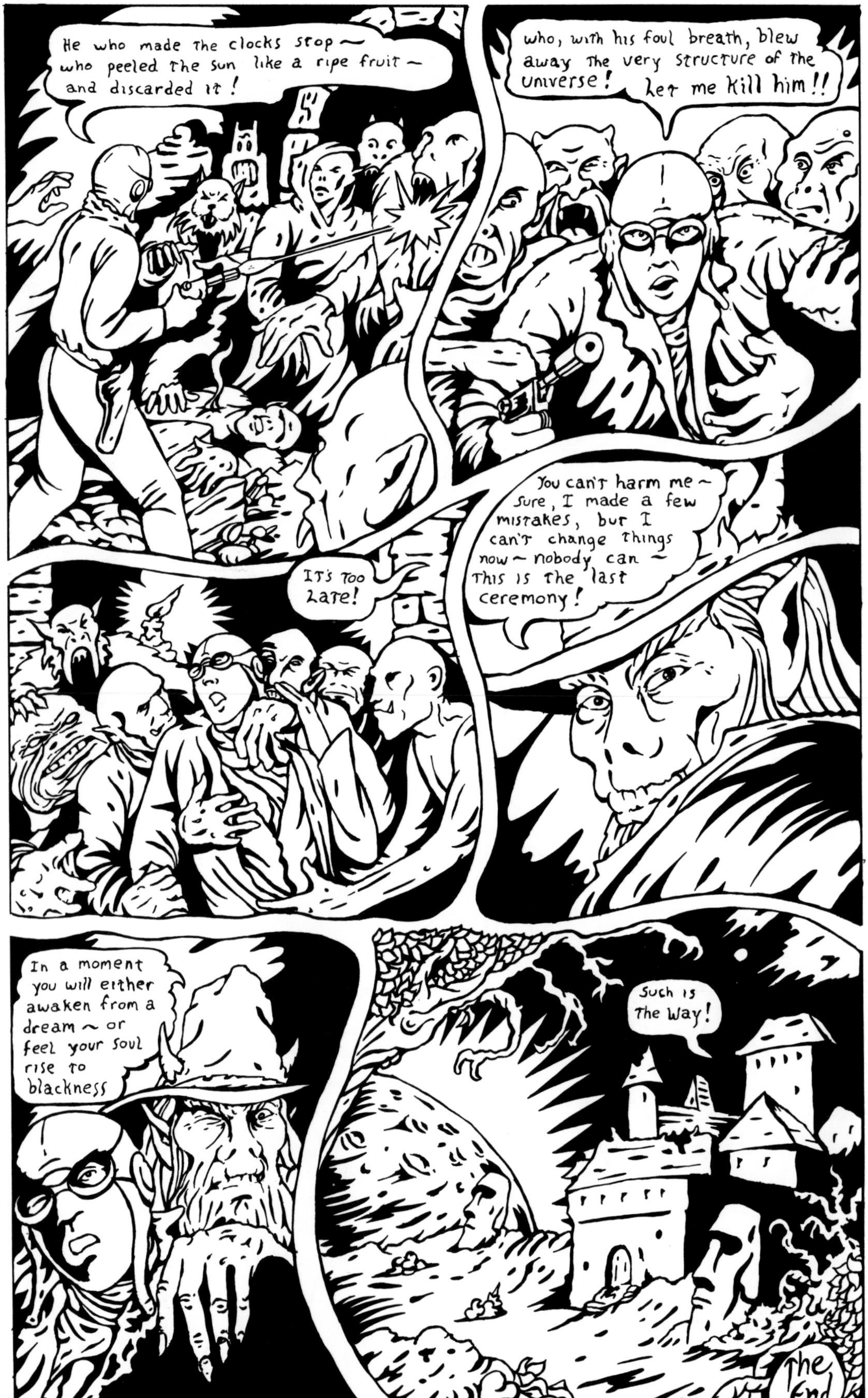
He who made the clocks stop ~ who peeled the sun like a ripe fruit ~ and discarded it!
who, with his foul breath, blew away the very structure of the universe!
Let me kill him!!
It's too late!
You can't harm me ~ sure, I made a few mistakes, but I can't change things now ~ nobody can ~ This is the last ceremony!
In a moment you will either awaken from a dream ~ or feel your soul rise to blackness
Such is the way!
The End

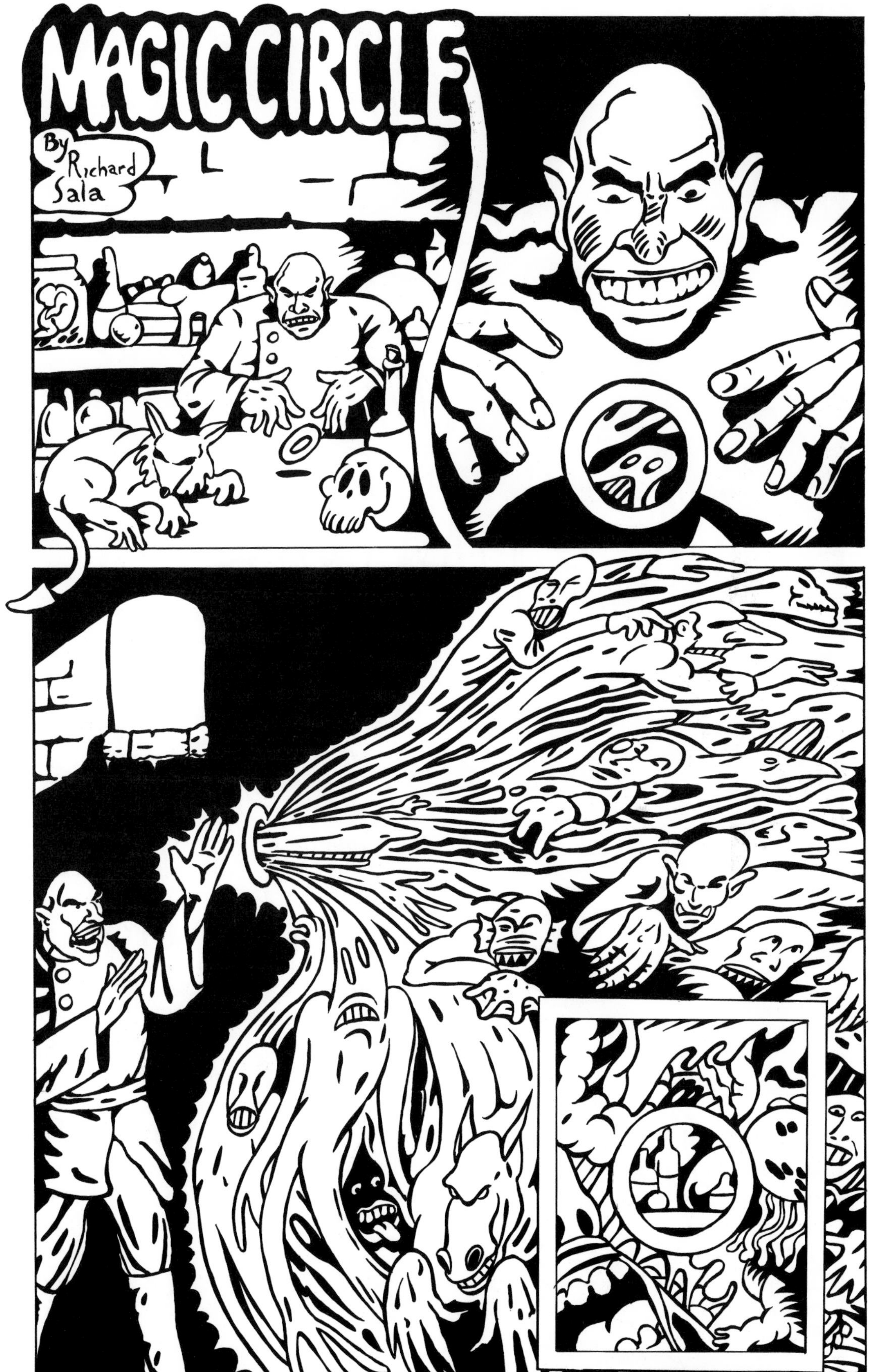
MAGIC CIRCLE
By Richard Sala

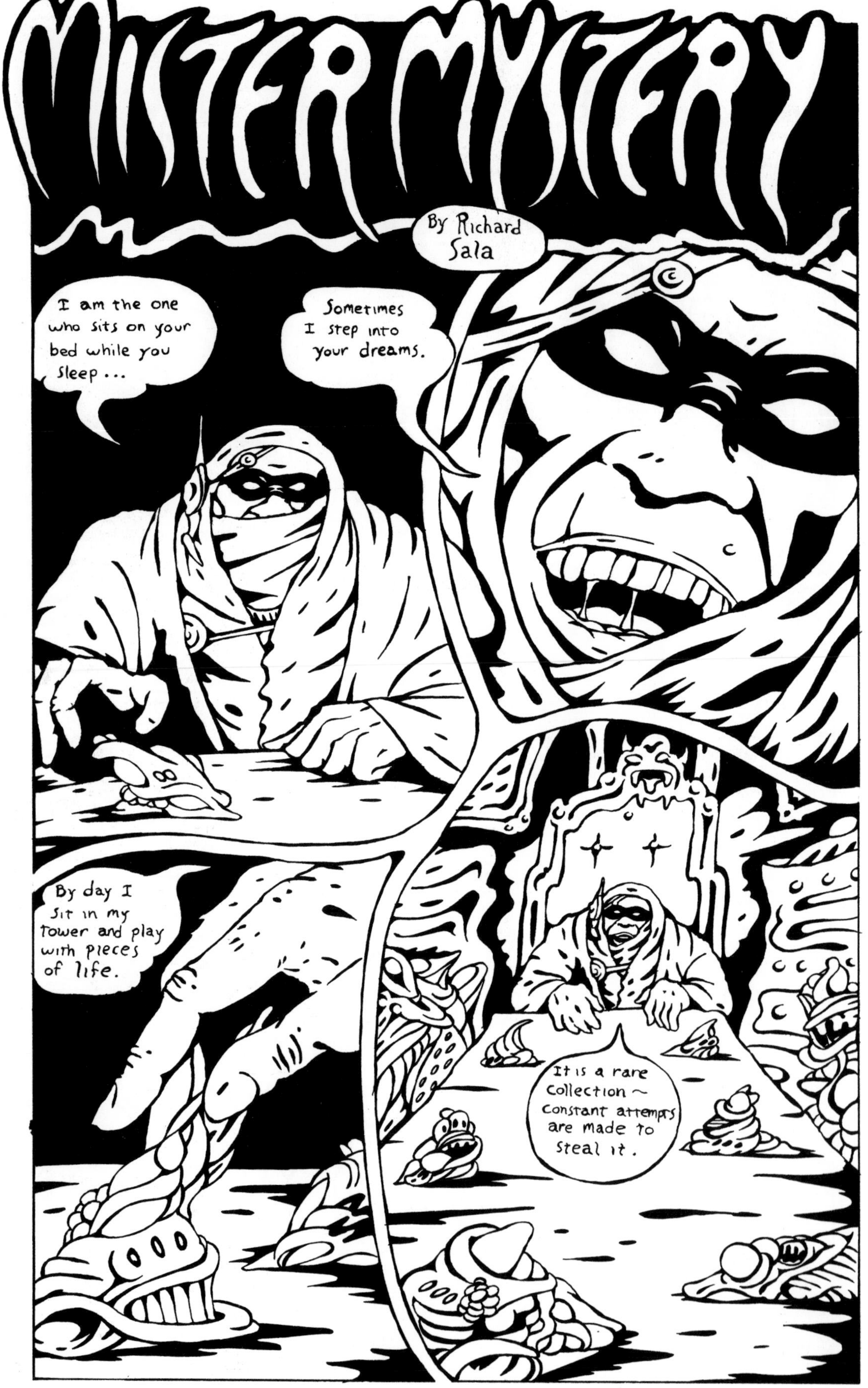
MISTER MYSTERY
By Richard Sala
I am the one who sits on your bed while you sleep...
Sometimes I step into your dreams.
By day I sit in my tower and play with pieces of life.
It is a rare collection ~ constant attempts are made to steal it.

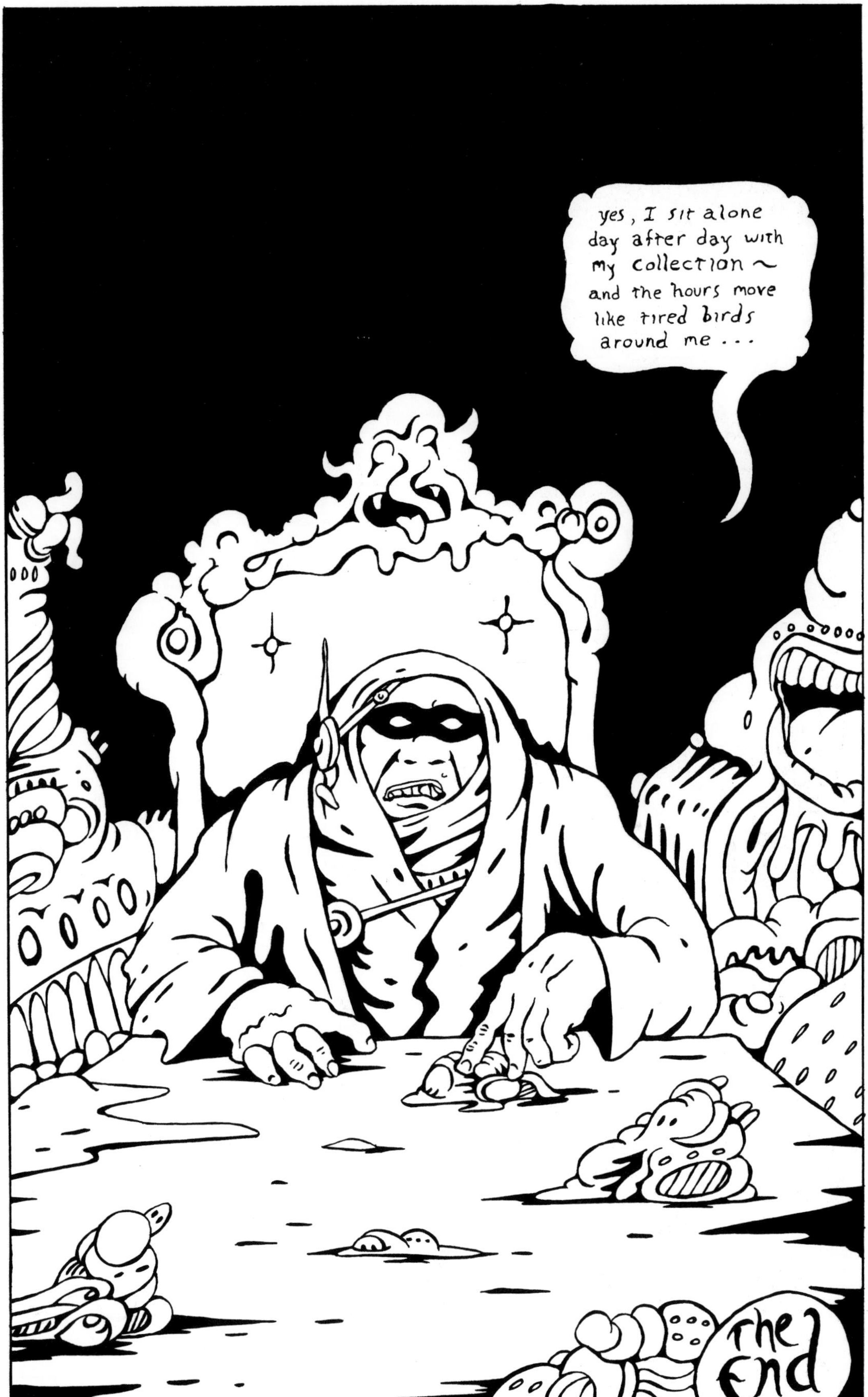
yes, I sit alone day after day with my collection ~ and the hours move like tired birds around me . . .
The End

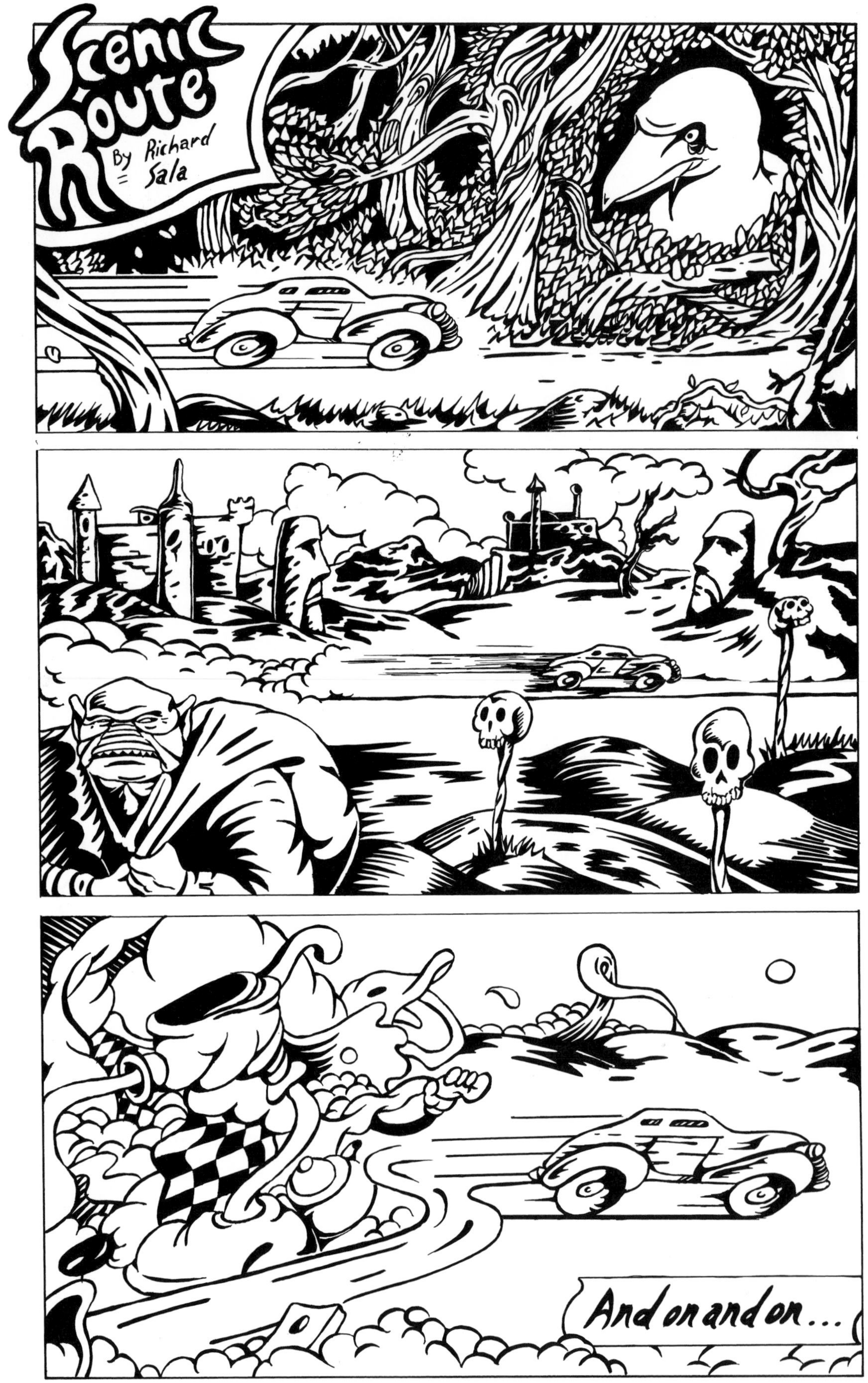
Scenic Route
By Richard Sala
And on and on...

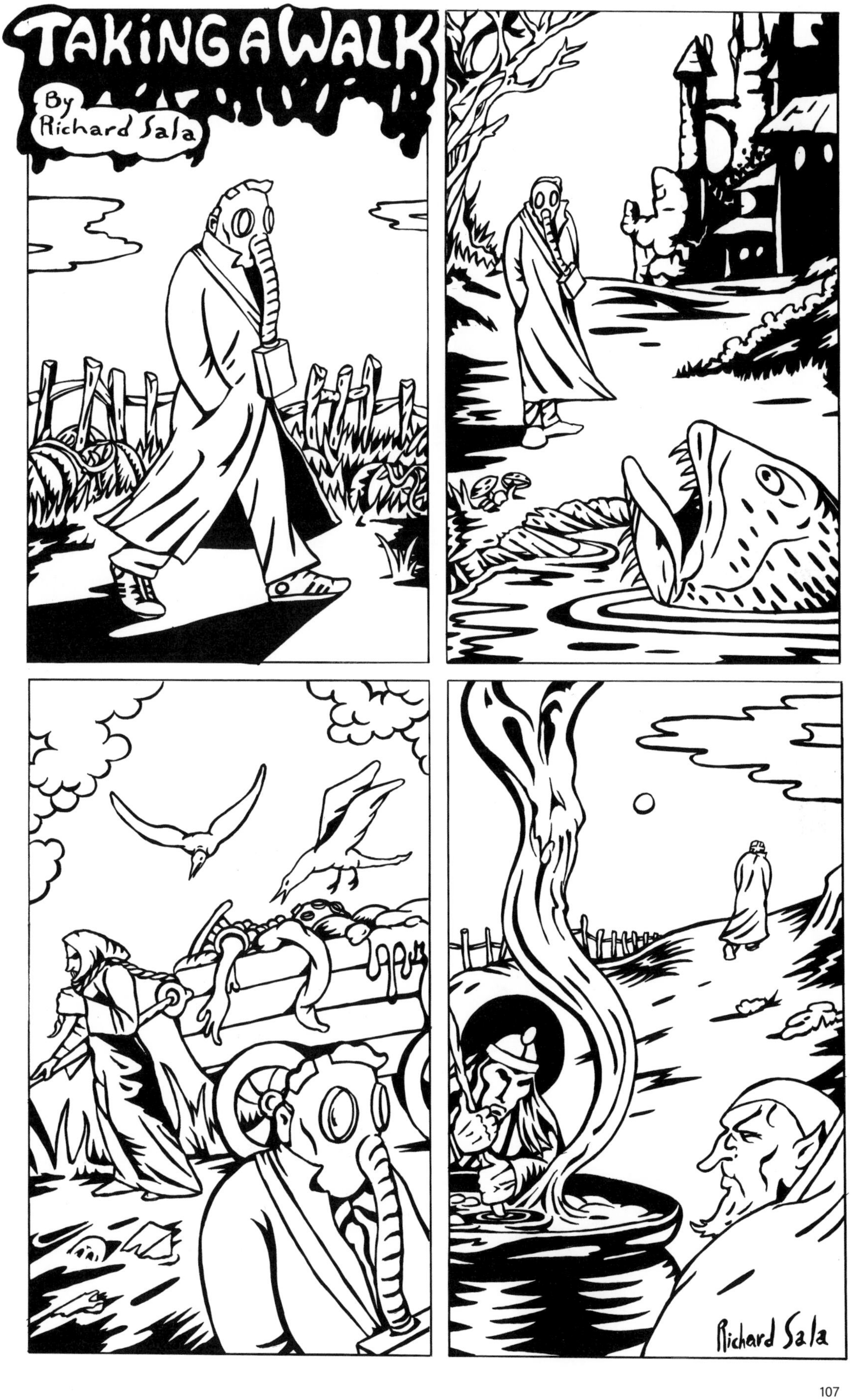
TAKING A WALK
By Richard Sala
Richard Sala

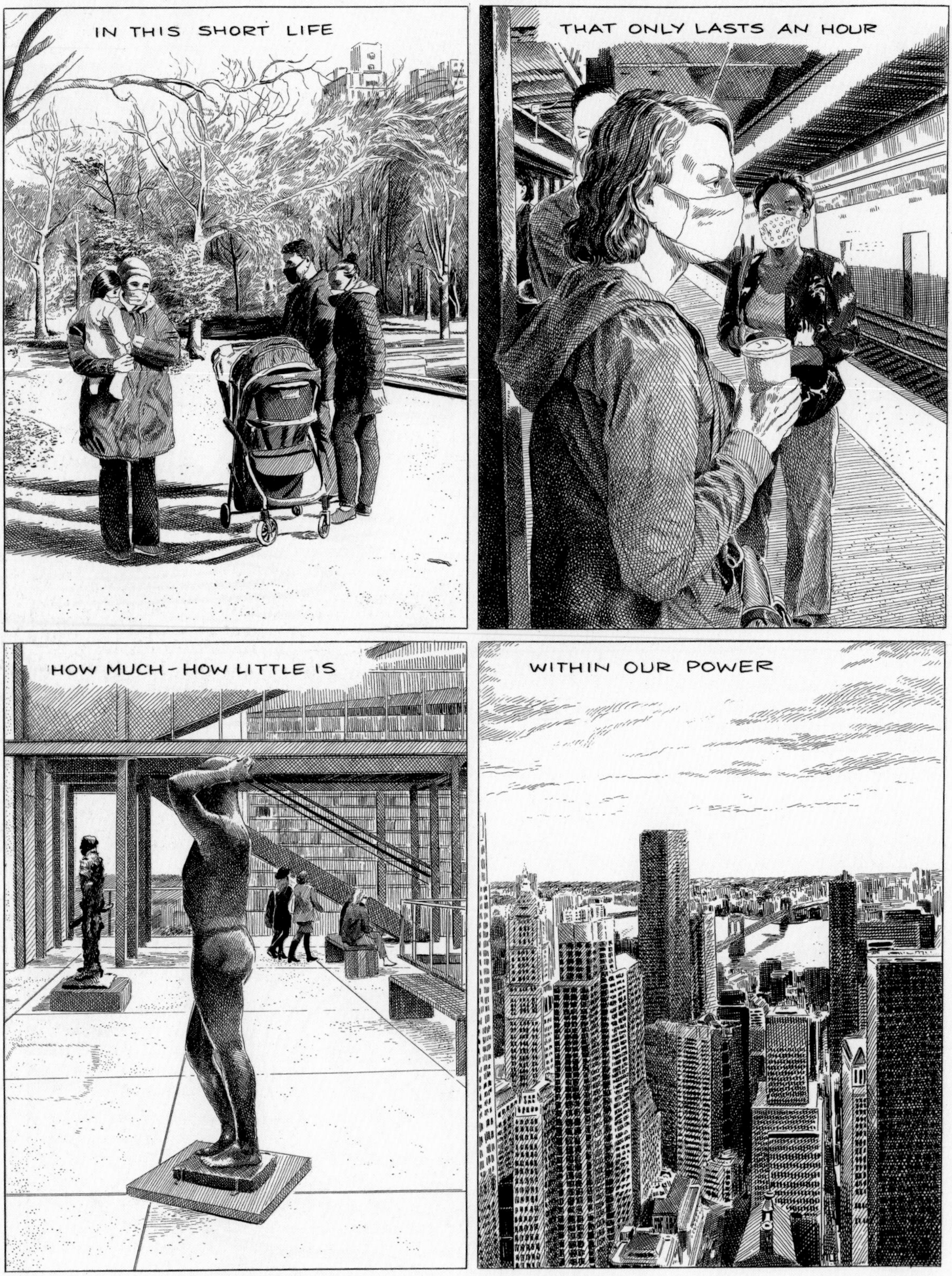
IN THIS SHORT LIFE
THAT ONLY LASTS AN HOUR
HOW MUCH - HOW LITTLE IS
WITHIN OUR POWER